DIGGING FOR VICTORY AT ROOKERY HOUSE

ROSIE HENDRY

For David, with love.

CHAPTER 1

Sunday, 22nd December 1940 – Manchester, England

'The holly and the ivy, when they are both full grown, of all the trees that are in the wood, the holly bears the crown...' Florence Butterworth sang her favourite, age-old Christmas carol in a hearty voice while she did the washing up, her hands plunged in the hot soapy water.

The warm kitchen was fragrant with the scent of spices and dried fruit from the freshly baked mince pies cooling on a rack on the table. Once they were cold, Flo would pack the pies away into a tin to be enjoyed over the coming festivities. There was something else in the air, Flo mused... a tingle of excitement that Christmas was almost here. She smiled to herself as she sang, enjoying the anticipation of the approaching holiday, her voice soaring upwards, filling the room with music.

'Are you getting in some practice for the carol singing tomorrow night?'

The voice made Flo jump, and she turned around from the sink to see her sister, Joyce, who at twenty was two years older than herself. Flo laughed. 'No, I've practised enough with the singing group in my dinner times at work. Tonight, I'm singing for the sheer enjoyment of it!'

'It sounded smashing, you've got a lovely voice.' Joyce put the two stone hot water bottles she was carrying down on the wooden table, unscrewed the lids, then took the kettle from the range and filled them up with hot water. 'I'm really looking forward to some time off over Christmas.'

Flo put the baking tray she'd washed onto the wooden drainer. 'Same here. Two days off work will be bliss.'

It would be a couple of joyous days away from the humdrum monotony of her job, Flo thought. Any time off from the mindless and endless typing of letters was a welcome relief, although she could never say as much to any of her family. Not after she'd won the scholarship to the Commercial College and the chance to train in shorthand and typing, which had enabled her to get clean, respectable office work. Her parents had been so proud of her and Flo hadn't the heart to let them down by telling them how she really felt about her job.

Her sister had never had the same opportunity, so for Flo to moan to Joyce about how boring her job was, and how much she disliked it, wouldn't have been fair or kind. No, Flo had to mind her tongue and bide her time as she knew she wouldn't be working there forever. The way things were going, sooner or later she'd have to do her bit for the war effort and then she could make her escape from the dreary world of typewriters. Where she would eventually go filled her daydreams at work. Would she get a job in the Avro plane factory like Joyce who worked there as a riveter and driller making bombers? Or she might join one of the women's services, but which one?

Joyce brought the kettle over to the sink and Flo moved to the side while her sister refilled it from the cold tap. 'I hope our Mam and Bobby are well enough to come down on Christmas Day.'

'So do I,' Flo agreed.

Their mother and brother Bobby had been struck down with the flu that was doing the rounds and had been poorly in bed for the past couple of days. Flo and Joyce had taken over running the house as well as caring for their mam and six-year-old Bobby.

'Even if they're not fully fit, they could come downstairs and sit by the fire on the day. I'm sure we can manage cooking Christmas dinner between us, can't we?'

Flo nodded. 'Of course, we can! We've got some smashing sprouts ready on the allotment. I know how much you love them!'

'Very funny, Flo. I'll let you have my share. I'll swap you for...' Joyce began, but paused as the back door opened and their father came in carrying a full coal bucket. He was dressed in his blue ARP overalls, ready to go on duty, and had gone out to refill the bucket from the coal hole in the garden before he left.

Closing the door behind him, he sniffed appreciatively. 'Those mince pies smell lovely. You sure I can't have one before I go on duty, Flo?'

'No, they're for Christmas Eve and not before!' Flo said, mock-sternly. 'Mam saved that jar of mincemeat for months and there's no hope of us getting any more at the grocers if you go and eat them all before Christmas Eve. I only made them tonight because I won't have time tomorrow. Remember

I'm going carol singing after work to raise money for the Red Cross. So, keep your hands off!' She met her father's twinkly brown eyes, which were the same colour as her own. 'And I've counted them. I know *exactly* how many there are. Just think, they'll taste all the better for waiting for them.' Flo gave her father a cheeky smile.

'Fair enough. I don't want to upset your mam since she's saved the mincemeat specially. I promise I'll wait!' Flo's father reassured her, before turning his attention to the hot water bottles standing on the kitchen table. 'Are they ready to go up?'

'Yes, I was about to take them up for Mam and Bobby,' Joyce said.

'Tell your mam I will be up shortly to see her before I go out,' their father said. 'I'll just make up the fire in the front room first. It's nippy out there so it will be a cold shift in the ARP hut tonight.' He went through to the front room, carrying the coal bucket with him.

'After I get Bobby tucked in, perhaps we can have a game of cards while we listen to the wireless,' Joyce suggested, picking up the hot water bottles.

'Good idea,' Flo agreed. 'I'll make us a pot of tea.'

While Joyce went upstairs, Flo put the kettle on to boil and finished the last bit of washing up. Then she packed the cold mince pies into the large red poppy-patterned tin which her mother used to store cakes and once more began to sing softly to herself, this time choosing another Christmas carol that she loved – O Little Town of Bethlehem. She'd just put the tin away in the pantry and poured boiling water from the kettle into the teapot when the air-raid siren started its loud wail, rising and falling over the Manchester rooftops.

'Not now!' Flo groaned, her stomach knotting as it always did at the sound of the siren. They'd had sporadic air raids this year, thankfully nothing as bad as what London or Liverpool had suffered, but each one had been unsettling. The last thing their poorly mam and brother needed tonight was to have to leave their warm beds and spend who knew how long in a cold, damp Anderson shelter.

The door from the hall flew open and Flo's father rushed in. 'Can you get things organised, Flo? Take the baskets out to the shelter and set up in there so your Mam and Bobby can get straight into the bunks when they get there. I don't want them getting cold. I'll go up and get your mam, make sure she puts on some warm clothes, then bring her down. Joyce can do the same with Bobby. We won't be long.'

'Yes Dad.' Flo's heart was beating hard as she got the flask out of the dresser and poured tea into it. It hadn't had a chance to steep properly as they liked it, but it would have to do – at least it would be something warm and wet to drink while they sat out the raid. There wasn't time to dither around if she was to get everything organised and ready in the shelter. With any luck, the planes would just pass over, and they'd soon be back indoors and could have a proper cup of tea then.

Flo grabbed her coat from a hook in the hall, rammed her warm knitted beret over her shoulder-length brown hair, then heaved the heavy baskets out from the cupboard under the stairs. Already packed with what they'd need to spend a night in the Anderson shelter, she added the flask of tea to a basket and hurried out of the back door.

The cold air nipped at her cheeks as she made her way to the Anderson shelter at the far end of the garden, using the faint cowled beam from her torch to light the way.

Once inside, Flo busied herself making up the wooden bunk beds her father had made. There were two, a set on either side of the Anderson, along with a smaller single bed which ran along the back wall where Bobby slept. Every time they had to seek shelter out here, the beds had to be made up with a pillow and some blankets brought from the house since it was too damp to leave bedding in here all the time. Instead, it was aired after each use and put back ready in the baskets to be grabbed and taken out when the next air-raid siren sounded.

Flo hoped that Joyce and her father would remember to bring out the hot water bottles to help keep Mam and Bobby warm, although if they needed support or even carrying out here, the bottles may well be left behind. She decided she should go back to the house and check to be sure.

As she climbed up the steps out of the Anderson, Flo glanced at the sky, where she could hear enemy planes fast approaching. She hated the sound of their engines, their beat uneven, coming in sinister, threatening waves, which made her heart race. Within seconds, the planes were overhead. Panic stabbed Flo in the stomach. Where were the others? They needed to hurry.

Flo headed towards the house but hadn't taken more than a few steps when there was a deafening roar, and she was pushed backwards as if by an invisible hand. Lying winded on the cold, damp concrete floor of the shelter, she heard heavy thumps against the roof and things clattering down, while gritty dust drifted down on her.

It took a few dizzying moments for Flo to realise where she was. Then some force inside her kicked into action and she pushed herself up into a sitting position and then scrambled to her feet as a surge of energy flooded through her. She looked around for her torch and, finding it, used its faint beam to guide her up the shelter steps, which were now partly blocked by chunks of brick and wood. Coughing in the powdery dust that filled the air, she shone the torch towards her home and gasped. The house had collapsed and crumpled in, leaving a pile of rubble with wooden beams sticking up at odd angles like discarded matchsticks. Their neighbour's house which joined onto Flo's home, had suffered the same fate. In front of her, the garden was littered with things from her home. She spotted a scrap of curtain from the bedroom she and Joyce shared.

Flo opened her mouth to call to her family, but no words came out. Where were they? They couldn't still be in there...

She began to scramble over the debris towards the house, finally finding her voice. 'Mam, Dad, Joyce, Bobby!' she shrieked. She was barely aware of the cold lines that smarted on her cheeks where her tears ran down.

'Stop!' a man yelled. Flo felt two strong arms grab hold of her. 'You can't go in there.'

'My family are in the house!' she screamed, wriggling against his arms to free herself. 'They were on the way to the shelter.'

'You need to keep back. Let us search for them. We know what we're doing.' The man's voice was firm, his hold tightening around her. 'Understand?'

Flo nodded as the fight drained out of her and she suddenly began to shake.

'Are you Reg Butterworth's lass?' he asked, loosening his grip on her.

She nodded, looking at the man who was dressed in the same ARP uniform as her father wore. 'Yes, Dad was due on duty tonight. He'd just gone upstairs to fetch Mam and bring her down to the shelter. She's ill...' Flo began but had to stop to gasp for breath.

'All right, lass, we'll find them. Are you hurt?'

'No.'

'You're shaking and in shock. You should go to the

communal shelter while we get organised here.' His voice was kind.

'No, I want to stay! Then I'll be here when you find them. Do you think they're still alive in there?' Flo asked.

'I hope so, there's *always* hope.'

'I promise I won't get in the way. I'll wait in the Anderson.' She nodded her head towards it.

'Very well if you insist, but make sure you *keep* in there. We don't want to have to worry about you.' He patted her shoulder and headed off towards the road where the voices of other men could be heard.

Flo stood still for a moment, closed her eyes and sent up a prayer that somewhere in that pile of rubble her family was alive. Opening her eyes, she looked up to where the planes were still going over. They were dropping more of their bombs judging, by the crumps and thumps that echoed across the city. Tonight, they hadn't passed over. Tonight, it was Manchester's turn to be the Luftwaffe's target.

Doing as the ARP warden told her, Flo made her way back to the Anderson, wrapped a couple of blankets over her shoulders and sat huddled on a bottom bunk looking out of the open shelter door. She didn't want to close it, shut herself in, not with her family out there. Flo would watch and wait until they were found.

Staring into the darkness, she noticed that the sky was gradually turning an eerie orange red, which was strangely beautiful. It was the colour of flame, of fire. The city was burning. The bombers must be dropping incendiary bombs as well, the fires they started lighting up the city, making Manchester a glowing target for more bombers to aim for.

Flo shuddered, pulling her blankets tighter around her, listening as the bombers kept on coming, wave after wave, the sound of their engines mixing with the cacophony of noise from a city under attack. Gunfire from the anti-aircraft guns. Bells ringing from fire engines and shouts from rescue workers. All the while, her family were somewhere trapped under the rubble. There was nothing she could do but wait and hope.

It was almost midnight when the all-clear finally sounded, its single note a relief after nearly six hours of bombing, but the damage done by the raid was ongoing. Flo stepped outside the shelter and watched as the rescue workers painstakingly worked their way through the debris of her home. Their shapes stood out as black silhouettes against the orange sky, which glowed from the raging infernos. The stench of burning drifted in the night air. She longed to go and help them but resisted, knowing her well-meaning attempts could cause more problems to her family trapped beneath. Flo's patience was being sorely tested as she waited, straining to listen to what the rescuers were saying. She could hear them calling out now and then, pausing and listening for any response from below the rubble. So far, there had been nothing. At least the glow from the fires was helping the search as it lit up the darkness.

Flo had never known a night pass so agonisingly slowly. What had begun as a pleasant evening with her baking for Christmas, singing carols and the promise of a game of cards with her sister sitting by the warm fire, had become a waking nightmare.

It was as dawn broke, the sky lightening to the east, that a shout went up from one of the rescuers. They'd found someone. Shrugging off her blankets, Flo began to pick her way over the debris-covered back garden towards the house, desperate to see who they'd found and get them out and to safety.

'Who is it?' she called.

'Stay there! It's not safe,' one of the rescue workers yelled.

Obeying him, Flo shouted, 'Who is it? Are they all right?'

She watched, her heart pounding hard as a small figure was lifted out of the debris.

'It's my brother, Bobby!' she shouted. 'How is he?'

'You'd best come with me, Miss,' a man's gentle voice urged her.

She turned to see a policeman beckoning her to him from the garden of their unattached neighbour's house where there was safe passage away from the ruins. Flo picked her way over the spill of bricks that littered the ground, clambered over what was left of the wall between the gardens and followed the policeman out to the street in front of the house. 'Is he injured? Can I see him?'

The policeman led her to where the rescuers had put a stretcher laid on the ground. 'Is this Bobby?'

Flo knelt beside him, noticing how still he was, how he was covered in brick dust, the tartan pattern of his dressing gown barely visible.

'Bobby?' She reached out and gently stroked his face. The skin was gritty and cool. 'Bobby, wake up, it's me, Flo.'

Flo felt a hand on her shoulder. 'I'm sorry, Miss, but your brother's gone. There was nothing anyone could do.' The policeman's voice was kind.

'No, he can't be.' Flo grabbed Bobby's hand and squeezed it. 'Wake up!'

Her brother, who was usually so full of energy, lay completely still, the life gone out of him. Flo's eyes flooded with tears as she struggled to comprehend what had happened, shaking her head, her hand over her mouth. He was dead.

Another shout went up from the rescuers – they'd found someone else. Who was it? How was she going to break the news to them about Bobby?

In the end, Flo didn't have to tell any of them because one by one, her sister, Mam and Dad were pulled from the debris of their home. All of them dead. Her mam was wrapped in the eiderdown from her parents' bed and must have been on the way out with her dad. Joyce had been found not far from Bobby.

'I'm sorry for your loss. None of them stood a chance,' the chief of the rescuers explained to a stunned Flo. 'The bomb fell on next door and with it being a semi-detached, your home got caught in the blast too.'

'But they were on their way to the shelter,' Flo said, her voice thin and reedy, her body feeling like it didn't belong to her. 'Another few minutes and they'd have been in there. Been safe even though a bomb dropped.'

She looked back at what remained of the house and something caught her eye, a pattern of familiar red flowers. It was Mam's cake tin wedged between two planks of wood in the rubble that spilt out onto the road. She hurried over and picked it up, brushing off the gritty dust to reveal the bright floral pattern. Flo bit her lip as hot tears slid down her cheeks.

'What is it?' the chief rescuer asked.

Flo sniffed. 'It's my mam's cake tin. I filled it with mince pies that I baked earlier.' She prised the lid off, which was harder than usual, as the tin was slightly dented. Inside, the mince pies were mainly intact. Their sweet, spicy fragrance scented the air. Her family wasn't here to eat them now so she would share them out to those who'd done all they could to rescue them.

'Would you like one? Pass them around to the others.' She handed the tin to the chief rescuer and left him and the other men to enjoy them. She needed to say her own private goodbyes to her family who now lay side by side on stretchers, their faces shrouded in blankets.

CHAPTER 2

New Year's Day 1941 – Lancaster, England

Flo drove the spade into the earth with far more force than she needed. Digging over a plot on her grandfather's allotment on her own was helping to calm her mind by putting her energy into something productive. The physical work had warmed her, and she'd discarded her coat, hanging it over the bench outside the shed at the end of the allotment. Her breath clouded in the cold air as she worked, methodically pushing in the spade, turning the soil over, repeating the process over and over.

It was a little more than a week since her parents, sister and brother had been killed in what had become known as the Christmas Blitz. Now they lay buried together in a Manchester graveyard. Afterwards, Flo had returned to the place she always thought of as home – back to Lancaster. It was the city she'd been born in, had grown up in, living all her life here until four years ago, when her father's job had taken him to Manchester and her family had upped sticks and moved there with him. Her grandparents were still here in Lancaster, and it was to them she had fled after the horrors of losing her family. Being here on familiar territory, within the comfort of her grandparent's home, was a balm to her shattered heart.

'The rate you're going, I won't have to do any digging on here myself this year!' Her grandad's voice broke into Flo's thoughts, and she stopped and looked at him, her breathing fast from the hard work.

He gave her a smile, his face moving in the way it should, but she could see that the deaths of his daughter, son-in-law and other grandchildren had hit him hard. His eyes had lost their usual sparkle. He and Flo's gran had welcomed Flo into their home with open arms and been grateful that she'd survived. Losing the others had left a vast hole in their family which could never be filled.

'It's good to be out here doing something...' her voice tailed off.

He nodded, an understanding expression on his face. 'Your gran sent me out with a hot drink for you. Thought you might be glad of it.' He held up a flask.

'I would, thank you.' Flo pushed the spade into the soil and followed her grandad to his shed. His little home away from home, a place where she'd spent many happy hours helping him with the allotment. Her love of growing things had been born here, her grandad patiently teaching her how to grow fruit and vegetables. Before they'd moved to Manchester, her family had had an allotment of their own on this same site. She glanced over to where it was on the far side, now tended by other people.

When her family had arrived in Manchester, they had taken on an allotment there, which she'd lovingly tended with her father, but it had never quite held the same place in her heart as this one did. Her grandad's plot was where she had been introduced to the joy of growing things and it would always mean a lot to her. Coming here, working on it, was a good way for her to distract herself from what had happened.

Inside the shed, her grandad settled down in the old armchair with patches on the arms where the material had worn thin. It had stood in here for as long as she could remember and was part and parcel of what she loved about this little wooden hut. Flo pulled out a stool from under the bench, which ran along one wall, where seeds were sown in pots or seedlings pricked out to grow on. The shed smelt of earth and fresh air – a potent combination which made her feel better. She moved the stool next to the armchair and perched on it.

'Here we are. Get this into you.' Her grandad handed her a mug of tea, which he'd poured from the flask.

'Thank you.' Flo took the mug, cradling it in her hands while she stared at the steam from the hot tea spiralling up into the air.

'Are you all right?' Her grandad's voice was gentle.

Flo lifted a shoulder and avoided looking at him, instead letting her gaze wander over the opposite side of the shed where a battered chest of drawers housed packets of seed and things like balls of twine, all neatly organised. Well-cared-for tools hung in their places on the wall. Spades, forks, rakes, each one she'd used many times as she'd worked here.

'As well as I can be, I suppose,' she said, her eyes meeting his. 'I still can't believe what's happened. It doesn't seem real…' She blinked hard as tears threatened. 'I know it is and we can never bring them back. We've just got to get on with things.'

'True enough. You know that you can stay with us for as long as you want.'

Flo bit her bottom lip and nodded. 'Thank you.'

'Have you thought what you're going to do now?' he asked.

Flo took a sip of her tea before answering. She'd lain awake at night working out what she would like to do. Her job in Manchester was gone, the office where she'd worked destroyed in the bombing, so she had not only lost her family and her home, but her employment too. That was by far the least of the losses, but it left her without work, and she needed to find new employment and soon. 'I don't want to get another job in an office... I didn't like it!'

Her grandad's mouth twitched at the corners. 'I never thought it was your sort of thing, to be honest. Though it was a good job, I suppose.'

'Yes, but very boring! And I was stuck indoors all day.' Flo gave a wry half smile. 'What I would like to do is something I enjoy, something outside...' She gestured with her hand towards the open shed door where the low winter sun was bathing the allotment in a pale light. She could see a robin hopping about on the earth she'd been digging over, looking for food. 'I reckon that sooner or later, women are going to be called up to work for the war effort. With my experience, I would probably end up in a WAAF or ATS office typing more letters only wearing a uniform. I don't want that!' She grimaced. 'I think the best thing for me to do is volunteer to join the Women's Land Army. I'd ask to do horticultural work so I could be outside growing plants. I'd love that! What do you think?' She looked at her grandad, waiting for his response.

He nodded and a smile spread over his face. 'I think you're

right. If you can do a job that you love, then it doesn't feel so much like work.'

'I'll go to the Labour Exchange tomorrow and volunteer to do my bit for the war effort by growing food.'

'You're very *good* at it too,' her grandad added. 'You've got the finest green fingers in this family, so best put them to use!'

CHAPTER 3

Sunday 2nd March 1941 – Great Plumstead, Norfolk

'What do you reckon?' Reuben asked, his breath clouding in the crisp, cold air. 'Do you want to buy it?'

Thea took a few moments to reply, her gaze following her evacuee children, George and Betty, as they chased each other around the field, laughing as Reuben's sheep dog, Bess, joined in.

'Yes,' she confirmed, turning to face her brother. 'But I'm not sure if I *should*, though.' Thea frowned. 'I want to, but it would be an enormous investment for me in terms of both money and work. If I bought this...' She swept her arm wide, taking in the expanse of the grass field where they stood, 'then I would use up most of my savings. The work on the three and a half acres that I've already got keeps me and Alice busy enough, so adding another five on top of that would more than double the workload. Am I crazy to even consider it?'

The corners of Reuben's mouth twitched into a smile.

'Since when did the craziness or otherwise of an idea stop you from doing something you wanted to? There's some would say that selling up your successful business in London to come back here and buy Rookery House was crazy!'

'Is that what you think?' Thea cut in, her hands on her hips.

'Of course not!' Reuben's face softened. 'I think that is one of the most sensible decisions you've ever made.' He turned his attention to the children for a moment who were enjoying their game, their joyful laughter mingling with the sound of rooks cawing in the tall elm trees down the lane, where they were busy tending their nests. 'In fact,' he continued, turning to Thea again, 'I'd be interested in buying this field *with* you. We could go halves on it and that way you don't have to spend all your savings. It's best to keep some in reserve because you never know when you might need it.'

Thea hadn't expected this. 'Are you *serious*? You want to buy half this field?'

Reuben nodded. 'I wouldn't have offered to unless I meant it. What do you think? It would solve the first problem you had with buying it.'

Thea narrowed her eyes against the pale early spring sunshine and looked across the field which backed on to Rookery House's garden. It was the perfect piece of land to add to what she already had if she were to expand. If she accepted Reuben's offer, then it would solve her dilemma about leaving herself with limited savings. In the long term, it would be good to increase the land she had to work with, simply because with more acreage she could produce more food. It was vital that Britain became more self-sufficient in feeding its people. Now Hitler had overrun so many countries on the European mainland, and his navy were attacking the Atlantic convoys bringing in supplies, the country had to grow much more food to ensure people had enough to eat.

The government was encouraging everyone to Dig for Victory. Thea's idea to turn this field to food production, in addition to what she already did, seemed like a good plan in theory. The farmer who owned it had given her first refusal before he put it on the open market. An opportunity such as this might not come along again. Should she take it? Should she accept Reuben's offer?

'Would you want me to pay you back for your half when I could afford it?' she asked.

'No. I've got savings and would be happy to spend some to help you. You won't accept any rent for having my railway carriage house on your land. You could say it's my way of paying for living here.' Reuben's eyes were earnest. 'And don't worry, I won't interfere with what you decide to do with the field or expect any money from what you earn from it. I will help with it if you want, but I'll be like a silent part-owner with you.'

'You know I'm glad to have you living here and that I don't want anything for it. You are family,' Thea reassured her brother. 'And I appreciate you saying you'd be a silent part-owner.' She bit her bottom lip. 'Do you think I should buy it then?'

'If it's what you want, then I do.'

Thea nodded. 'All right, if you're willing to pay for half of it, then I will.' She gave him a grateful smile. 'And there's a way of getting help with the extra work. I'll apply to the Women's Land Army for a Land Girl.' She held out her hand. 'Shall we shake on a new partnership?'

Reuben took her hand in his work-roughened one. 'Here's to a long, and happy, silent partnership.'

'Auntie Thea, Auntie Thea!' George called, catching Thea's attention as he and Betty came charging towards them, their breaths coming out like puffs from a steam engine in the cold air. Bess bounded along beside them, her tail waving high in the air, its white tip like a feathery flag. 'Did you see how fast we ran?'

Thea threw her arms wide to greet them and the children ran in for a hug. 'I did. You were both so quick that Bess could hardly keep up with you.' Her eyes met Reuben's above the children's heads, and his eyes twinkled with amusement. 'How about we all go indoors? Hettie made some crumpets yesterday and we could have some toasted with some of Primrose's butter on top? Will you join us, Reuben?'

'I'd be a fool to turn down an offer of Hettie's crumpets and butter. So yes, please,' Reuben agreed.

The warmth of Rookery House's kitchen was most welcoming after the cold, Thea thought as she ushered the children inside. She'd helped them take off their coats and boots in the scullery, then made sure they washed their hands so they'd be ready to eat.

'I didn't think you'd be much longer, so I've just put some milk on to heat up to make cocoa. That will help warm you up.' Hettie stood by the kitchen range, where she was watching over a saucepan of milk. 'Evie and Marianne are toasting crumpets on the fire in the sitting room. They'll soon be ready.'

'Auntie Thea said we could have some crumpets.' Betty went over to Hettie, wrapped her arms around the older woman's waist and gave her a hug.

'She was right.' Hettie winked at Thea as she put an arm around the little girl and returned her embrace. 'Having toasted crumpets on a cold, wintery day is just what we need.'

'It certainly is.' Thea took some blue and white patterned

plates and cups from one of the dressers which lined the walls of the kitchen and set them out on the wooden table. 'Even Reuben's been tempted in by the thought of them.' Thea gave her brother, who'd just come in carrying a basket of logs for the range, a cheeky grin.

Reuben laughed. 'It's true, Hettie, I admit it.'

When everyone was settled around the table tucking into hot buttered crumpets and mugs of milky cocoa or tea, Hettie asked the question that Thea had been waiting for. 'Have you made up your mind up about the field?'

Thea nodded at the older woman, who'd been her mother's best friend and was like an aunt to Thea and her brothers and sisters. 'I have. I'm going to buy it.' She glanced at Reuben, who gave a nod of his head in agreement. 'Reuben and I are paying half each.'

Hettie's eyes widened with surprise. 'Well, that is good news!' She gave Reuben a beaming smile.

'He's going to be a silent part-owner,' Thea explained.

'Doesn't Reuben want to be involved?' Evie asked.

Thea looked across at the young woman who sat opposite enjoying one of her few days off from her work as a nurse at Great Plumstead Hall Hospital. 'He's interested and will help out from time to time but is happy to let me get on with using the field however I want. I'll be in charge of what we do with it.'

'And what are you planning to do?' Hettie said, spreading butter on a crumpet and handing it on a small plate to George who sat beside her.

'I'll use part of it to make hay and then as grazing for Primrose after we have harvested it. The rest of it will need to be ploughed up and used to grow more vegetables. We'll be able to plant a lot more potatoes and other veg with the extra land. I plan to grow sunflowers for the seeds to feed the chickens as well and we must start producing our own meat by keeping rabbits and pigs, too. I've been wanting to get started with that for a while now.'

Hettie raised an eyebrow behind her round glasses. 'And how are you going to manage all that with just you and Alice working here? You're both busy enough as it is.'

'I'll do the ploughing,' Reuben said. 'I can borrow a horse and plough from the Great Plumstead Hall estate. I'll get it done as soon as possible.'

'Thank you.' Thea gave her brother a grateful smile. 'And as for the rest of the work, I'm going to apply to have a Land Girl to come and work with us. I'll give Lizzie a ring tomorrow to find out what I need to do.' Having her younger sister working for the Women's Land Army at their office in Norwich would be a help, Thea thought.

'Good idea, but are you planning to have her live here?' Hettie asked.

Thea swallowed her mouthful of crumpet before replying, 'Of course.'

Hettie put down the cup of tea she'd just taken a sip from. 'But where are you going to put her? We don't have a spare bedroom.'

'There's the dining room,' Marianne said, cutting a crumpet into fingers for her one-year-old daughter, Emily, who was sitting on her lap. 'It could be turned into one.'

'Then you wouldn't have anywhere to do your sewing. I know you don't do as many dressmaking jobs as you did when you first came here, but you still need somewhere to work,' Thea said. 'We already use the dining room for visitors staying a few nights on a camp bed. I wouldn't want it used as a bedroom full time. I've had another idea.' She looked at Evie. 'I was wondering if you'd mind sharing your room with a Land Girl. It's big enough to fit another single bed in there.'

'Of course not,' Evie replied. 'I shared a dorm with five other girls all the years I was at boarding school. Sharing with just one person will be a huge improvement on that.'

'Thank you,' Thea said. 'Rookery House is going to be bursting at the seams.'

'It certainly is, but I reckon a house like this one is made to be filled.' Hettie chuckled. 'It's going to be another busy year.'

Bess, who'd been lying quietly beside Reuben's chair, suddenly got up and went to stand by the back door, wagging her tail.

'Looks like someone's coming,' Reuben said.

Moments later, a figure passed the kitchen window, the door opened and Prue, Thea and Reuben's sister, walked in.

'Afternoon,' Prue greeted them cheerfully. 'I was hoping you'd all be here. I have some news.'

'So have we!' Hettie got up from her seat. 'Sit yourself down and help yourself.' She nodded at the plate of toasted crumpets in the middle of the table.

Prue sat down next to Evie.

'What's happened?' Thea asked as Hettie took a cup off the dresser, poured tea into the cup and passed it over to Prue, along with a plate, then sat down in her place again.

'Thank you, Hettie.' Prue leaned back in her chair and looked at everyone sitting around the table. 'It's quite a shock... there's going to be an aerodrome built between Great Plumstead and Geswick! Victor heard about it at a council meeting last night.'

There were a few moments of silence as the news sank in before Hettie burst out. 'An aerodrome! Near here? But what about the houses and farms between the two villages?'

'The government's requisitioning them so the owners and tenants have to move out,' Prue said. 'It's for the defence of the nation and they'll receive compensation.'

'What about my sister Ada's cottage?' Hettie asked. 'She lives between Great Plumstead and Geswick.'

'I'm afraid she'll be one of those told to leave,' Prue said. 'It's not nice, but there are new aerodromes planned in lots of places and they need a lot of land. Unfortunately, that means that people are going to lose their homes.'

'It will cause a lot of disruption around here as well. Building an aerodrome is no small business,' Reuben added.

'And once the aerodrome is operational we'll have planes flying in and out,' said Marianne, whose husband Alex was in the RAF training to be a pilot. 'Do you know what sort of aerodrome it will be? Is it for bombers or fighters?'

'For heavy bombers, that's all I know.' Prue stirred some milk into her tea. 'It feels like the war's coming ever closer to home if bombers are going to be flying in and out almost from our doorsteps.'

'We'll cope with it. We have no choice,' Thea said matter-of-factly. 'It won't be the first change we've had because of the war and certainly won't be the last.'

Prue nodded. 'Of course, but it feels different putting people out of their homes and farmers off their land.'

'What about the woodland, trees and hedges?' Hettie asked. 'There are plenty of them in that area.'

'They will rip them out,' Reuben said. 'They'll have to make room for the long runways and all the other buildings needed.'

'When are they starting on it?' Evie asked.

'As soon as possible, so Victor said. The surveyors are mapping out the land.'

'I must go and see my sister.' Hettie's face was full of concern. 'Find out what's going on.'

'What's your news?' Prue asked, before taking a bite of buttered crumpet.

'Nothing as dramatic as yours,' Thea said. 'Reuben and I

have decided to buy the field behind here, and I'm going to apply to have a Land Girl to work here alongside Alice and myself.'

'That is good news,' Prue said. 'It saves ships having to bring supplies in and men's lives being put at risk to feed us. The more food we can grow in this country, the better.'

'I agree.' Thea gave her sister a warm smile. 'That's exactly what I plan to do!'

CHAPTER 4

Tuesday 4th March

Hettie propped her bicycle up against the garden wall then
unstrapped her wicker shopping basket from the carrier on
the back. She'd bicycled over to Geswick, the next parish to
Great Plumstead, to visit her sister Ada. She walked up the
path to the front door of Ada's small cottage and raised her
hand to knock, but before Hettie had touched the wooden
door, it opened – her arrival had already been noticed. Ada
didn't miss a thing going on around her cottage.

'Hello, Ada,' Hettie said cheerfully.

'You'll have heard I'm being thrown out of my home then,'
Ada said, skipping any greeting.

'Yes, news about the new aerodrome has spread far and
wide. Along with how the government is requisitioning land
for it and any homes that stand in the way. I've come to see
how you are and what you're going to do. And I've brought

you some things.' Hettie held up the basket packed with produce from Rookery House.

'Come in then. I don't want to let the heat out. Make sure you shut the door properly behind you!' Ada turned and headed towards the kitchen at the back of the cottage. Hettie stepped inside, closed the front door and followed her sister, noticing the pleasant fragrance of lavender and beeswax polish scenting the air.

In the kitchen, Ada pushed the black kettle onto the hot plate of the range to come up to boil before turning to face Hettie. 'I've got to be out of here by noon on the 31st of March. In just four weeks' time!' Ada's face wore a pinched look. 'I came here as a young bride and now I'm being thrown out to make way for bombers! I don't know what Walter would say if he were still here!' Ada's voice caught and she swallowed back tears.

Hettie reached out to her sister, but Ada stepped sharply to the side, went over to the dresser, grabbed two teacups and plonked them down with a thud onto the wooden table standing in the middle of the kitchen.

'It must be harder to deal with this without Walter,' Hettie said, her tone gentle. She suspected that underneath Ada's prickliness, her sister was worried sick about what was going to happen to her. Walter, Ada's husband of forty-six years, had died suddenly last June, and since they didn't have any children, her sister had no family close by except for Hettie. Hettie and Ada had two brothers, but both had gone abroad to Canada and they hadn't seen either of them for many years, although they kept in touch by the occasional letter.

'I haven't got a say in the matter. No choice! They say I must go, but I don't *want* to live anywhere else.' Ada looked around the kitchen of the little cottage, which was cosy and homely. 'This is my home! I like where it is, and I don't want another one!'

Hettie sympathised with her sister, knowing how well this cottage suited Ada. Set out on its own in the countryside, three quarters of a mile from the heart of the village, it had been perfect for Ada and Walter, who liked the peace and quiet, but it now stood in the way of the new aerodrome.

'Do you know what you're going to do?' Hettie asked as she took off her coat and hung it on a peg by the back door.

'I am staying put! That's what I'm doing.' Ada folded her arms across the wrap-around apron which hugged her thin, bird-like frame. 'They might be requisitioning it, but that doesn't mean I'm going quietly. They'll have to carry me out. I am not leaving of my own accord.'

Hettie stared at her sister for a moment. 'But the law is on their side. You can't fight the government on this.'

Ada pursed her lips. 'That's as maybe, but as I said, I'm not going quietly.'

'They might put you in prison!' Hettie exclaimed. 'You'd still lose your home *and* be locked up.'

'Why here?' Why do they want to build an aerodrome here?' Ada threw her arms out wide. 'There are plenty of other places they could do it.'

'I suppose they've decided this is a good place, enough flattish land for a runway and suitable with the prevailing winds. I heard surveyors have been around checking the lie of the land.'

'I saw them! Told them to clear off!' Ada snapped as she spooned tea leaves into the teapot.

'I'm truly sorry that you're going to lose the cottage, but maybe there's a chance you'll come back to it after the war.' Hettie's voice was tentative.

'They're pulling it down to make way for the main runway.'

Tears glistened in Ada's brown eyes, and she quickly turned away to wait over the kettle while it came to the boil.

Hettie watched her sister for a moment, noticing her thin slumped shoulders, so different from her usual upright stance. She wished she could put her arms around Ada and hug her. It wouldn't stop her from losing her home, but it might just provide a bit of comfort to her. But she knew Ada would never thank her for it, and rather than try and be batted off, Hettie respected her sister's feelings and busied herself unpacking the basket. She put the butter, cheese and a jar of honey on the table. Then she unwrapped the apple cake she'd made for Ada, set aside the greaseproof paper wrapping to reuse, and positioned the cake on a large plate she took from the dresser. It would be nice to have a slice with their tea.

By the time the kettle came to the boil, Ada had recovered herself and as she carried the kettle over to the table and poured the steaming water into the teapot, all signs of her tears were gone.

'You'd best get two small plates as well for our slices of cake,' Ada instructed Hettie. 'There's a sharp knife in the table drawer.'

Hettie did as she was told, knowing better than to ask Ada if she was all right, and then sat down at the table and cut them each a slice of cake and passed a plate across to her sister.

'I don't want to go to prison,' Ada said, her face creased with anxiety as she sat opposite Hettie. 'But I won't be leaving until the last day, the very last minute.'

Hettie nodded. 'Have you looked for somewhere else yet?'

'I've made a few enquiries but haven't found anything suitable. There's not much available, but I'll find something. I don't want to go and live in Wykeham. Too busy there for my liking.' Ada sighed. 'I enjoy living in the countryside.'

Hettie appreciated Ada's love of the countryside, but she had also worried about her sister being here on her own since Walter had died. Living in such an isolated cottage wasn't, in Hettie's opinion, a good place for Ada to be. However, her sister had refused to even consider moving into the village or elsewhere after she'd been widowed. Only now such a move was being forced on her.

Ada picked up the teapot and poured out two cups of tea and then pushed a cup over to Hettie.

'I'll keep an ear out for anything for you. Ask around. Would you be interested in something in Great Plumstead?' Hettie took a bite of her apple cake.

'Perhaps, though when it comes to it, beggars can't be choosers,' Ada said, glumly, as she stirred milk into her tea.

'Something will come up, there's time yet and I'll help,' Hettie said, with a note of optimism in her voice. 'Try the cake. It's a new recipe I tried out.'

Ada took a bite and chewed slowly. 'It's tasty.'

Hettie gave her sister a warm smile. 'Glad you like it.' She watched as Ada sipped her tea, thinking about what she could do to find her sister a new home in time. Hettie wanted to help Ada, and she owed her sister for what she had done all those years ago. This would be a chance for Hettie to repay Ada for the sacrifice she'd made for their family, although it might prove to be easier said than done.

CHAPTER 5

Monday 10th March

Prue stared at the thicket of twisted brambles, her heart sinking. Victor had informed her last night that the village Women's Institute could take over what had been old Mrs Appleton's allotment after they'd been waiting months to get one. Now they finally had, Prue hadn't expected it to be in this awful state. No wonder he'd had a smirk on his face when he'd told her that the parish council, of which he was chairman, had agreed to the WI becoming the new tenant. Victor *must* have known how bad it was.

Gingerly making her way across the plot, Prue took care not to trip on trailing bramble suckers or on one of the many thick tussocks of grass. It was obvious that it was some time since Mrs Appleton had done any gardening here. Not surprising, as the poor woman had become crippled with arthritis and had recently left the village to live with her daughter in Wykeham. It was going to need a lot of work to get the allotment cleared and in good order before they could even begin planting vegetables.

Growing more food was vital to help the country and Thea's expansion at Rookery House had inspired Prue's plan for the WI to take over this allotment. They would sell crops grown here at the WI's stall at Wykeham market, and the profit made would be ploughed back into growing more food or used to fund other projects for the war effort. It wasn't an option to fail before they'd even begun!

Prue poked at the emerging green leaves of a nettle with the toe of her shoe. It was one of many beginning to sprout now spring was here, the days gradually growing longer and the sun warmer. Before long, the whole fifty yards of the allotment would burst into growth again and it needed dealing with and quickly.

'Are you taking that on?' a man's deep voice broke into her thoughts.

Prue turned to see Percy Blake, one of the old boys who spent many hours on their perfectly tended allotments, watching her, a concerned look on his weather-beaten face. 'Yes, the village WI are the new tenants. We're going to grow vegetables on here to sell.'

'Then you've got a heck of a job to sort that lot out,' he scoffed, nodding towards the allotment. 'It will take a massive amount of work.'

'I was just thinking the same,' Prue agreed. 'I don't suppose you'd like to help us?' she asked.

Percy took a step backwards, holding up a gnarled hand, palm towards her. 'No! I've got enough to do on my allotment. I wouldn't touch that one even if you gave me five pound to clear it.'

'Do you think any other allotment holders might lend a hand, or be paid to do it?'

He shook his head, his lips pursed into a thin line. 'Not if they've got any sense, they won't. I reckon you're wasting your time there, missus. The WI best stick to making jam. That's at least something they *can* do!' Before Prue could reply, Percy turned on his heels and headed off to his own neatly tended plot on the far side of the allotments, his scruffy little terrier trotting behind him.

Prue stood open-mouthed, her hackles rising. How *dare* Percy say jam making was all the WI women were good for? There was no reason why they couldn't clear the allotment themselves. They didn't *need* men to do it for them. She'd only asked, thinking it would save some time.

She wandered over the allotment again looking carefully at what needed doing – cutting back the brambles and digging out the roots, along with those of plants such as dock, dandelions, nettles and foul grass. It looked like one end of the plot had become a dumping ground from the pile of bricks and bottles that littered it. That would all need clearing up too.

At the far end of the allotment, behind an overgrown elder bush, she spotted a shed. Prue squeezed past the bush and saw that the shed was still in reasonable order and looked watertight. She opened the door and peered in. There was a bench running along one side by the window, under which were stacks of terracotta pots waiting to be used. There were also lots of cobwebs and a thick layer of dust, but nothing a thorough clean-out wouldn't fix.

Outside, to one side of the shed, was a large compost heap that had been there for some time from the state of it. Prue bent down and picked up a handful and rubbed it between her fingers releasing a wonderful earthy smell. The vegetation had broken down into a brown, crumbly mixture, which was perfect for sowing seeds in or for repotting seedlings. It could also be used to fertilise the soil as well. This compost along with the pots in the shed were a real bonus, Prue thought, and they would put them to use getting their vegetables off to a good start.

Prue squared her shoulders. There was no doubt that clearing this allotment was going to be a huge amount of work, but Percy had sorely underestimated the women of this village if he thought they should stick to making jam. Prue liked a challenge and had never let a setback stop her from achieving what she wanted. She knew exactly who to ask to start with.

~

'He said that?' Gloria's eyes grew wide. 'Well, 'e ain't got no idea what us women are capable of!'

Prue was at The Mother's Day Club the following morning and had just described her visit to the allotment. The mothers, most of whom were also members of Great Plumstead's Women's Institute, were indignant at what Percy had said they should stick to doing.

'We can get that plot cleared and ready for planting!' Nancy, who was billeted at Prue's house, declared. 'There's plenty of us to pitch in. We can do it between us and will show that fella just what we can do when we put our minds to it!'

'Hear, hear!' Marianne called out.

Prue looked around proudly at the women. Since their arrival in Great Plumstead as evacuee expectant mothers back in September 1939, or as bombed-out refugees from the London Blitz last autumn, they had become well integrated into village life and were firm friends.

'I hoped you'd think that. What Percy said took me by

surprise,' Prue admitted. 'And he cleared off before I had a chance to pull him up on it.'

'The best thing to do is show 'im that 'e's wrong, by doing it ourselves,' Annie declared. 'We don't need a man to do it for us!'

'Put your 'and up if you're willing to help clear the allotment.' Gloria held up her own hand and the other women in the room all followed, each one of them prepared to put in the work.

'Thank you.' Prue smiled gratefully. 'We will show him he's underestimated us. I'll ask at next week's WI meeting for other volunteers to join in too. Between us, we'll make it happen and, with hard work, our allotment will grow wonderful vegetables.'

'When do we start?' Nancy asked.

'How about on Saturday morning?' Prue suggested. 'It will give me time to organise some tools. I'll ask Victor to donate some from the shop.' It was the least he could do, she thought, having known what a terrible state the allotment was in. His hardware and seed merchant business in Wykeham could afford to give them some gardening tools to help them.

'I'll be there,' Gloria said.

'And me,' other women chorused.

'Excellent!' Prue beamed at them. 'We'll show the doubters what we are capable of.'

CHAPTER 6

Wednesday 12th March

As the train came to a halt alongside the platform in Norwich station, Flo stood up, checked her hat was on straight and then reached for her brown leather suitcase and Land Army greatcoat from the overhead luggage rack. After setting off early this morning, and having spent several long hours sitting on trains, she was glad to be here in Norfolk. Now all she needed to do was find the train which would take her out to Great Plumstead, and then she'd be on her last leg of her journey.

The platform was busy with people as she stepped on to it, and she made her way along towards the guard who stood at the far end of the train near the engine, which hissed and steamed like some great metal beast.

'Could you tell me which platform the train to Great Plumstead goes from, please?' she asked him.

He shook his head. 'There's none from here! You need to

go to City Station. All trains out to Great Plumstead go from there on the M&GN line.'

'But this is Norwich…?' Flo began, feeling confused.

'Yes, and we've got *two* stations, this one and City Station. If you want to go to Great Plumstead, then you need to go to City Station.'

'How far is that?'

'About half an hour walk. You can have a look at the castle and the cathedral as you go,' the guard said kindly.

'Thank you.' Flo gave him a smile and headed across the wide forecourt of the station towards the exit. The unexpected news that Norwich had *two* stations and she needed to transfer between them would mean that it would take longer to get to Great Plumstead than she'd thought. On the positive side, she could do with a walk after sitting on the train for so long.

Before she did anything, Flo decided she would buy a cup of tea from the mobile WVS canteen parked outside the station entrance.

Joining the end of the queue, she looked across the city rooftops, where she could see the spire of Norwich Cathedral soaring up into the clear sky. Its pale brown stone contrasted against the blue, and it was much taller than the cathedral back in Lancaster. Thinking of Lancaster sent a pang of longing darting through Flo. She missed her grandparents and being on familiar territory.

'What can I get you?' The WVS woman asked, interrupting Flo's thoughts.

'A cup of tea and a…' She scanned the food on offer, which was set out on trays to the side of the counter. Her stomach rumbled, reminding her it was a long time since she'd had breakfast. 'A spam roll, please.'

'There you are.' The WVS woman poured tea out of the

urn into a white cup and placed it on the counter. 'Help yourself to a spam roll,' she added as Flo handed over some money. 'They were freshly made this morning.'

Flo helped herself and moved out of the way, going to stand to the side of the canteen, cup of tea in one hand and the sandwich in the other, while the woman dealt with the next person in the queue. The hot tea and roll were warming and filling. By the time Flo had finished them, she felt ready for the walk to City station, wherever that was.

With no one else now waiting to be served, Flo placed her empty cup on the canteen counter. 'Can you give me directions to City Station please? I didn't know there were two stations in Norwich and have no idea where the other one is.'

'This your first time here then?' the woman asked.

'Yes, and it's my first job for the Land Army.'

'You should call in at the Land Army office on your way to City Station, introduce yourself so you know where it is if you need anything. It's above the Women's Institute Federation office at number three Castle Street.' The WVS woman leaned out of the hatch of the mobile canteen and pointed to where Flo could see a bridge. 'You need to cross the road there, go over the river, then walk up Prince of Wales Road towards the castle. You can't miss that. Once you get to the castle, ask someone to point you towards Castle Street. They'll be able to direct you to City Station from the Land Army offices. If I try to tell you all the way from here, you'll only end up in a muddle.'

Flo thought that sounded like a good plan. Finding the Land Army office could be useful in case she needed to go there in the future. 'Thank you, I'll do that.'

The woman gave her a warm smile. 'Good luck in your new job.'

Flo followed the directions, crossing over the river, then headed up the street towards the castle, which, as it came into sight, made her think of the one back home in Lancaster. Norwich's castle looked different to what she was used to. It sat on a high mound, a square building, topped with battlements which towered above the street. It's pale, sandy-coloured stone looked smooth and a complete contrast to the darker-grey mottled, rough stone of Lancaster's castle, but she liked it.

After asking for more directions, Flo found her way to 3 Castle Street and the Norfolk office of the Women's Land Army. Taking a deep breath, she opened the door and went in.

A woman with ash-blonde hair, fashioned into a roll around the nape of her neck, and cheery red lipstick looked up from the desk where she was working and gave her a welcoming smile. 'Good afternoon! How may I help you?'

Flo put her suitcase down and held out her hand to the woman, who she thought must be in her thirties. 'I'm Florence Butterworth... Flo. I've just arrived in Norwich on the way to my new position and thought I'd call in and say hello and ask for directions to City Station.'

'Welcome to Norfolk, Flo! I'm Lizzie Thornton, county secretary.' Lizzie stood up and shook Flo's hand. 'Why don't you sit down and tell me where you're heading to.' She indicated a chair between her desk and a filing cabinet.

Flo did as she was asked. 'To a Land Army hostel in Great Plumstead. I was told at the station where I arrived that trains only go there from *City Station*.'

'That's right.' Lizzie sat down behind her desk again. 'You must be heading to Rookery House.'

Flo nodded. 'Yes, do you know it?'

Lizzie laughed. 'I certainly do, but it's not a hostel. It's my sister Thea's house. You'll be working for her.'

Flo's stomach dropped. She hadn't expected that. 'Because it wasn't called a farm, I assumed it was a hostel for Land Army girls.' And she would have preferred that, Flo thought. Living in a hostel was more impersonal than staying in someone's house with a family. Flo didn't want to become involved with a family, not after what had happened.

'No, I suppose it's not a farm *officially*, but my sister recently bought more land to grow even more vegetables and needs help. That's where you come in.' Lizzie gave her a smile. 'Look, I'm heading out that way in a little while as I need to go to a farm on the other side of Wykeham, so I can take you to Great Plumstead on the way if you like. Then you won't have to bother with getting to City Station.'

'Thank you, I'd like that,' Flo accepted gratefully. 'It's very kind of you.'

'You're welcome. It will give me a chance to see Thea and catch up with the latest goings-on at Rookery House.'

Half an hour later, Flo was heading out of Norwich in Lizzie's Austin 7 car, thinking she'd been lucky to find a lift to her new billet.

'Tell me about yourself,' Lizzie said as she drove along. 'Where's home for you?'

'Lancaster,' Flo said. She didn't want to talk about her home that was no more in Manchester, or what had happened to her family there.

'You're a long way from home then.' Lizzie glanced at her. 'It must seem different around here, not so hilly. Although Norfolk isn't as flat as some people think it is, especially on the north coast. It's the fens which are flat. Anyway, I'm sure it feels odd, but I hope you'll soon get used to it and feel at home. Rookery House is a welcoming sort of place. Everyone who goes to stay there likes it.'

'Are there many people living there?' Flo asked.

'There's my sister, Thea, who owns Rookery House. Hettie, who was Cook at Great Plumstead Hall, and who's now retired. She was our mother's best friend and has always been like an aunt to us. She's a fabulous cook, so you can be sure of having lovely meals.' Lizzie changed gear and slowed as they approached a bend. 'Marianne's from London and she's got little Emily. Evie is a nurse at Great Plumstead Hall Hospital. My brother Reuben has a railway carriage house in the garden, and my niece Alice works in the garden with Thea, though she lives in the village with my other sister, Prue. Last year, Thea took in two refugee children from the London Blitz, to add to them all.' Lizzie gave a laugh. 'I realise that must sound like a lot! Most of them aren't blood related, but they still feel like family.'

Flo's heart squeezed. She missed her family so much, but she had made a promise to herself that she must keep going, start afresh, and try to put the past behind her. Her plan was to work hard to help bury the pain and grief. Flo forced a half-laugh. 'Is there room for me as well?'

Lizzie looked at Flo and grinned. 'Of course. Though you might have to share a bedroom.'

'That's all right. I had to sleep in a dormitory with all the other girls while I was doing my training.' And she'd always shared with her sister, Joyce, Flo thought and quickly pushed the memory aside.

'Where did you train?' Lizzie asked.

'Shipton Court in Shipton-under-Wychwood in Oxfordshire,' Flo explained. 'The head gardener there was good. He taught us a lot. Though I had some experience before I went there as I've worked on family allotments since I was little. I love growing things, that's why I asked to work in horticulture.'

'Then you sound like the perfect person to help Thea get her new acres into production. Speaking as County Secretary,' Lizzie said, in a more serious tone, 'if you have any problems let me know. That's what I tell every Land Girl we have in Norfolk. I'm always there to help.'

'Thank you. What's Great Plumstead like?'

'It's a typical village, everyone knowing each other. I grew up there, but I prefer to live in Norwich now. Suits me better.' Lizzie brought the car to a halt at a junction and checked the road was clear before turning the car to the right. 'But I enjoy visiting when I can. You'll find there's lots going on in the village if you want to get involved. I hope you will be happy there.'

CHAPTER 7

Thea smoothed out a wrinkle on the blue eiderdown covering the bed that she'd made up with fresh linen. Then she checked that everything was ready for Rookery House's newest resident who'd be arriving sometime this afternoon. Lizzie, Thea's youngest sister, had telephoned earlier to say that she was bringing the new Land Girl, rather than her coming on the train as expected.

'Is it ready?' Hettie's voice came from the open doorway. Thea turned around to see the older woman standing looking in at her.

'I think so. I'm glad Evie's happy to share her room, otherwise I don't know where we would have put the new Land Girl. Mind you, an extra bed in here means there's less space.' Thea rested her hand on the black iron bedstead of what would be the Land Girl's bed, looking at the gap between the two beds, where there was just enough room for a bedside table and a rag rug.

'It will be fine,' Hettie reassured her. 'Evie always keeps it nice and tidy, and she's made space in the drawers.' She gestured towards the chest of drawers that stood on the other side of the room to one side of the window. 'At least there are only two sharing in here. I was talking to Grace Barker in the shop the other day and her daughter, the one who's joined the WRAF, is sleeping in a Nissen hut with eleven other girls.' Hettie tutted. 'I'm looking forward to having another person in the house and getting to know them.'

Thea nodded. 'So am I and I definitely need more help.' She glanced out of the window, which looked over the back garden towards her new field in the distance, which was now ready for planting after Reuben had ploughed three quarters of it. He'd then harrowed it to smooth out the ridges created by the plough. There was a lot of work to be done and having another pair of hands to help her, along with Alice, would make a big difference.

'Although it's always a bit unsettling having someone new move in,' Thea admitted. 'What happens if they don't fit in or get on with everyone?'

'We've managed having new people here just fine so far,' Hettie said. 'We didn't know Marianne, Anna, Evie or George and Betty before they came to the village, and they all settled in well. There's no reason why the Land Girl shouldn't be the same.'

'I know. I hope she'll soon feel at home.'

'You've always said Rookery House should be filled with people,' Hettie reminded her.

'You're right, and it is!' Thea acknowledged. 'So much better to have the rooms occupied than to be rattling around in an empty house. Only at the rate we're going, it's almost bursting at the seams!'

'We'll manage whatever comes our way,' Hettie said sagely. 'It's no good fretting over what hasn't happened yet because it might not. Now if there's nothing else to be done in here, why don't you come down to the kitchen and read the letter that's just arrived for you in the afternoon post? It has a London postmark on it. Could be from Violet.'

Thea's spirits rose at the thought of a letter from her dear friend, Violet Steele. Violet was station officer at an ambulance station close to the Tower of London and the pair of them had become firm friends when they'd worked together as ambulance drivers during the Great War. They had kept in contact ever since.

Downstairs in the kitchen, Thea was delighted when she saw the letter lying waiting for her on the table as she recognised the handwriting at once – it *was* from Violet.

'Do you want a cup of tea?' Hettie asked.

'Please.' Thea sat at the table while Hettie busied herself making some tea.

Thea slit open the envelope, pulled out the letter and began to read it.

10th March 1941

Dear Thea,

I hope all is well with you and all those at Rookery House. It's been a difficult few days here at Station 75 (I'm writing this in the middle of the night, while all is quiet and thankfully there's been no air raid so far tonight – and I hope it will remain that way!) as we've had a stark reminder of how thin the line can be between surviving an air raid or not. I'm not sure if you have heard about the bombing of the Café de Paris two nights ago here in London. Well, Winnie, who you've met on a couple of occasions, was there with her brother, Harry.

Thea remembered Winnie from her visits to Station 75. She knew that Violet thought highly of the willowy, blonde-haired young woman with the pillar-box red lipstick and cheery manner. Winnie was a lovely person but her disregard for rules was something that often sorely tried Violet's patience. She read on.

He's a pilot in the RAF and was shot down last autumn and terribly burned, lucky to survive at all. The outing to the Café de Paris was a long-awaited evening out for them in what was supposed to be the safest restaurant in town some twenty feet below ground. Only it wasn't! They were dancing when the bomb went off and frankly, it was a miracle they survived when those within a short distance of them did not. Harry was knocked unconscious and has a broken arm and Winnie has some scratches and bruises but is otherwise unhurt. Although it's shaken her up badly.

I know we're living in a city under attack and Winnie and my other crew members take their lives in their hands every time they go out on call during an air raid. Unfortunately, we've lost a crew during raids, so understand how it can happen. Getting caught in such a horrific bombing in a place that was deemed safe and during a much longed for outing has made it far more shocking and harder to come to terms with. We came close to losing a valued and important member of our station that night.

But we'll get through it. We must. We will.

Thea could picture her friend squaring her shoulders. Violet would do what was necessary to support the ambulance station crew members who relied on her guidance. Being in charge of the station was a heavy burden for Violet, who had to make decisions under difficult circumstances. Thea did her best to bolster up her friend through her letters. She encouraged Violet to let off steam in those she sent back to Thea in a way that she never could do at work, having to always maintain a strong, calm presence as station officer.

Tell me how you're getting on with your new land. News of your life in the countryside is a welcome distraction and I treasure reading your letters.

With fondest love,
Your friend,

Violet.

Thea sighed as she put the letter down on the kitchen table. Hearing what her friend and others in London were going through was a reminder of how hard life was for so many people right now. Thea's concerns over the new addition to Rookery House were minor in comparison.

'Bad news?' Hettie's voice broke into her thoughts.

Thea explained about what had happened. 'Winnie and her brother were lucky to survive. It's really shaken them and the crew at Station 75. They're a close-knit bunch and Violet looks out for them like a mother hen.'

Hettie poured some tea from the cosy-covered teapot and pushed the cup across the table to Thea, before pouring one for herself and sitting down opposite her. 'This bloomin' war! When will it be over? How many more people will be hurt or killed before the end?'

Thea's eyes met the older woman's, which were glittering with tears behind her round glasses. 'I know.' She reached over and took hold of Hettie's hand and squeezed her fingers gently. 'We'll get through it together.'

Hettie sniffed and managed a smile. 'Course we will. We did the last one and we shall this one too!'

~

'That's Rookery House up ahead,' Lizzie said as they rounded a bend in the road, having driven through the centre of the village and out the other side.

Flo stared at the building standing on its own further down the lane, the upper storey visible above the hedgerow. The sight of her new home set butterflies dancing a jig inside her stomach.

'What do you think?' Lizzie asked as she slowed the car, turned in at the gateway and brought it to a halt.

Flo looked at the red brick Victorian house, with a bay window on either side of the front door. 'It looks nice.'

'My sister always loved this place, right from when she was a child. She dreamed about living here one day and bought it nearly two years ago. Dreams can sometimes come true!' Lizzie turned to Flo. 'Are you ready?'

Flo nodded.

'Good.' Lizzie patted Flo's arm. 'Now don't worry, you'll be fine here. Rookery House is a *much* better billet than some of the places our Land Girls live in, and I'm not just talking about the house, I mean the people who live in it too. I don't think you'll have any problems working for Thea, but if you do, you must come to me. It won't matter that she's my sister. I am there for *all* the Land Girls under my watch.'

'Thank you.' Flo managed a smile. 'I'm sure I will be fine here.'

After collecting her suitcase and great coat from the back of the car, Flo followed Lizzie around to the rear of the house, taking in the extensive garden with a greenhouse, sheds and a barn, as well as large vegetable plots. Over to one side she noticed there was a single-storey building with a veranda built around it.

Lizzie noticed Flo staring at the building. 'That's my brother Reuben's railway carriage house, the one I told you also lives here. It's cosy in there. Anyway, we always go in this way,' Lizzie explained as they headed for a door at the back of the house.

Before they reached the door, it was opened from the inside by a woman with brown curly hair, cut into a bob, around which was tied a red and white spotted scarf. She gave a wide, welcoming smile. 'Hello.'

'Flo, this is my sister, Thea Thornton,' Lizzie introduced her. 'Thea, this is Flo Butterworth, your new Land Girl.'

'Welcome to Rookery House!' Thea stepped forward and held out her hand to Flo. 'We're delighted to have you come and work with us.'

'Thank you.' Flo shook her hand. She could see the resemblance between Lizzie and Thea. Their hair might be different, but they shared the same shade of blue eyes – the colour of bluebells – and had a similar-shaped nose and mouth.

'Is the kettle on? I'd love a cup of tea?' Lizzie said, heading indoors.

'You're in luck. We've just made a pot. After you...' Thea gestured for Flo to go inside.

Stepping into the kitchen, Flo was struck by the warm, homely feel. It wasn't only the heat that came from the range standing at one end of the room, which was sunk into the chimney breast. It had a strong sense of a family home.

'Hello, my dear,' an older woman with curly grey hair and round glasses, behind which her blue eyes twinkled, greeted

Flo, coming across the kitchen to meet her. She held out her hand. 'I'm Hettie.'

'I'm Florence Butterworth, Flo.' She shook Hettie's hand.

'Come and sit down and have some tea.' Hettie ushered Flo towards the large, scrubbed wooden table that stood in the middle of the kitchen, where Lizzie was already sitting.

'Would you like some cake?' Hettie asked.

'Yes please,' Lizzie said. 'Remember I told you that Hettie was Cook at Great Plumstead Hall, Flo? Anything she cooks is always delicious.'

Flo put her suitcase down, took off her coat and hung it over the back of a chair before sitting down at the table opposite Lizzie.

'I can second that,' Thea said, putting two cups and some small plates on the table that she'd taken from one of the dressers lining the wall.

'What sort of cake is it, Hettie?' Lizzie asked.

'An apple one, made with some apples I dried from last autumn's harvest,' Hettie said. 'I'll just fetch it from the pantry.' She went through a door at the far side of the room and came back a few moments later with a large tin. She cut generous slices from the cake inside it and put them on the small plates.

'Help yourself to milk.' Thea poured out two cups of tea from the teapot, which, Flo saw, was covered with a colourful knitted tea cosy rather like the one her grandma had.

Lizzie handed a cup to Flo and took the other for herself. 'Are you trained to milk cows?' she asked as she added some creamy-looking milk from the flower-patterned jug to her tea and stirred it in.

Flo's stomach lurched. 'No, my training was for horticulture. I've never milked a cow in my life! I thought they sent me here to help grow vegetables and fruit!'

'And you will be, don't worry!' Thea threw Lizzie a look. 'We have a house cow, who's milked by hand, and you can learn how to do it if you'd like to, but if you don't want to, that's fine,' Thea reassured Flo. 'You'll be helping with growing fruit and veg, just as you thought. I've recently bought some more land, so we're expanding what we grow and need more help to do that.' She gave Flo a warm smile. 'We're pleased to have you come and join us here at Rookery House.'

Flo returned her smile. 'Thank you.'

'Here you go.' Hettie placed a slice of cake in front of Flo before sitting down next to her, with a slice for herself. 'Where are you from? You don't sound like you're from round here.'

Flo laughed. 'No, I'm not.' She knew that her accent must sound very different to theirs. She was already enjoying how they stretched out their vowels, adding an 'r' to 'last' so it sounded like 'larst'. 'I'm from Lancashire,' she said, a little self-consciously. 'My relatives are in Lancaster.'

'You're a long way from home.' Hettie put her hand on Flo's arm. 'You must write and let them know where you are now, so they won't worry. Tell them we'll look after you.'

Flo's chest tightened, and she squeezed her hand into a fist under the table, holding back the sudden tears that threatened. She didn't want to explain what had happened, that her immediate family was gone and no longer around to worry. She was grateful to still have her grandparents and knew they'd be waiting to hear from her to know she was here and safe. 'I will. I'll write to them tonight.'

'This cake is delicious,' Lizzie said. 'I'm glad to say that rationing hasn't had a detrimental effect on your cooking, Hettie!'

'It hasn't hit us so hard as most people, not with us having eggs from our hens, making butter from the milk and honey from the bees. We can produce a lot more of our food here, and that makes a huge difference,' Hettie acknowledged.

Flo took a bite of her cake and agreed with Lizzie. It was delicious, the apple complemented with a touch of cinnamon. As she savoured the mouthful, she gazed around the room, taking in the red quarry tiled floor with its colourful rag rugs, and the pretty yellow curtains patterned with blue flowers that hung at the window above the stone sink. The two dressers that stood against the wall displayed fresh looking blue and white cups and plates.

'Where are you off to next?' Thea asked Lizzie.

Lizzie put down her cup, having just taken a sip of tea. 'Home Farm in Barham. The Land Girls are having trouble with their billet. I need to sort it out. I...' She paused at the sound of running feet outside and, seconds later, the kitchen door burst open.

'Is she here yet?' a boy called as he rushed in, closely followed by a slightly older girl.

Flo had to stop herself from gasping at the sight of the little boy who made her think of Bobby. They had the same colour hair and were about the same age. But this wasn't her brother, Flo chided herself. Although living in a house with a child who reminded her of Bobby and his loss would not be easy. Not for the first time that day, she wished they had sent her to live in a more impersonal Land Army hostel than with a family.

A woman with shoulder-length curly brown hair had come in behind, holding the hand of a much smaller child who was toddling along beside her. The boy had halted as his eyes fell on Flo. He came over shy and dashed across to stand beside Thea.

Thea put her arm around the boy. 'This is our new Land Girl, Flo. Flo, this is George and Betty, who've been evacuated from London, and Marianne and her daughter, Emily.' Thea gestured to each of them as she made the introductions.

'Hello!' Marianne came over and held out her hand to Flo, smiling warmly. 'Welcome, I hope you'll be happy here.'

Flo returned her smile as she shook her hand. 'Thank you.'

'I'm just going upstairs to change Emily. I won't be long.' Marianne picked up her daughter and headed through a door at the far end of the kitchen.

'Are you from London?' Betty said, coming to stand by Flo and staring at her.

'No, I've never been there. I'm from the north, from Lancaster,' Flo explained.

'I ain't never 'eard of Lancaster.' Betty pulled out the chair next to Flo and sat down.

'It's on the other side of the country to here,' Flo told her.

Betty looked Flo up and down. 'I like your clothes and your 'at. I ain't seen any like them before.'

Flo laughed. 'It's my Land Army uniform, part of it anyway.' She loved her uniform, from the brown corduroy breeches and green pullover she was wearing now, to her bib and brace overalls and thick greatcoat and hat. Wearing them made her feel proud to be helping the war effort.

'Perhaps Flo will tell you more about where she lived another time,' Hettie said, putting a cup of milk and a plate with a slice of cake on it in front of Betty. 'You need to have something to eat and drink now as you'll be hungry after a day at school.'

Hettie gave the same to George, who was now sitting on Thea's lap, and he tucked in. Flo was aware that the little boy was watching her as he ate, and she did her best to avoid looking at him. The sight of him was too unsettling and the last thing she needed.

'Right, I'd better go,' Lizzie said, getting to her feet.

'Thank you for the tea and cake. It was lovely.' She looked at Flo. 'If there's anything you need, just get in touch, won't you?'

Flo nodded. 'I will and thank you for bringing me here.'

'My pleasure. I'm off to sort out this billeting mess in Barham.' She headed towards the door and then stopped and turned back. 'I don't suppose you've got room for any more Land Girls, have you, Thea, even if they don't work for you?'

'No, we've no spare room any more,' Thea said. 'Sorry.'

Lizzie laughed. 'Oh well, it was worth a try. I'll see you all again soon.'

After they'd said their goodbyes and Lizzie had gone, Flo felt strangely alone and adrift to be in this house, nice as it was, but with people she didn't know. This was her new home for the time being, the place she would work, but it felt odd to be here. A knot had tied itself around her stomach. Being on her month's training had been different. Then, lots of new people had all been thrown together. They were all in the same boat. Here, everyone was familiar with each other, and *she* was the stranger among them. It was going to take some getting used to, but she must if she was to succeed as a Land Girl.

'Shall I show you to your room?' Thea's voice broke into Flo's thoughts.

Flo nodded. 'Yes, thank you.'

'Can I come?' Betty asked.

'You stop here and finish your cake and milk,' Hettie said firmly. 'You can help show Flo around outside in a little while, all right?'

Betty nodded, took a large bite, and chewed it, watching Flo as she got up and picked up her suitcase and took her coat from the back of the chair.

'Thank you for the cake and tea, Hettie,' Flo said and then

followed Thea out through the doorway which Marianne had gone through earlier.

It led into a hallway which ran the length of the house and from which the stairs rose up. At the far end, the front door had a pane of colourful stained glass and the floor was covered with a chequered pattern of black and white tiles.

Thea pointed to an open doorway. 'That's the sitting room.'

Flo looked in and liked what she saw. The room had French doors at one end and a bay window at the other.

'There's a dining room at the other end of the hall,' Thea told her, gesturing to a door to the right of the front door. 'We always eat in the kitchen, so Marianne uses it for her sewing. It's somewhere we can put up temporary visitors too. You're going to be sharing a bedroom with Evie,' Thea explained as she climbed the stairs. 'She's a nurse at Great Plumstead Hall Hospital and works long hours there. She won't be home till tonight, so you'll meet her then.'

Flo followed Thea up the stairs. 'Is Evie one of your family?'

'She's not a relation, but she is part of our Rookery House family.' Thea halted on the landing and turned to face Flo. 'None of us, except for Reuben and I, are related here, but that doesn't matter. I hope you'll come to think of us as a sort of family away from home too in time. We all look out for each other.'

Flo nodded and did her best to smile. She wasn't looking for another family. She hadn't come to terms with losing the one she'd had and wasn't in need of a new one. 'Where did Evie come from?'

'From London. Marianne did too. She was evacuated here as an expectant mother at the start of the war, and Evie came here last autumn. We've also had Anna. She's a Jewish German refugee. Though she's teaching at a boarding school in

Wiltshire at the moment. She comes home when she can. Don't worry, you'll soon get to know who's who.' Thea gave her an understanding smile. 'Right, this is my room,' she pointed to a doorway to the left at the front of the house. 'And Hettie is in here.' She gestured to the door opposite, then led the way along the landing, pointing out rooms as they went. 'Marianne and Emily are in here, George and Betty are in this one, and this is yours and Evie's bedroom.'

Thea opened the door and stepped back for Flo to go in.

Flo went inside and liked what she saw. There were two beds with a bedside cabinet between them, a chest of drawers and a bookcase packed with books. The room was tidy and smelled of lavender and beeswax polish. The window looked out over the back garden. She turned to Thea, who stood in the doorway, and smiled at her. 'It's lovely, thank you.'

Thea stepped into the room. 'That's your bed nearest the window. Evie has emptied half the drawers for you.' She pulled out an empty drawer to show her.

'I'm sure that will be enough room for my things. I don't have that much stuff.' Flo held up her suitcase, which contained more of her uniform and the few other items of clothes she had. She'd lost everything except for what she'd been wearing in the bombing. Her gran had helped her replace a few necessary things when she was in Lancaster but she'd still been grateful to be given her Land Army uniform.

'I'll leave you to settle in and will show you the rest of the house later. The bathroom's downstairs. You get to it through the kitchen and scullery. We don't have electricity or gas here so it's oil lamps and candles after dark. I'll give you a guided tour outside before it gets dark, too. I must go and do the milking now. If there's anything else you need, let me know. It's good to have you come to help and I hope you'll be happy living here with us all.'

'Thank you.' Flo gave her a smile. 'I'm looking forward to starting work.'

'That's good to hear – there's lots to do. I'll see you later.'

Left on her own, Flo sat on the bed and sighed. Everyone she'd met here was kind and lovely, so why did she have this awful knot squeezing her stomach so tight? She had her job as a Land Girl and would be doing the sort of work she loved. That wasn't the problem. No, it was the thought of living here with people who were as good as a family to each other that upset her. It scared Flo. She didn't know how she'd cope with that. It made her miss her own family even more, stabbed at her grief. But what choice did she have? The Women's Land Army wouldn't be impressed if she didn't try. The best thing to do was focus on her job, Flo resolved. Do what she was here to do. Work hard, keep busy and tire herself out so that she slept at night. Flo would be polite but must maintain her distance. It was the only way to keep the pain of her grief in check.

CHAPTER 8

Thursday 13th March

A sudden clanging bell broke into Flo's dream, and she woke with a start trying to work out where she was. Then she remembered. She was here in Norfolk, at Rookery House, and the ringing was from Evie's alarm clock. Aware of Evie getting out of her own bed, Flo turned over to face her.

'Morning,' Flo said.

'Good morning, I'm sorry if my alarm woke you. It's a nuisance having to wake up so early,' Evie spoke in a hushed voice.

'Don't worry, it's fine,' Flo reassured her. Evie had been most apologetic last night when she'd warned Flo that she had to be up at twenty past six to give her enough time to get herself ready and have breakfast before leaving to start her shift at the hospital. 'I'll get out of bed soon but will wait until after you've dressed and gone downstairs – otherwise we'll be getting in each other's way.'

'Do you mind if I open the blackout curtain to let a bit of daylight in?' Evie asked. 'Then I won't have to light the candle.'

'Not at all.'

Flo snuggled down in her warm bed and closed her eyes while Evie opened the blackout and dressed in her nurse's uniform, which hung on the back of the door. Flo had been surprised when she'd met Evie last night after she'd returned from her shift at the hospital. Evie clearly came from a wealthy background going by her plummy accent and yet she was working as a VAD nurse. Nursing was hard work and involved unpleasant tasks that Flo wouldn't expect a young upper-class woman would want to do. Evie seemed like a lovely, caring person and sounded dedicated to her work. She had made Flo feel welcome and didn't appear to mind having to share her room.

'I'll see you downstairs,' Evie said before going out of their bedroom, closing the door quietly behind her.

Left on her own, Flo lay in bed for a few more minutes, thinking over the day ahead. She was keen to get started on her work. Thea and the children had given Flo a tour around the grounds before it got dark yesterday, and she'd liked what she'd seen. There were large vegetable beds, an orchard with beehives and chickens, a meadow where Primrose the cow grazed and the new five-acre field which had prompted Thea to employ a Land Girl. Thea had also told her about her plan to raise rabbits and pigs for meat. It was exciting to be part of expanding what they already did here.

Flo threw back her covers, ready to get dressed and start her day.

A few minutes later, Flo headed downstairs wearing her uniform. She had chosen her bib and braces dungarees as they were comfortable to work in and she wasn't yet sure what she'd be doing today. In the kitchen, Hettie and Evie were sitting at the table, eating their breakfast.

'Good morning,' Hettie greeted Flo. 'Would you like some porridge?'

'Soon, please, I'm going to the bathroom first and then I'll join you.' Flo made her way into the scullery, which was in the single-storey annexe off the kitchen, and then through into the bathroom, which Thea had explained she'd had put in after moving into the house. Otherwise, they'd have had to go outdoors to use the outside toilet.

When Flo returned to the kitchen a short while later, Hettie went to get up from her place.

'Please don't disturb your breakfast,' Flo told her. 'I can help myself.'

'The porridge is keeping warm on the range,' Hettie said. 'I'll pour you out a cup of tea.'

Joining Hettie and Evie at the table with a bowl of thick, creamy porridge, Flo followed their lead and added a spoonful of honey and tucked into it.

'Did you sleep well?' the older woman asked.

Flo nodded. 'I did, thank you. Though when I woke up, I wasn't sure where I was to start with.'

'My alarm clock startling you awake probably didn't help,' Evie said apologetically.

'Don't worry about that,' Flo reassured Evie. She noticed how her roommate had pinned her beautiful long, auburn hair up into a bun after wearing it in a long plait at night. 'As the days get longer, we'll want to make the most of the light to work earlier, anyway.'

'I can't sleep any later than six,' Hettie said as she scooped up a spoonful of porridge. 'After so many years of having to rise early working at the Hall it's become too much of a habit to change. But I enjoy having a slower start to the day now, everyone gradually getting up and coming down, and making sure they've had a nutritious breakfast inside them.'

Evie laughed. 'Dear Hettie feeds us so well. You are lucky to come to Rookery House. It was a fortunate day when I was billeted here.' Evie glanced at the clock on one of the dressers. 'I must get a move on or I'll be late and Matron Reed will be on the warpath.' She got up from her place and put her empty bowl and cup in the sink, before heading upstairs again.

'What are you going to be doing today?' Hettie asked Flo, as she poured herself another cup of tea from the large brown teapot with its colourful tea cosy.

'I'm not sure yet, but I'm very much looking forward to getting started.'

'We're delighted to have you here. You working alongside Thea and Alice will make a big difference.' Hettie reached over and patted Flo's arm. 'It's good to have another person in the house, too. You're most welcome.'

Flo smiled at the older woman. 'Thank you.'

By the time Alice arrived at eight o'clock, Thea had come downstairs with George and Betty and was closely followed by Marianne and Emily. Hettie had been busy getting everyone fed and ready to start the day. While Marianne took the children off to the bathroom to wash their hands and faces, Thea grabbed the opportunity to speak to Flo and Alice, who'd joined them at the table for a cup of tea, about what the plans were for the day's work.

'I'm out with the WVS canteen this morning, so will have to leave you two to get on,' Thea said. 'It's bad timing on your first day here, Flo. I'm sorry it's worked out like that, but they draw up the rota for the canteen several weeks in advance and I can't pull out when servicemen and women rely on us,' Thea explained, apologetically. 'But I'll be back as soon as I can this afternoon.'

'Don't worry, I'm sure we'll be fine.' Flo looked at Alice, who nodded in agreement.

'What do you want us to do?' Alice asked.

'Plant the early potatoes in the part of Five Acres that we marked out yesterday. You know where it is, Alice. The potato chits are in the greenhouse and ready to go in. Just make sure you use the row markers to plant them in a straight line. Have you set potatoes before, Flo?'

Flo nodded. 'Plenty of times.'

'Excellent.' Thea stood up. 'I need to get ready and put my WVS uniform on, then head off to Wykeham to pick up the canteen.'

'Is Prue working with you today?' Hettie asked.

'Yes, I'm meeting her at the station. I'll see you both later.' She smiled at Flo and Alice and then added, 'If you get all the potatoes planted, then you can sow some broad beans and peas in the greenhouse.'

'How are you settling in?' Alice asked as she pushed a wheelbarrow filled with the boxes of chitted potatoes towards the five-acre field.

'Good so far, though I've only been here since yesterday,' Flo said pushing another wheelbarrow holding the tools they'd need, along with more boxes of potatoes to plant. 'Rookery House is lovely, and everyone's been friendly.'

'They are, but I supposed I'm biased with Thea being my aunt. Everyone who's come to live here has been happy. I love working here.'

'How long have you worked for your aunt?' Flo asked.

'Since last summer. I started helping here after I left school, while Anna was interred.'

'Interred?'

'Yes, Anna was taken into custody because she's German and was put in Holloway Prison in London and then ended up in a camp on the Isle of Man. She hadn't done anything wrong! She is a Jewish refugee who'd fled from Germany, not a spy.'

'Poor Anna, that must have been awful.'

'It was. Thea needed help because Anna worked in the garden and with her gone, there was so much to do,' Alice explained as they pushed their barrows through the gateway and towards the area in the field where they'd be planting. 'When Anna was eventually released last September, she came back here to work again, but was then offered a job in a school as she's a teacher. Thea asked me if I'd like to take over Anna's job for as long as I wanted it and I've been here ever since.'

'What persuaded the authorities to let Anna go? Flo asked.

'Thea helped to get her released, but it took a while. Before Anna came here to work for Thea, it was my brother Edwin's job. He's a conscientious objector. He left to join the Friends Ambulance Unit and now works in the East End of London in a hospital and out doing first aid in air raids as well. And now you've come to help! This is where we need to plant the potatoes.' Alice parked her wheelbarrow beside an area marked out with thick sticks pushed into the ground.

Flo positioned her wheelbarrow next to Alice's. 'What about you? Are you planning on moving on to another job sometime?'

'Perhaps at some point, but I'm not sure what I'd do though. I would like to see other places and if I joined one of the women's services, it would be a way of doing just that while helping with the war effort.'

'You've got time to decide; I don't think the war will be over for a while yet.' Flo took the row marker tool out of her barrow and handed one of the wooden ends to Alice. 'If you stick that in at this end, I'll go down the other end and mark out a line.' Flo strode off to the far end of the area that had been marked out for the early potatoes, unravelling the string from around her wooden marker as she went. Reaching the end, she pushed it into the soil, creating a long line which they could use to guide themselves along as they planted.

Flo headed back to where the wheelbarrows stood and took a box of chitted potatoes and a hand trowel, the same as Alice. Then the pair of them got to work, one working on each side of the string line. First making a small hole in the soil with the trowel, gently putting a potato in taking care to keep the green shoots uppermost, then covering them up before moving on and repeating the process over and over.

'What did you do before you joined the Land Army?' Alice asked.

'I worked in an office. It was very boring,' Flo said, glossing over what had happened to that job. 'I decided I'd much rather work doing something I enjoyed, and here I am.'

'Though working in an office probably didn't give you backache,' Alice said, straightening up and rubbing her back.

Flo laughed. 'No, it didn't, but I wouldn't swap this for being back typing letters all day long.' She popped a potato in the hole she'd just made, thinking there was no comparison with how bored and frustrated she'd felt stuck indoors all day. She would rather be out here working in the fresh air, even if it made her muscles ache sometimes.

CHAPTER 9

Saturday 15th March

'Victor's been *most* generous!' Nancy eyed the wheelbarrow filled with gardening tools which Prue was pushing towards the WI allotment on Saturday morning.

Prue snorted. 'And so he should be after giving us the *worst* allotment on the site!' She glanced at Nancy, whose two daughters, eight-year-old Marie, and seven-year-old Joan, were skipping along ahead of them, hand in hand. 'It also gives him a chance to crow at his various committee meetings about how he's helping good causes. It's all for show, Nancy, nothing more.'

'He won't be coming to actually help us do any work on the allotment, then?' Nancy asked.

Prue barked out a laugh. 'Definitely not!' Victor didn't like getting his hands dirty. He preferred to give orders for others to do the work. 'I wouldn't want him anywhere near our allotment. He would only put a damper on things. It might be hard work, but I hope we'll still have fun and enjoy ourselves.'

They weren't the first ones to arrive at the WI's overgrown plot. A group of eight women from The Mother's Day Club had already turned up and stood chatting, their prams lined up with their infants inside. Children who were sitting up wore the security harnesses to stop them from falling out and each one was warmly dressed and wrapped in blankets but looking around bright-eyed. A few were lying down, tucked under covers, and having a nap. The sight of all the women and their children was causing a stir among the other allotment holders. Many of them had gathered at the ends of their plots next to the path that ran through the middle and were eagerly watching what was going on.

Prue spotted Percy Blake, who was puffing on his pipe, an amused expression on his face, his scruffy terrier sitting at his feet. 'Good morning, Percy,' she said brightly.

'Mornin' missus.' He nodded to her.

'If you've nothing planned, you're welcome to come and join us.' She gestured to the waiting group of women who'd spotted her and Nancy and were waving at them, calling out greetings.

Percy's face blanched. 'No, no, I've got taters to plant.' He turned and strode off towards his shed at the far end of his allotment. His dog looked at Prue, its eyebrows waggling, and then followed its master.

A chortle of laughter came from two other men who stood side by side on a nearby plot.

Prue smiled sweetly at them and called out, 'You'd be welcome to come and join us, too.'

They mumbled something she couldn't make out and shot off to do some work on their own allotments.

'The natives ain't very welcoming!' Nancy commented.

'Remember what Percy said to me the other day when I first came here? About how we should stick to making jam?' Prue reminded her. 'He and no doubt the other men here don't think much of us having this allotment or rate our chances of being successful in growing things. But we'll prove them wrong!'

Nancy grinned. 'We certainly will. They ain't going to recognise our patch when we're done.'

'Good morning!' Prue greeted the gathered women as she and Nancy reached the WI allotment. 'Thank you all for coming. It appears that our presence has caused quite a stir.' She nodded her head towards Percy and the other allotment holders.

'You can say that again!' Gloria raised her eyebrows. 'They've been watching us from the minute we got here.'

'They ain't used to such colourful folk around 'ere as you, Gloria,' Annie, one of the mothers, said.

'They could do with a bit of brightening up!' Gloria put a hand on her hip, the violet colour of her dress showing below her coat standing out against the duller shades of the soil and stems. 'If I get 'ot and need to take off my coat, then they'll see my colourful outfit in all its glory. Though I've 'ad to make some adjustments to my usual wardrobe. Working on an allotment ain't no place for my 'igh heels.' Gloria stuck out her foot, which was encased in a rubber wellington boot. 'Don't look nowhere near as nice but needs must!'

'You're showing true dedication indeed.' Prue gave Gloria an appreciative smile. Turning to face the group of women, she addressed them all. 'As you can see, our allotment is in rather a wild and unkempt state. It looks like nothing has been done to it for some time. The best thing to do is clear back the brambles to start with. Then we can dig out the roots and work our way across the plot, digging it over and getting rid of nettles, docks, dandelions and so on. We've got a good supply of well-rotted compost, but we'll leave that where it is for now until we're ready to dig it in. Help yourself to tools from the wheelbarrow and be careful how you work. Watch out for thorns on the brambles and stings from the nettles.'

'Where shall we put the stuff we cut down?' Nancy asked.

'If we pile it up over there but not right next to the hedge,' Prue pointed to the end of the plot, 'then we can have a bonfire.'

The women got to work with great enthusiasm. As Prue tackled some brambles, hacking the plant down at the base with a pair of shears, she listened to the chatter that went on around her. Gloria soon began to sing, her beautiful voice soaring across the allotment, and the others joined in as they worked.

Prue noticed their activities had once again attracted the attention of the older male allotment holders. Many of them had found a job to do on their own patch where they could watch from. She smiled to herself, thinking they had probably never seen anything like this on the allotments before. If their collective attitude was anything like Percy Blake's, who thought the WI women should stick to making jam, then they needed a thorough shaking up.

By the time the women stopped for a drink before they went home, they'd made excellent progress. They had cut the brambles back and raked them into a pile to make a bonfire, which now made it easier to move around the plot. They had also begun to tackle digging out the invasive plants, surprised at the butter-yellow nettle roots and how deep the bramble roots went down.

'We've got off to a marvellous start, thank you everyone.' Prue beamed at the women whose cheeks were glowing from the hard work. 'It looks so different already and the soil is good.' She poked at it with the toe of her boot. 'We should get bumper crops from here.'

'I enjoyed myself. I ain't done anything like this before but it's very satisfying,' said Gloria. She'd taken off her coat and her violet dress glowed in the warm sunlight making her look like an exotic flower.

'My girls 'ave enjoyed themselves too,' Nancy added, nodding to where Joan and Marie were still excavating a network of yellow nettle roots.

'If the weather's fine, I'd like to have another session here in the week during a Mother's Day Club meeting,' Prue said. 'I think with so many of us working on it we might be able to clear out the rest of the roots and foul grass in a couple more work parties. Then we can get digging and adding compost, so we'll be ready to sow seeds when the weather is right. We also need to tackle clearing out and cleaning the shed too.'

'I'll help,' Nancy said.

'And me,' Gloria added.

The other women agreed.

'Splendid. Thank you...' Prue began, but halted as she spotted Percy Blake and the two men who'd laughed at them earlier approaching.

'You giving up already?' Percy asked.

'Not at all,' Prue retorted. 'We're finished for today, but we will be back in the week to carry on. We've made good progress.'

'You looked like a lot of old hens scrapping about on there,' Percy mocked and the two men standing behind him guffawed.

Prue glared at him and was about to respond, but Gloria got in first.

Puffing herself up, Gloria took a step towards Percy, her hands on her ample hips. 'We looked like 'ens did we? Well, you should remember that 'ens 'ave sharp beaks, so you'd best watch what you say!'

Percy stepped back, his cheeks flushing. 'I didn't mean no harm. Hens do a good job turning over the ground.'

Gloria narrowed her eyes and looked him up and down. 'I think you owe these wonderful, hard-working ladies an apology.'

'I'm sorry I didn't mean no offence,' Percy stammered. 'You took on the worse allotment of the lot.'

'It's the one the parish council *gave* us,' Prue said. 'But we're not letting that stop us. We can turn it around, as you can see.' She gestured at the cleared plot. 'It's best not to underestimate what women are capable of, Mr Blake.'

Percy nodded. 'We'll let you get on.' He touched the rim of his hat, his fellow allotment holders followed suit and the three of them turned and hurried off back to their own plots.

'That told 'em.' Gloria said and burst into laughter.

The rest of the women joined in. Laughing alongside them, Prue thought what a strong team they made. Individually, they were all fine, hard-working women, but together they were amazing!

CHAPTER 10

Saturday 22nd March

'The rabbits are 'ere! The rabbits are 'ere!' George shouted as he came running around the house at full pelt to where Thea and Flo were sowing seeds in the greenhouse in the March sunshine.

'Auntie Thea, they're 'ere!' The little boy's face was alight with joy as he skidded to a halt by the greenhouse door. 'Come on! Come and see them.'

Thea smiled at George. He'd been waiting at the front of the house with his sister, watching out for Reuben to arrive. Since he'd got up this morning, George had been bursting with excitement about the new arrivals to Rookery House and had helped get everything ready for them in the hutches and runs which Reuben had made for them.

George stepped into the greenhouse and grabbed Thea's hand. 'Please come and see them. Both of you.'

Thea turned to Flo, who was gazing at the little boy, a look of sadness on her face. 'Flo? Are you all right?'

The young woman turned her gaze to Thea, her expression quickly returning to normal. 'Yes, I'm fine. You go with George. I'll carry on here.'

'No, you come too. You've said you've kept rabbits before so I'm hoping you'll be able to help look after them,' Thea said. 'We can come back to this later.'

Flo dusted the soil off her hands and nodded. 'Let's go then.'

With George holding on tightly to Thea's hand, he led her out of the greenhouse and they met Reuben and Betty coming the other way. Reuben was carrying two wooden crates in his arms and the little girl was skipping along beside him, a beaming smile on her face.

'Come and see the rabbits, Auntie Thea and Flo,' Betty called.

'The hutches and runs are ready and have been since half past seven this morning. George and Betty were eager to get everything sorted out,' Thea said to Reuben, her eyes meeting his.

His blue eyes crinkled with amusement. 'That's good to hear. The rabbits will be glad to run free again after being stuck in these crates.'

Reaching the hutches, with their runs which could be moved around the garden providing fresh food for the rabbits to feed on, and a grass-cutting service at the same time, Reuben put the crates down gently on the ground.

'Now,' he said in a hushed voice, addressing George and Betty, who'd crouched down near the crates peering in through the gaps between the wooden bars. 'You need to keep quiet and calm. The rabbits will be scared and don't understand what's happening or where they are.' George and Betty nodded, their eyes wide.

Slowly and carefully, Reuben opened the lid of a crate and lifted out a large brown rabbit, holding it securely in his arms. 'This is the buck, the daddy,' he explained. 'You can stroke him gently.'

Both children reached out their hands and, with the greatest of care, stroked the rabbit's back. He seemed calm, his nose quivering and whiskers twitching as he sniffed the air.

'He's ever so soft,' George whispered, his face rapt with delight.

'Let's get him settled into the hutch and he can get to know his new home.' Reuben stood up and carried the rabbit over to one of the hutches and put him inside, then Flo quickly attached the run to it so he couldn't escape.

Reuben lifted out the other rabbit, who was white with brown splotches on her back and had brown ears and nose. 'This is the doe, the mummy, and she's going to have babies in a few weeks' time,' Reuben explained as the children gently stroked her fur.

'How many baby rabbits?' Betty whispered.

'We'll have to wait and see.' Thea bent down to stroke the doe. 'Her babies won't be staying with us for ever though – just until they're grown up and ready to leave.'

'Where will they go?' George asked.

Thea's eyes met Reuben's and he raised his eyebrows.

'They will go for food, for meat. Remember I told you that's why we're having them here.' Thea regarded the children who she'd already talked to about what would happen to some of the rabbits in a few months' time. It was important that they understood from the start that the babies wouldn't be staying on. It was a harsh thought, but best to be clear about it from the beginning.

George nodded. 'But before then we can 'elp look after them?'

Thea smiled at him. 'Of course, I hope you will help a lot. You'll need to gather food for them and clean them out.'

'I will.' His face was serious. 'I want to.'

'So do I,' Betty added.

'Good, now we'd better get our mummy rabbit in her new home.' Thea stood up.

After Reuben had carefully put the doe in her hutch and attached the run, they stepped back to watch. It wasn't long before she was outside, chewing on the grass, like the buck rabbit was already doing over in his run.

'Looks as if they're settling in well,' Reuben said. 'What are you going to call them?'

'Can we call the daddy Benjamin?' George asked.

'And the mummy rabbit Flopsy,' Betty suggested. 'Like in the book.'

'Those are perfect names for them.' Thea put her arms around the children who stood watching the rabbits, knowing how much they liked the Beatrix Potter books with her rabbit characters, which she often read to them.

'Is this one all right?' George asked, holding up a long, pointed leaf with parallel veins running through it.

'Yes, can you remember what it's called?' Flo asked.

'Plan...tain.' George's face was serious, looking up at her.

Flo gave him a warm smile. 'Excellent! You're learning fast. Let's add some more plantain to the sack. Rabbits love it.'

Flo and George were out foraging for fresh food for the rabbits along the hedgerow on the lane near Rookery House. Now spring was here, the warmer weather was making vegetation shoot up, painting the countryside in growing greenery. Flo was teaching George how to identify different plants which the rabbits would enjoy, taking the time to show him the various leaf shapes so that he could learn what to look for, along with each plant's name. It reminded her of her grandfather showing her how to do the same and what to look for, as he'd kept rabbits on his allotment in Lancaster where she'd helped him forage for them.

Now she was here with George, who was taking his rabbit keeping seriously and had wanted to come with Flo this morning. She couldn't spoil the little boy's enthusiasm by refusing, but spending time with him was difficult. He was a lovely child – happy, kind and gentle – but he reminded her of Bobby and that made it hard for her to be with him. Because of that, she reasoned, it was best to keep her distance from him. However, that was sometimes impossible. When Thea had asked her to take George foraging with her Flo couldn't say no, as her boss would have wanted to know why.

'Is this a dandelion?' George asked, holding up another leaf. 'It's got the pointy edges like you said. *The teeth of a lion*, you said.' He ran a finger along the bumpy leaf edge.

'It certainly is. Pop it in the sack. You're getting good at recognising the plants,' Flo praised him.

'I ain't seen some of them before. I never knew what they were 'cause there weren't any where we lived in London. If I'd 'ad a rabbit when I lived there, I wouldn't have known what to feed them.' He frowned. 'But my mum wouldn't let me. We couldn't have *any* animals in our flat. But I always wanted a dog or a cat or a rabbit!'

'Now you can help look after rabbits and chickens and a cow.'

George smiled. 'I like living 'ere with Auntie Thea and

everyone. I miss my mum, but she writes to us every week. We write back to her with Auntie Thea's 'elp.'

Flo's eyes suddenly prickled for the little boy who'd been taken away from all that he knew and his family and moved to live with strangers. It was a difficult thing to deal with for anyone let alone someone his age. She couldn't imagine how his mother must feel with her children so far away. How would her mother have felt if Bobby had been evacuated? Her parents hadn't accepted the offer, as they'd wanted to keep the family together. But if Bobby had been sent to safety, then he wouldn't have been killed in the Christmas Blitz, and she'd still have one member of her family left.

Taking a deep breath, Flo concentrated on finding more rabbit food, picking a huge handful of hogweed leaves and stuffing them in the sack.

'I think we've got enough for now.' Flo held up the brown hessian sack, which bulged with all they'd collected. 'The rabbits will enjoy this.'

'They need to eat well. Especially Flopsy because she's having babies,' George said.

Flo threw the sack over her shoulder and they set off down the lane, heading back to Rookery House. Flo felt a little hand take hold of her free one and she blinked away tears. George's hand in hers reminded her of Bobby, and how he'd liked to hold on to her whenever they went out together. Her instinct was to let go, drop George's hand as she would a hot pan, but it wouldn't be fair to the little boy. It wasn't his fault he reminded Flo of her dead brother. That was Flo's problem and hers alone. She had to deal with it, keep it locked away inside and get on with living here and doing her job.

Back at Rookery House, they took some of the plants out of the sack, put them in Benjamin and Flopsy's runs and stood watching as the two rabbits tucked in.

'They love the dandelion leaves.' George gazed intently as Benjamin chewed on a leaf, starting at one end, his jaws moving rapidly from side to side as the leaf gradually disappeared inside his mouth. 'We must get more of them next time we go collecting.' He looked up at Flo and gave her a beaming smile. 'I'll know what to look for better then, won't I?'

Flo returned his smile. 'You certainly will.'

CHAPTER 11

Tuesday 25th March

Hettie was glad to see that Thea was alone in the greenhouse, as she needed to ask her something in private. It wasn't something she'd have chosen, but after another night of broken sleep, Hettie had decided it must be done because time was running out.

'It's a lot warmer in here,' Hettie said, stepping into the greenhouse where the air smelled of earth and plants. She closed the door behind her to keep in the heat.

Thea turned around from the bench which ran along one side, where she was sowing seeds into pots of compost. 'Some sunshine makes such a difference, warms it up nicely in here. Hopefully, these peas will germinate quickly with the heat.'

'Have you got a minute?' Hettie asked.

'Of course.' Thea's face was full of concern. 'Are you all right, Hettie? You looked tired.'

'I've not been sleeping well. My mind keeps going round

and round about Ada and what will to happen to her.' Hettie frowned. 'You know I went to see her again yesterday afternoon and she *still* hasn't found anywhere to move to. Ada must be out of her cottage by next Monday. She only has a few more days to find somewhere to live and says it's impossible to find anything suitable.'

'I suppose a lot of new people have moved into the area through being evacuated or having been bombed out. But Ada's not the only one having her home requisitioned. Everyone moving out to make way for the aerodrome is having to find somewhere else.' Thea's voice was sympathetic.

'I'm worried come the 31st of March she'll be turned out of her cottage and have nowhere to go...' Hettie paused for a moment, biting her bottom lip. 'I was wondering if she could stay here? But only *temporarily* until she finds somewhere else more permanent. I know we haven't got a spare bedroom so she could share my room. We used to share when we were children.' Hettie managed a smile. 'I owe it to Ada to help her because she helped me and my brothers when our mother died.'

'You were only young then, weren't you?' Thea asked.

'I was eight and Albert and Sidney were ten and twelve. Ada was fifteen, and she'd already left home and been working as a milliner's apprentice in Norwich for a year. It was something she had always wanted to do, but she gave it up and returned home to look after our family. She had to step into our mother's shoes, care for us all and run the house for our father. It can't have been easy for Ada and I'm grateful for what she did. She made sure we were always well fed, had clean clothes to wear and lived in a well-run home.' Hettie's eyebrows drew together slightly. 'It must have hurt Ada deeply, having to give up her apprenticeship and with it her dream of becoming a qualified milliner.'

'She never went back to it then?' Thea asked.

Hettie shook her head. 'No. Not long after I left to go into service as a scullery maid at Great Plumstead Hall, Ada married Walter and went from caring for her father's home to her own. She never had her own career – she sacrificed it to look after her family. I think seeing me rise the ranks to become Cook irked Ada. I had a job that I loved and she didn't. We've never talked about it, but I've sensed it there, festering away. Ada's not an easy person and she's got pricklier over the years, and even worse since she lost Walter.'

Thea reached out and touched Hettie's arm. 'It's not your fault your mother died and Ada came home to look after you all. If she'd really wanted to, she could have found another apprenticeship to train after you'd left home.'

'I know. Nevertheless, I feel I should help her now. I want to.' Hettie's eyes met Thea's blue ones. 'What do you think? Could she come and stay here temporarily? It probably won't be easy, but she's my only family nearby and...'

'Of course, she can,' Thea interrupted and gave Hettie a reassuring smile. 'As long as you're willing to share your bedroom with her, because there's nowhere else for her to sleep unless she goes in the barn.' Thea raised an eyebrow. 'And I don't suppose she'd like that!'

'Definitely not!' Hettie chuckled. She was relieved that Thea had agreed to her request despite being warned of Ada's prickliness. 'Is there anywhere we could store her belongings? There's some furniture and other things, but not a huge amount as it's only a small cottage. Ada won't want to leave anything behind and will need them again sometime.'

'If we push the table to one side in the dining room, then we can get some furniture in there, and her bed will go in your room and some other bits. There's the attic as well. Don't worry, we'll manage. Ada's going to need help to move it here, though.'

'I thought I'd ask Alf Barker if he would transport her things. The van he uses for the grocers is big enough.'

'I'll help, and I'll ask Flo as well.'

'Thank you. I appreciate it.'

And I hope you won't come to regret your generosity, Hettie added for herself silently. It was only a temporary measure, as she'd keep on looking out for something more permanent for her sister. In the meantime, Hettie vowed to do whatever she could to make Ada's stay a smooth and a short one!

CHAPTER 12

Wednesday 26th March

Thea steered her bicycle in through the gate of Rookery House and was surprised to see a dark green Morris van parked in front of the house. She brought her bicycle to a halt, dismounted, and pushed it around to the shed in the back garden where they kept their cycles, wondering who was visiting. As far as she knew no one was expected today while she'd been out doing a shift on the WVS mobile canteen. With petrol being rationed most people who had cars, like herself, had taken them off the road for the duration of the war.

Going through the back door into the kitchen, the mystery was solved by the sight of Marianne's husband Alex, seated at the table looking after their daughter, Emily, who was sitting on his lap. Seeing Thea he got to his feet and held out his free hand.

'Alex!' Thea gave him a welcoming smile as she shook it.

'This is a lovely surprise. I was wondering who was here when I saw the van.'

'It's good to see you, Thea. I've borrowed the van to take my wife and daughter away on holiday with me.' Alex sat down again and settled Emily on his lap. 'I've got a week's leave and a fellow pilot has loaned me a cottage near the Norfolk Broads.'

'Did Marianne know you were coming?' Thea took off her green WVS coat, folded it over the back of a chair and sat at the table opposite Alex.

'No, I wanted to surprise her.' He grinned, his conker brown eyes bright with happiness. 'She's upstairs packing. Hettie's helping her.'

'I'm sure Marianne must be delighted. It's hard for you both being married but living apart.'

Alex nodded, his expression suddenly serious. 'We've been married just over a year and only spent a little time together because of me being away training.' His face brightened once more. 'But now that's finished and as soon as I'm at my operational base it will be easier for us to see each other.'

'Do you know we're you're being posted to?' Thea asked.

'I do.' He gave a rueful smile. 'But I can't tell you that!'

Thea laughed. 'Fair enough. Wherever it is, if it means you're closer and can see your wife and daughter more, then that's a good thing.'

Alex gently stroked his daughter's brown curly hair. 'Emily's grown so much since I last saw her. I thought she might not want to wait here with me while Marianne went to pack.'

'Emily's used to lots of people here. We all help look after her sometimes. She's a happy soul.' Thea watched the little girl playing with the gold buttons on Alex's blue air force uniform tunic. 'She loves your buttons.'

'Is it still all right for Marianne and Emily to stay living with you while I'm in the RAF?' Alex asked, his voice serious. 'I do appreciate you having them here and it was a big help to me while I was away training, knowing that they weren't alone.'

'I love having them here. We all do. They are part of our Rookery House family and can stay for as long as they want,' Thea reassured him.

Alex gave her an appreciative smile. 'Thank you.'

Hearing voices and the sound of footsteps coming down the stairs, Thea got up and hurried across the kitchen to open the door leading into the hall.

'You're back!' Marianne said. 'I hoped you would be before I left.'

Thea reached out and took one of the suitcases Marianne was carrying. 'I hear you're going on an unexpected holiday.'

Marianne smiled, her eyes dancing with happiness. 'I thought I was dreaming when Alex turned up. And now Emily and I are off for a whole week with him. Our family will be together at last.'

'You'll have a wonderful time,' Hettie said coming down the stairs behind Marianne, carrying two baskets packed with things for Emily.

Marianne beamed. 'We certainly will!'

Outside, with everything they needed packed into the van, including Emily's pram, Alex settled Marianne into the passenger seat with her daughter in her arms.

'It's a good job you borrowed a van,' Hettie said, as Alex closed the passenger door.

'I know how much Marianne uses the pram so thought we definitely must take it with us on holiday,' Alex said.

'Have a lovely time,' Thea said. 'We'll see you back here in a week's time.'

Alex gave her and Hettie a wide smile. 'Thank you. We'll see you next week.'

He went round to the driver's side, got in and started the engine. Marianne and Emily waved to them out of the passenger window both looking so happy.

Thea and Hettie returned their waves, watching as Alex drove the van through the gateway and turned towards the village, off on their holiday.

'I wasn't expecting that when I came home,' Thea said, turning to Hettie. 'What a lovely surprise for Marianne and Emily. It will give them precious time together as a family. We can look forward to hearing about their holiday when they get back next week.'

'Ada will be living here by then, that's unless she finds somewhere else to live in the meantime.'

'She still hasn't?'

'No.' Hettie frowned. 'And I'm not so sure she's been looking that hard either, not now she knows she can come here if she doesn't find anything in time.'

Thea put her hand on Hettie's arm. 'Don't worry yourself about it. If she hasn't got anywhere then she can come here until she finds something else. We're not going to see her out on the street.'

'I couldn't do that to her. We'll manage,' Hettie said in a positive tone.

'Of course, we will,' Thea agreed. 'In the meantime, the house will feel emptier with Marianne and Emily away.'

CHAPTER 13

Arriving at the village hall with Hettie, Flo wasn't sure if she'd made the right decision to go to tonight's Women's Institute meeting or not. It might have been better to volunteer to help Thea who was running a children's evening club at the school while their mothers went to the WI. George and Betty and Emily had gone with Thea. But Hettie had been so keen for Flo to try the WI meeting, and she didn't want to let the older woman down as she had been so kind and welcoming to her since Flo had arrived at Rookery House.

Taking a deep breath, Flo followed Hettie in through the door where the sound of women chatting filled the hall.

'This way.' Hettie took hold of Flo's arm and steered her towards the front where chairs had been set out in rows facing forwards. 'I'll introduce you to Prue.'

Flo had heard about Prue, who was Alice's mother and Thea and Reuben's sister, but hadn't met her yet.

'Prue,' Hettie called, approaching a smartly dressed blonde-haired woman who was sorting through a pile of papers on the table at the front.

Prue turned around and her resemblance to Thea was striking. She might have blonde hair rather than Thea's dark brown, but her facial features were very similar, just like Flo had noticed Lizzie's were.

'You must be Flo.' Prue held out her hand, a warm smile on her face. 'Welcome to our village WI. I'm delighted to meet you and that you've come along tonight. Alice will be pleased you're here.' She gestured to the side of the hall where Alice was helping to set out teacups on a table.

'It's nice to meet you.' Flo shook Prue's hand. 'I've never been to a WI before.'

'I hope you'll enjoy it, although tonight's meeting isn't going to be as planned,' Prue explained. 'Our speaker has had to postpone her demonstration, as she's unwell. I didn't find out until this morning.'

'What are we doing instead?' Hettie asked.

'Talking about something important!'

'What's that?' Hettie asked.

'You'll see.' Prue's blue eyes twinkled mischievously. 'It might be fortuitous timing actually that the speaker had to postpone.' She glanced at her watch. 'We'd better get started. If you'll excuse me.'

'Come on, let's take a seat,' Hettie said, heading for some free chairs in the front row.

'I wonder what Prue's going to talk about?' Flo mused as she sat next to Hettie.

'We'll find out soon enough. One of her good causes, perhaps,' Hettie replied.

'Good evening, ladies, if we can make a start.' Prue's voice cut through the chatter and those women who weren't already in their seats quickly sat down. Those who were chatting fell silent and directed their attention to the front of the hall where Prue stood behind the table, facing the audience.

'Prue's the vice-chair and that's our WI president, Mrs Baden, sitting beside her,' Hettie whispered to Flo. 'Though Prue does most of the work!'

Prue sat down and the president stood up to address the women.

'Good evening, everyone. Welcome to this month's meeting. I'm sorry to inform you that our speaker for the evening is unwell and we were unable to find a replacement at short notice,' Mrs Baden explained. 'However, Prue has offered to tell us about the latest WI initiative that's recently started in the village. I think you'll agree what an important project it is.' She gestured to Prue, who stood up as the president sat down.

Prue made her way out from behind the table to stand in front of the audience. 'Some of you know about and are already involved in our new WI allotment. We have taken it on in response to the extended call to Dig for Victory and produce more of our own food rather than rely on imports coming in by sea from other countries. Our aim is to grow as much as we can and sell our fresh produce at our weekly stall at the Wykeham market.'

'I'm already Digging for Victory in my back garden,' one woman called out.

'So am I and so are most of our members,' Prue acknowledged. 'The WI allotment is to grow extra food for other people rather than just our immediate families. The aim is to grow fruit and vegetables, sell them and plough the profit back into growing more food or for other uses such as buying wool for our knitting for the troops or other worthy causes.'

'Tell 'em about the state of the allotment,' a woman with peroxide-blonde hair in a pompadour style called out from the front row on the other side of the aisle.

'That's Gloria,' Hettie whispered to Flo. 'I'll introduce you to her at the tea break. She's a good friend of mine.'

'As Gloria and other members who were at the allotment last Saturday can tell you, we haven't been given the best plot on the site but the *worst*. It hasn't been tended for some time and was rampant with brambles, docks, nettles and in a terrible state. When I asked one of the other allotment holders if he might be interested in helping to clear it, the answer was no. He also suggested that we wouldn't be able to sort it out either and it would be best if we stuck to making jam!'

The women gave a collective gasp.

'He underestimated us!' Gloria called out. 'We'll show 'im.'

'We certainly will show him and all the other allotment holders who doubt us,' Prue agreed. 'Last weekend we made a good start and have cleared back the brambles, so at least we're now able to walk across our plot without getting our legs scratched. Next, we need to do further work on digging out roots so that we can dig it over properly and add the plentiful supply of compost from the site's own heap.' Prue paused and looked around at the women. 'Preparing and nurturing our allotment is a task that is going to take time and hard work, but we, as a collective, are very capable of doing an excellent job. It's like our own vegetable gardens, but on a bigger scale. For this to be successful, and the burden not to fall upon just a handful of members, I'm appealing to you to volunteer to help if you can. Our next work party there will be this weekend. Who can help then or on other occasions?'

Flo looked behind her as some hands went up. She could help, she reasoned. She had the skills and experience. Without a second thought, Flo raised her hand.

Prue beamed at the response. 'Are there any questions?'

'My back's no good for digging,' one woman said. 'Can I still be of use?'

'Of course, there will be many jobs over the coming year, from sowing seeds and hoeing to harvesting. All help is much appreciated.'

By the end of the meeting, the second half of which had been a fun game of musical statues following by a sing song, Flo left thinking she was glad she had gone tonight. The women she'd met, Prue, Gloria and others, had been lovely and welcoming. She was looking forward to helping with the WI allotment too. It was working on allotments that had borne her love of growing things and led her to join the Land Army. The WI's plot sounded like a good community-based place to work and a chance to get to know more people by doing what she loved. Flo knew she'd be busy helping on the allotment along with her doing her job for Thea, but she was sure she could manage both.

CHAPTER 14

Saturday 29th March

After she'd finished her half day's work, Flo rode to Great
Plumstead allotments on Hettie's bicycle. Bumping along the
track through the site, she smiled and waved at some of the
other allotment holders who'd stopped what they were doing
to watch her pass by. Seeing the land divided up into separate
areas, many with sheds and makeshift greenhouses, reminded
her of her grandad's plot back home in Lancashire. Flo might
be in a different part of the country now but the feeling of a
community space where people grew fruit, vegetables and
flowers was the same. It gave her a warm glow in her chest to
be somewhere familiar again.

She wasn't the first to arrive, as there were already some
women at work on the WI plot at the end of the track. Prams
were parked close by so the infants sitting up inside could see
their mothers. Flo spotted Prue and waved to her as she
leaned Hettie's bicycle against a hedge.

'I'm pleased you could come,' Prue called, walking across to Flo. 'We've had a few more WI members come along today after hearing about it on Wednesday night.' She nodded to the women who Flo recognised from the meeting.

'What shall I do?' Flo asked.

'If you can dig out roots, it would be a big help. The sooner we get them cleared, the sooner we can dig the allotment over properly. There are tools in the wheelbarrow.' Prue gestured to where the barrow was parked by the shed. 'Help yourself to what you need.'

Flo took a fork from the wheelbarrow and got to work, breathing in the wonderful earthy smell that was released as she dug. It was hugely satisfying removing roots, especially those that plunged down deep, burrowing into the soil. She might be doing gardening tasks during the rest of the working week, but Flo couldn't imagine ever tiring of it. Spending her free Saturday afternoon working the allotment was a pleasure.

'I was thinking I might make myself a pair of bib and braces dungarees like you're wearing,' Gloria, whom Flo had met at the WI meeting, said, wandering over to where Flo was working. 'Only, if I'm going to keep coming 'ere, I don't want to spoil my dresses.' She looked down at her violet, close-fitting dress, which showed off Gloria's curvy figure. 'Are the dungarees comfy?'

'Yes, very. There's no waistband, which is good when you're bending over doing jobs. I like them a lot.'

Gloria nodded. 'I would 'ave to make them out of something nice and colourful though. I prefer to dress colourfully, as you can see!' She laughed a throaty laugh. 'No offence at your dungarees. Only brown definitely ain't my colour.'

'No offence taken,' Flo reassured her. 'Probably one of the reasons for choosing this colour for our Land Army uniform is because of the dirty jobs we do. Dirt won't show up so much on brown cloth.' She dusted her soil-covered hands off on the leg of her dungarees. 'See, it doesn't stand out so much.'

'Fair enough.' Gloria nodded. 'I never would 'ave dreamed I'd be doing this sort of thing back at 'ome.'

'You're from London?'

'The East End of London. I lived in a terrace 'ouse with just a back yard, no garden. All this is new to me,' she gestured with her arm. 'But I must admit I'm enjoying it. It's lovely to be out in the fresh, clean air doing something productive.'

The pair of them fell into working alongside each other and when Gloria began to sing *Daisy Bell*, Flo joined in too. Soon all the women on the allotment were singing together, their voices filling the air. After that they went on to other favourite songs, women calling out suggestions. All the while they worked, their singing aiding the effort.

When they stopped for a break, Flo welcomed a cup of tea from one of the flasks which Prue had brought to share out.

'We're making good progress,' Prue said, standing by Flo and surveying the plot. 'It's so much better already than how we found it.'

'Many people working together makes a difference,' Flo said. 'Once the roots are out and it's been dug over, it will be easier to look after it and keep on top of the weeds.'

'You sound like you know what you're talking about,' Prue said.

'I've been working on allotments as far back as I can remember. My grandad taught me about how to care for one and grow things on his allotment. It started my love of gardening,' Flo explained.

Prue's face was thoughtful. 'You might be just the person to help us with this one. I've got a vegetable garden at home, but this...' she waved her hand to include the plot, 'it's much bigger and we need to make the most of it, grow the best crops from it to sell. Can you advise us how to do that?'

Flo's cheeks grew warm. 'I'm no expert, but I can tell you what I know and have learned, if that will help.'

'Yes please.' Prue's tone was enthusiastic. 'If we're putting all this time and effort into this allotment, it's important to do it right.'

Flo considered for a moment thinking about all she'd been taught by her grandad and practised over the years on their family plot, along with her more recent training after joining the Land Army.

'The first thing is to decide what crops you want to grow. Then you need to plan a three-year rotation on the allotment growing different sorts of crops in a new area each year and rotate them around.' Flo paused, aware that several other women were listening as well as Prue. 'So, if you divide the plot into three areas and call them A, B and C.' She counted them out on her fingers. 'In the first year, you use area A for root crops and potatoes, area B for growing green crops like beans and cabbages, and C for any others such as onions. The following year you grow the root crops and potatoes in area B, the greens in area C and other crops in area A. In the third year...' Flo noticed Prue frowning and stopped. 'It's easier to show it written out on a piece of paper.'

'I'll get my notebook.' Prue dashed off to rummage in her handbag, which she'd left hanging on the handle of the wheelbarrow, and returned with a notebook and pencil and handed them to Flo. 'If you can draw what you mean it will help.'

Flo took them and quickly drew a diagram explaining how the rotation would work and showed it to Prue.

'Is this better?'

'Much. It's far easier to see on paper. We can do that.

Thank you.' Prue gave Flo a grateful smile. 'I'll make a list of what we should grow and check that there's something to harvest all year round for us to sell.'

'Rotating your crops around will help prevent pests too,' Flo said. 'We need to start another compost heap with any bits of plants not used. Once they've rotted down, they can be dug into the soil to fertilise it. The heap you've already got is ready to use now.' She nodded towards the heap to the side of the shed. 'It's good stuff and will add nourishment to the soil. It would be a good idea to get a load of well-rotted manure, too.'

'I'll ask Reuben about that,' Prue said. 'We might be able to get some from the Hall's estate.'

'With Flo's advice, we'll 'ave a smashin' allotment,' Gloria said. She'd been quietly listening to them talking. 'It will prove them old fellas wrong to doubt us.' She drank the last of her tea, shook the drops out of her cup and returned it to Prue's basket. 'Let's get back to work!' With a wide smile, Gloria marched off across the plot to where she'd left her fork in the ground, humming loudly.

Prue looked at Flo, their eyes meeting. 'Thank you for your advice. I really appreciate it. I hope you'll keep coming along when you can and advising us so we can produce the best crops.'

'I'm glad to help and am enjoying myself. I will definitely be back.' Flo drank the last of her tea, put her empty cup in the basket and returned to work, thinking that she'd write and tell her grandad about this allotment and what they were doing here. He'd be delighted to know that she was putting all he'd taught her to good use.

CHAPTER 15

Monday 31st March

'That's the last box.' Hettie passed it to Alf Barker and he loaded it into the back of his van, which was packed with Ada's furniture and belongings from her small cottage. One load had already been taken to Rookery House earlier, with the larger items like Hettie's sister's bed, chest of drawers, kitchen table, dresser and chairs. This was the second load, the final farewell to Ada's home of almost forty-seven years.

'Just fits in nicely.' Alf clambered down from the back of the van. 'Is your sister ready to go?'

Hettie glanced towards the cottage. 'She's taking a minute to say goodbye...'

Alf nodded, his face sympathetic. 'It's a wrench for her. I'll sit in the cab and wait; there's no hurry.'

'Thanks Alf.' Hettie gave him a grateful smile and he headed around to the front of the van.

'We'll meet you back at Rookery House,' Thea said,

collecting Ada's bicycle, which was leaning against the side of the van. There wasn't room in the cab for Thea and Flo along with Ada and Hettie, so Thea was cycling Ada's bicycle the three miles back to Rookery House with Flo, who'd ridden over on Hettie's bicycle. 'See you soon.'

Left on her own, Hettie watched the pair of them cycle off down the narrow lane, glad that they'd volunteered to help as some of the furniture had been heavy to move. It would have been a struggle for her and Ada to carry it on their own with Alf. Hettie took a deep breath and went to find her sister.

Ada was in the kitchen, staring out of the window above the stone sink. She didn't turn around as Hettie walked in, her footsteps sounding hollow on the quarry tile floor now that all the furniture was gone.

'It's all loaded in and we're ready to go when you are.' Hettie went to stand beside her sister.

Ada gave a nod of her head but remained silently staring out of the window.

Hettie gently touched her sister's arm. 'Are you all right?'

'Of course, I'm not!' Ada snapped, turning to glare at Hettie. 'How would you feel if you were being *forced* out of your home?'

Hettie ignored her sister's harsh tone. She was understandably upset and had every right to be. 'I know this is hard for you.' Her voice was gentle.

Ada sniffed and crossed her arms over her bony frame. 'It's criminal that they're going to bulldoze a perfectly good cottage.' She shook her head. 'I never thought in all the years I stood here looking out of this window and across the fields that it would come to this.'

Ada ran her hand along the smooth edge of the stone sink. 'This cottage is my last link with Walter.'

'You'll still have your memories of him,' Hettie said. 'No one can take them away.'

Ada's brown eyes narrowed. 'What do *you* know? You've never been married.'

Before Hettie had a chance to respond, Ada took a final glance around the room and swept out, down the short hall and out of the front door.

Hettie let out a long, slow breath, shaking her head. Ada was bristling for a fight, but Hettie wasn't going to bite. Her sister was in pain and lashing out. Hettie wouldn't normally let *anyone* speak to her like that but, on this occasion, she would turn the other cheek, she decided as she made her way outside, closing the door behind her for the last time. What Ada had said was true, Hettie had never married, so she couldn't know how it felt to have first lost a husband and then the home they'd shared. But she *did* have empathy for her sister's losses and would do all she could to support her and help her through this difficult situation.

They had unloaded everything from Alf's van and Thea and Flo had just carried the last boxes into the house.

'How much do I owe you, Alf?' Hettie asked, taking her purse out of her bag.

He waved his hand as if swatting away her question. 'Nothing! I was glad to help. It doesn't feel right your sister being turned out of her cottage. I know what it's for, but...' Alf shook his head. 'It's a hard day for her.'

'What about the petrol you used? At least let me cover that,' Hettie urged him.

'No, I don't want anything, honestly.' Alf's voice was firm.

'When Ada finds a new home, I'll be happy to help her move again.'

Hettie put her purse back in her bag. 'Well, if you won't take any money, then I will bring you some butter and cheese as thanks.' She raised her eyebrows. 'I dare say you'll enjoy them.'

Alf laughed. 'I certainly will, thank you. I'll be seeing you, then.'

'Thanks Alf,' Hettie called as he went around to the driver's door and got in. She stayed outside and watched him leave, waving to him as he turned the van towards the village.

Turning to go inside, Hettie glanced up at the window of her bedroom, which she'd now be sharing with her sister. They'd shared a room as children, but that was many years ago. Being back together again, for however long it happened to be, was going to be strange.

'You're in perfect time for a cup of tea,' Thea said as Hettie let herself in the door to the kitchen. 'I've just poured hot water into the teapot.'

'I think we all need one after hauling all that furniture and those boxes around,' Flo said, putting clean cups on the table that she'd taken from a dresser.

'Where's Ada?' Hettie asked.

'Upstairs,' Flo said. 'Said she wanted to unpack and settle in.'

'I'll go and see if she's all right. I won't be long.' Hettie went out into the hall and, before going up, decided to check the state of the dining room. Going into the large room at the front of the house, which was directly under her bedroom, she regarded the stack of furniture over on the far side. It had been piled up and slotted in rather like a puzzle to make the most of the space. The furniture, along with many boxes of things, including kitchenware, now took up just over half of the room. They had reduced Thea's dining table to its smallest size, the extending leaves having been taken out of it. There was just enough room left for a camp bed for when visitors came to stay.

Hettie sighed. It wasn't ideal but the only practical solution because if the furniture or boxes were stored out in the barn or a shed, they could get damp or be damaged by mice. This was a temporary measure, she reminded herself.

Leaving the dining room, Hettie made her way upstairs to her room... or *her and Ada's bedroom,* as she should now think of it. She hesitated outside the door before going in as she hadn't yet seen it with Ada's bed in place. Bracing herself, she took a deep breath and went in.

'There you are.' Ada turned to glance at her before returning to her unpacking, removing neatly folded clothes from a suitcase and placing them in the chest of drawers that she'd brought from her old bedroom.

'How are you getting on? I hope it's all right in here for you,' Hettie asking gazing around and trying not to blanch at how different it looked with the addition of Ada's double bed and chest of drawers. Hettie's own single bed, her wardrobe and set of drawers had been shifted over to make space and she couldn't help thinking how squeezed in it now felt in here. After years of sharing a bedroom, first at home, then as a servant at the Hall, when she'd finally graduated to having her own room when she became Cook it was such a luxury. Hettie had fully appreciated having her own private space. Having someone else now sharing that with her was going to be hard!

'It will *have* to be all right, won't it?' Ada declared in a shrill voice. 'There's no choice in the matter, having been thrown out of my home!'

Hettie ignored her sister's outburst. 'Can I help with your unpacking?'

'No, I'll manage.'

'There's room in the wardrobe if you want to hang anything up and spare hangers.'

Ada nodded her head but said nothing, her shoulders hunched as she continued to put clothes in a drawer.

'Thea's just made some tea, so come down when you're ready.' Hettie went towards the door and then stopped. 'I hope you'll be comfortable here while you're with us.'

Ada spun around and glared at Hettie. 'What in here, with us squeezed in together? I hope you don't snore. It's going to be bad enough with barely room to swing a cat, but if you keep me awake...' Her voice tailed off, her lips pressing into a tight line.

Hettie forced a smile. 'It's only temporary, Ada, until we find you a more permanent home. I'm sure we can manage till then.'

Ada snorted and returned to her unpacking.

Hettie left her to it, reminding herself not for the first time that day how upset her sister must be feeling and that she was just lashing out. Things would settle down in a day or two – Hettie hoped!

CHAPTER 16

Thursday 3rd April

'What do you think?' Thea asked, glancing at Flo who, like her, was standing by the wall of the pigsty watching the antics of the latest arrivals at Rookery House.

'They're lovely!' Flo smiled. 'I've never had anything to do with pigs before, but these two have made a big impression on me already.'

'They are lovely, but we mustn't forget they are being kept for meat.' Thea watched the newly weaned piglets chasing around, going in and out of the straw-strewn bedroom part of the pigsty. They seemed delighted with their new home. At two months old, the young female saddleback piglets were prettily marked. Their heads and three quarters of their bodies were a rich charcoal black, while their front legs and shoulders were a pale pink. 'These will make a huge difference to our meat supply. Hettie has plans for making sausages and curing bacon and hams when the time comes.'

Flo winced. 'I know it's what pigs are kept for, but it seems so harsh looking at them now.'

Thea nodded. 'I understand, but it is the reason we've got them. We'll look after them well – give them a good life while they're here.'

The sound of a distant explosion made them both jump.

'Not another one!' Flo put a hand to her chest. 'I wish we knew when they were going to go off. Every time it catches me out.'

Reuben had told them that the explosives were being used to quickly remove tree stumps, the trunk of the tree having already been cut down.

'At some point all the stumps will be gone and they'll stop.' Thea hated the thought that each of the bangs that had been going off over the past few days marked the demise of another large tree ripped out to make way for the new aerodrome. Creating the aerodrome was cutting a swathe of destruction through the countryside before building had even begun.

'I'll be glad when that happens, and we're not surprised with loud bangs any more. But they're for a good cause. The sooner the aerodrome's ready the sooner it will be operational.' Flo reached down and held out her hand to the two piglets who came over to investigate, sniffing at her fingers with their blunt noses and then allowing her to scratch behind their ears.

'I'm not sure if it's a good thing or a bad thing having an aerodrome on our doorstep and bombers flying off to drop bombs on the enemy,' Thea said.

'It will only be doing back to them what they're doing to us!' Flo said vehemently, putting a hand on her hip.

Thea regarded the young woman, surprised at her strong reaction. 'I suppose so, but it's all out of our hands.' Turning back to the piglets, she changed the subject. 'George and Betty will be delighted to see these two when they get home from school.'

'They certainly will.' Flo gave a smile. 'Did they know they were coming today?'

Thea shook her head. 'I didn't say or they would have wanted to stay at home to see them. It will be a lovely surprise. I'm going to tell Hettie the piglets have arrived. She's keen to see them too.'

Leaving Flo watching the piglets, Thea headed to the house. She was pleased with how the animals had taken to their new home so quickly after a local farmer had delivered them a short while ago. They were another step in Thea's plan to produce more food and would eat scraps, as well as things foraged from the surrounding area like acorns, beechmast and chestnuts when they were in season. For centuries, the autumnal nuts and seeds had made a good food source to help fatten pigs and Thea had plans to collect them for their pigs later this year. It was especially important now the amount of pig meal that could be bought was limited.

Opening the kitchen door, Thea popped her head inside so she didn't have to take her rubber boots off. Hettie and Ada were sitting at the table. Hettie was busy peeling apples while her sister sat doing nothing, her arms folded across her skinny body. Marianne, who'd returned from her holiday yesterday, was at the sink washing up, with Emily sitting on the rag rug on the floor beside her playing with some wooden blocks.

'The piglets are here, if you want to come and have a look,' Thea announced cheerfully.

'I didn't realise they'd arrived!' Hettie got up, an enthusiastic expression on her face. 'Are you coming, Ada?'

'Why would I want to do that?' Ada retorted. 'I'm not interested in pigs.'

'They're very sweet and lovely,' Thea said. 'Come and have a quick look.'

'No, I'm fine where I am,' Ada said, curtly.

'Fair enough,' Thea replied, her eyes meeting Hettie's as she headed towards her.

'You'd like to see them, wouldn't you, Emily?' Marianne asked as she dried her hands on a tea towel.

At the sound of her name, Emily held up her arms to her mother, who picked her up and followed Hettie and Thea outside.

Hettie let out a heavy sigh. 'I'm sorry about that.'

'There's no need to be,' Thea reassured her friend as they walked towards the pigsty. 'If Ada doesn't want to see the piglets, it's up to her.'

'I know, but she didn't have to be so rude about it.' The older woman frowned. 'She's not doing herself any favours behaving like this I'd hoped she might ease up a bit after she left her cottage. It's five days since she moved here and she's *still* prickly and…' Hettie tutted. 'Ada has never been easy to be around but it's worse now. I'm sorry she's such a misery.'

Thea halted and put her hand on Hettie's arm for her to stop too. 'I've noticed you've not been yourself either since Ada arrived. Please don't worry that she's upsetting me because she isn't. My concern is if Ada's upsetting *you*. Is she?'

'No more than she usually does when I used to go to see her. At least then I only saw her in small doses. Now she's here all the time and being snippy to everyone. And Ada's snoring is keeping me awake at night as well and that's making me tired.' Hettie's eyebrows knitted together. 'But she has just lost her home on top of losing Walter last year. It's a lot for her to cope with.'

Thea nodded. 'I know. Ada's comments can only get to us

if we allow them to. Try to ignore them, Hettie. Don't let them affect you.'

'I'll try.' Hettie raised her chin. 'If Ada doesn't want to see the piglets, then it's her loss. Come on, let's have a look at them.'

Reaching the pigsty, Thea, Hettie and Marianne, with Emily in her arms, joined Flo who was still watching the piglets. The little pigs were now pulling on either end of a cabbage stalk, squealing at each other. When one succeeded in getting the stalk, it would be chased around by the other till it dropped it and the whole game would begin again.

'What do you think?' Thea asked.

'They're very sweet,' Marianne said holding on tightly to Emily, who was leaning forwards, her arms outstretched wanting to reach the piglets.

'Marianne's right. Now I see them, I feel awful thinking of them in terms of bacon, ham and sausages!' Hettie admitted.

'That's what they're here for eventually, I'm afraid,' Thea replied. 'Flo said the same thing, but we can't keep them as pets.'

'I know,' Hettie said. 'It's what farmers do all the time. We need to remember we're doing our bit for meat production here.'

'That's the plan,' Thea agreed. Although when it came to it, she had the feeling saying goodbye to the pigs wouldn't be easy. But that was some months off yet. In the meantime, she would enjoy looking after them.

CHAPTER 17

Friday 4th April

Prue checked the envelopes, one addressed to Jack, the other to Edwin, before dropping them in the red post-box. Her weekly letters to her sons were no substitute for seeing them but were the best she could do at present. At least Edwin wrote back regularly, but Jack's letters were less frequent, although he would occasionally telephone. Prue was grateful that they were both in the country, Jack with his engineering unit in the North of England and Edwin in London. So many other mothers had sons hundreds or even thousands of miles away overseas.

Picking up her shopping basket, Prue headed for Barker's grocery shop. The bell above the door jangled loudly as Prue opened it, meeting another customer coming out.

'Good morning,' she said, holding the door for Percy Blake, who had a newspaper tucked under his arm.

'Morning.' He nodded to her.

'You not at your allotment today?' Prue asked.

'I shall be later. There's always something to be done, as you'll be discovering,' he said pointedly.

She raised an eyebrow at him. 'Indeed, we are learning all the time.'

Percy gave another nod of his head and walked off in the direction of his cottage.

Prue rolled her eyes. Clearly the WI allotment, and the women who worked on it, still had a long way to go in Percy's opinion. Closing the shop door behind her, Prue saw that Grace Barker was serving a woman who Prue didn't recognise and who must be a newcomer to the village as she was registering her ration book with Grace.

'You must be Hettie's sister, Ada.' Grace gave a welcoming smile across the wooden counter.

'Yes, I am,' Ada replied.

'Welcome to the village. I'm Grace Barker. Are you settling in well at Rookery House?'

'As well as can be expected,' Ada said sharply.

So *this* was Hettie's sister, Prue thought. Alice had told her that Ada had moved in, but Prue had yet to meet her.

Prue stepped forward, so that she was level with the older woman. 'Hello, Ada. I'm Prue, Thea's sister and Alice's mother. I'm pleased to meet you.' She held out her hand, smiling warmly.

Ada glanced at Prue's hand, hesitated, and then shook it briefly, her handshake soft. 'Hello.'

'I hope you'll be happy here in Great Plumstead,' Prue said. 'There's plenty going on in the village if you'd like to join in. We've got our village WI and have recently taken on an allotment. There's The Mother's Day Club with our evacuee mothers and their children, salvage collections and—'

'I'm not one for joining in,' Ada cut in. She folded her arms over her skinny frame, her expression anything but friendly.

Prue's eyes briefly met Grace's across the shop counter.

'Well, if you change your mind, you'd be welcome at any time,' Prue said keeping her tone warm. 'If you want help with finding a new place to live, I could assist you. I'm the billeting officer for the area. Although I should warn you, it's much harder now than it was to find new accommodation as we've had so many evacuees arrive in the village. I might be able to find you a room in a house.'

'I'm looking for another cottage of my own. That's what I had. That's what I want again.' Ada pursed her lips into a thin line.

'I understand,' Prue said sympathetically. 'But there's just not that sort of housing available around here right now. With the influx of evacuees and the aerodrome being built, there's more demand for the limited housing in the area. At least you've got a place to live at Rookery House for the time being.'

Ada sniffed. 'I had to share a room with my sister when I was a child. I didn't expect to have to do it again at my age!'

'If I hear of anything suitable, I'll let you know,' Prue said.

'And so will I. I'm sure something will turn up for you,' Grace added optimistically. 'Is there anything else I can do for you?'

'I'd like three ounces of mint humbugs, please.' Ada pointed to one of the jars of sweets on the shelf behind the counter.

While Grace weighed out the humbugs, Prue wondered what else to say to Ada, thinking anything she said was likely to be rebuffed. Ada was *nothing* like her sister. Not in appearance or attitude. Whereas Hettie was jolly, rounded and a joy to be around, Ada was all angles, spikes and sourness and, Prue suspected, wasn't a woman who'd be easy to live with.

'There we are.' Grace handed Ada the paper bag of humbugs and took the money, which the older woman had counted out exactly and placed on the counter.

'Thank you.' Ada put the bag into her coat pocket and, after a curt nod at Prue and Grace, she went out, the bell above the door jangling loudly.

'Well...' Grace's eyes met Prue's. 'Her and Hettie are as different as chalk and cheese! I don't envy your Thea having Ada living with them if that's how she is.'

Prue nodded in agreement. 'It can't be easy being forced to leave your home. It's enough to make anyone prickly.'

'That's true,' Grace acknowledged. 'But something tells me that Ada's never been the jolliest of people.'

'Perhaps staying at Rookery House will knock some of the sharp edges off her,' Prue suggested optimistically.

Grace laughed. 'Let's hope so. Either that or Ada finds a new home soon. Now, what can I get you this morning?'

CHAPTER 18

Saturday 5th April

Flo had never been this close to a cow before. Until she'd come to Rookery House, she'd had nothing to do with cows. She hadn't considered she would even want to be involved with the milking when she'd first arrived but after seeing Thea and Alice doing it, Flo had decided that she wanted to try it herself. Now here she was, sitting on a three-legged stool, her face inches away from Primrose's flank. She was so close she could feel the warmth from the cow on her cheeks.

'All set?' Thea asked, standing to the side just behind Flo and briefly placing her hand on Flo's shoulder to reassure her. 'Take it slowly, pull and squeeze the teat like I showed you.'

Flo glanced up at Thea and nodded. 'I'll do my best.'

She took hold of one of Primrose's soft teats between her thumb and index finger, then pulled and squeezed at the same time. Nothing happened; not even a single drip of milk appeared. Primrose carried on munching from the hayrack at the front of her stall. Flo tried again. This time she applied more pressure and, to her delight, a small stream of milk spurted out and clanged into the bottom of the metal pail that she held in place underneath with her legs.

'That's it, you're doing it!' Thea said in a delighted voice. 'Keep going and try with your other hand.'

Flo took hold of another teat with her left hand and repeated the process, but it was harder with this hand. She tried again and again and finally some milk appeared. The next step was to use two hands at once and get into a steady rhythm like she'd seen Thea doing so many times, making it look so easy. Flo concentrated, and the milk flowed, as she pulled on first one teat and then the other, one after another. It was hard work on her hands. They weren't used to this motion and it wasn't long before they began to ache. Flo had to stop.

'It's painful on your fingers.' Flo shook her hands and then wriggled her fingers to ease the throb.

'They'll get stronger the more you milk, but it's hard at first,' Thea admitted. 'Do you want me to take over?'

'Not yet.' Flo took hold of the teats again and milked, letting her shoulders sink as she gradually relaxed. Keep going, she told herself; if she wanted to be able to do a whole milking, just as Thea and Alice did, then she mustn't give up. If her grandparents could see her now, she thought, they'd be thrilled. She'd write and tell them about it later.

But the pail was only half full of creamy milk when Flo was forced to stop. Her hands felt like they couldn't go on.

'Will you take over now?'

'Of course, you've done really well for your first time.' Thea gave her a beaming smile. 'I didn't manage as much as that when I started learning. Reuben had to step in after I'd only milked a quarter of a pail. If you do some each day, then your hands will get stronger, and it won't be long before you can do the milking all by yourself.'

'I'll keep practising. I wasn't sure if I'd be able to get any milk out at all. I enjoyed doing it.'

Flo was now looking forward to being able to take responsibility for some of the twice daily milking sessions herself – something she'd never expected to happen.

'Being able to milk is a good skill for a Land Girl to have,' Thea said, swapping places with Flo. 'It's helpful to me to have someone else who can milk Primrose if I'm not here to do it. Running Rookery House is a team effort.'

'It's good that we all contribute. Although I was expecting to be sent to a hostel with lots of other Land Girls, not a family home,' Flo admitted.

Thea glanced up at Flo, as she milked. 'This place must have come as quite a shock then; it couldn't be more different to a hostel. I hope it hasn't disappointed you.'

Flo shook her head. 'Not at all. I like it very much and enjoy my job.'

'I'm glad.' Thea gave her a warm smile. 'We all love having you here and you've settled in so well. I know it's difficult coming to a place you don't know and living with strangers.'

'You don't seem like strangers to me now,' Flo said. Over the weeks since she'd arrived, she had settled in well, getting to know the rhythms of the household and the people who lived there. Their kindness and friendliness had helped her feel comfortable here. Although they still had no idea of Flo's past and what had sent her to Rookery House. That was something that she had to keep to herself. It was the right thing to do, wasn't it?

CHAPTER 19

Sunday 6th April

It was early evening and, after a busy afternoon's work at the WI allotment, Prue was on her way home. She was tired and dirty and in need of a long soak in a hot bath to ease her aching muscles. But she had thoroughly enjoyed herself. Prue smiled, thinking that although bringing the WI plot up to scratch was proving to be hard physical work, she was also finding it hugely satisfying. Working with other women was fun and there was always a good atmosphere, with plenty of chatter and laughter. Each time she went, Prue came away feeling happy and that she'd achieved something worthwhile.

Turning into the road where she lived, she spotted a familiar figure walking towards her from the opposite direction. It was Victor. He was on his way home from the railway station, strolling along with a self-satisfied look on his face. He looked like a cat who'd got the cream and gone back for second helpings. Prue's happy mood instantly evaporated.

Victor had gone to Norwich this morning, as he usually did on Sundays for his so-called meetings, although of course Prue knew the truth, that he had, in fact, gone to see his mistress.

Spotting Prue, Victor's step faltered for a moment, but he quickly recovered and carried on, picking up his pace and striding towards her, a look of disgust on his face. They both neared their front gate at the same time and halted, staring at each other.

'Look at the state of you!' Victor hissed, keeping his voice low. 'You look like a tramp. And you're wearing trousers!'

Prue looked down at the dungarees she'd borrowed from her daughter Alice. They were far more practical than a skirt at the allotment and Prue rather liked them. She was thinking of getting some slacks of her own. 'I've been working at the WI allotment,' she said, keeping her voice steady.

'You are filthy! You ought to think about what sort of message that sends to the village, going around looking like that.' He gestured with his hand towards her, looking her up and down, his nose wrinkling above his narrow moustache as if it had a bad smell under it. He narrowed his icy blue eyes. 'You *never* would have presented yourself in public like this before, but now you're spending so much time with those East End women it's clearly rubbing off on you. You've let yourself down, Prudence.'

Prue's heart rate quickened. How *dare* he speak to her about letting herself down when he'd just come back from committing adultery in Norwich!

'*I've* been working for the community, for the war effort!' she snapped.

'So have *I*, but I don't go around looking a mess. I have some pride,' Victor retorted.

'So you say. How was today's meeting?' Prue stared at

Victor until he quickly looked away. She wanted to tell him that she knew where he'd been but held back, holding onto that nugget of ammunition for when she really needed it.

He gave a dismissive turn of his head. 'You wouldn't understand such committee matters, Prudence.'

'Let me be the judge of that and tell me what they were,' Prue offered.

Victor snorted. 'I suggest you get yourself indoors and cleaned up before anyone else sees you. I'm going to my study. I have work to do.' Without waiting for a response, he went in through the garden gate and let himself in the front door, slamming it shut behind him.

Prue stood in the road, hands on her hips, glaring after him. The nerve of the man. How could he have the bare-faced cheek to stand there mocking a bit of honest dirt on her when he was lying about where he'd been? He was a hypocrite. But then she knew that. It was nothing new. Victor was a man who was all show, caring about putting on an act out of the house, while indoors he was a dominating bully.

She took a deep breath and blew it out slowly, feeling her shoulders drop. So what if she was wearing trousers and a bit dirty? It would wash off! Perhaps her appearance was a shock to him after being with his mistress, a woman whom Prue had often wondered about. What was she like? Prue imagined her as someone glamorous, dressed in fancy clothes. A woman who didn't have any qualms about messing around with someone else's husband. All at once Prue was curious to find out, to see Victor's mistress for herself. She'd never wanted to before, but his reaction had infuriated her. It was something she would have to think about. Right now, she needed a bath.

CHAPTER 20

Thursday 10th April

'Why don't you come with me to The Mother's Day Club this morning, Ada?' Hettie asked as she packed her knitting into her wicker basket. 'You'd be welcome and we're always glad of another pair of hands to help out.'

Ada turned from where she stood staring out of the kitchen window. 'No, I'd rather stay here.'

'What are you going to do then?' Hettie's eyes met her sister's.

Ada gave a shrug of a shoulder.

A spark of annoyance flared inside Hettie. She'd had enough of this. It was ten days since Ada had moved into Rookery House and in all that time she hadn't lifted a finger to help. Not even clearing her plate from the table after a meal or helping with *anything* to do with the running of the home. Her sister had taken but given nothing back. It was time to put an end to that.

'If you don't have anything planned, then I'd be grateful if you would sweep and mop the floor in here while I'm out. Then if you could prepare the vegetables for the stew, it will save me time when I get home. I'll be able to put it in the oven and give the stew time to cook nice and slow and make the meat tender.' Hettie pointed to the basket of fresh vegetables that Thea had brought in for her earlier.

'But…' Ada began.

Hettie held up her hand to silence her. 'I think it's about time you started pulling your weight around here. I appreciate that you've lost your home but sitting about doing nothing isn't helping you. Keeping busy will keep your mind off it and will contribute to you living here. Thea isn't charging you rent when she has every right to, you know. Apart from paying towards your food you're living in this house for free, so it's about time that you gave back don't you think?' Hettie put her hands on her hips giving her sister a hard stare.

'Well, I…' Ada began. She raised her chin. 'You only had to *ask* me to do something, and I'd do it.'

'I'm asking you now. You've run a home for many years Ada. You know there are always jobs to be done and with nine of us living here, there is plenty to do. You don't need to wait to be told to do things. If you're not sure what, then ask me.'

Ada's cheeks flushed. 'Very well.' She folded her arms across her body. 'I'll get those things done by the time you get home.'

'Thank you.' Hettie nodded. 'I'll be back by half past twelve.' She picked up her basket and headed out of the door, closing it quietly behind her.

As Hettie walked to the shed where she kept her bicycle, she realised she was shaking. She had never challenged her sister like that before. With Ada being seven years older than Hettie, her sister had always been the one in charge, and especially when she'd returned to take over after their mother had died. But Ada had to be pulled up on her behaviour now she was living in Thea's house. It was time for her to do her bit, contribute like everyone else who lived there. They all did what they could to help, even the children by doing small jobs. Hettie was sympathetic about Ada losing her home and knew how deeply upset she was, but the time had come to put that behind her and move on. Sometimes people needed a prod in the right direction and that was what Hettie had just done.

CHAPTER 21

Friday 11th April

Thea glanced at Prue, who'd been unusually quiet since they'd met at Great Plumstead railway station earlier that morning. Together they had got the train into Wykeham to collect the WVS canteen and begin their shift. Now, heading off to their first stop of the day, Prue was staring out of the window of the cab.

Thea spotted one of the many heavy lorries full of supplies heading to where the new aerodrome was being built. She changed down to a lower gear, preparing to stop so it could squeeze past. They often met the lorries these days while out doing their round as there many of them going to and fro from the aerodrome site each day. Thea pulled the canteen over in a gateway to let the lorry pass, the driver putting up his hand to thank her.

'You're quiet today?' Thea glanced at her sister again.

Prue didn't answer for a moment, continuing to look straight ahead.

Thea sensed something was amiss. 'What's wrong?'

Her sister turned to face her. 'I'm curious about this woman who Victor's involved with.'

Thea looked at Prue, who stared back at her, her expression serious. 'What's brought that on?' She checked her wing mirror to see if anyone was coming up behind them and, seeing it was clear, switched off the engine to save petrol. Thea needed to give her whole attention to Prue. 'Has something happened?'

'I met Victor when I was going home from the allotment on Sunday. He was coming back from the station. He had this look on his face, like the cat that got the cream. When he saw me... well, he wasn't complimentary about how I looked.' She threw her hands out wide. 'I know I was messy and dirty, but I'd been working all afternoon on the plot. I was wearing a pair of Alice's bib and brace dungarees and he *hates* women dressing in trousers.'

Thea snorted. 'Then I shall keep on wearing mine!'

'Be serious, Thea!' Prue snapped.

'I'm sorry, but that man has ridiculous views. I thought you were fine with him having this mistress of his?'

'I was. I *am*!' Prue sighed, shaking her head. 'But I can't get it out of my mind wondering what she's like. Who *is* this woman that makes Victor look so pleased with himself after he's been to see her? What does she look like? Let's face it, Victor is no Errol Flynn, is he? He never was and now... well he hasn't improved with age the way some men do. The thing is I...' She hesitated for a moment before finishing, 'I want to see her for myself!'

Thea stared at her sister, incredulous. 'Are you serious?'

'Absolutely,' Prue confirmed. 'I'm going to go to Norwich

to discover what she's like. It sounds crazy, but I must! It's become an itch that needs to be scratched.' She bit her bottom lip. 'She really is quite welcome to him, but I need to fill in this gap, know the truth of who he goes to visit every Sunday. In a way, I'm grateful to her, because the more time he spends with her, the less he's at home.'

Thea nodded slowly. 'I understand. When are you going?'

'This Sunday, only I don't want to go alone. Will you come with me, please?' Prue's voice was uncertain.

Thea reached out and took her sister's hand. 'Yes, of course. How about Lizzie, too? She knows where this woman lives.'

'Thank you.' Prue squeezed her hand. 'I thought we could go in on the same train as Victor, without him seeing us. Then we can follow him.'

'Like some private eyes, you mean?' Thea grinned. 'It could be fun.'

Prue gave a half-laugh. 'I suppose. I don't want to confront them or anything, just sate my curiosity. Put a face to this woman.'

'Shall I give Lizzie a ring and ask her to meet us at the station on Sunday morning, then?'

'Please. I know she will think I'm daft.'

'No, she won't,' Thea reassured her. 'She'll enjoy it. You know what Lizzie's like, always up for a bit of mischief.' She took hold of both of Prue's hands. 'And don't let Victor get to you, Prue. He should have been ashamed of *himself* coming home from seeing his mistress, instead of belittling you for what you were dressed in, or for being dirty from honest work doing something for the community. The man is a hypocrite!'

Prue nodded. 'I know, but it caught me off guard.' Her lips

curved into a smile. 'I rather liked wearing dungarees. I think I might buy some of my own *and* some trousers.'

Thea laughed. 'Good for you, Prue. Now we'd better get a move on. We have soldiers waiting for their canteen visit.' Thea started the engine, checked her mirrors, then pulled out into the road, thinking that Sunday was going to be an interesting day.

CHAPTER 22

Saturday 12th April

*The drone of bombers overhead was growing louder by the
second, the unsynchronised beat jarring Flo's nerves. She
hurried, but her fingers and thumbs refused to do her bidding
and she dropped the blanket to the floor of the Anderson.
Bending quickly, she picked it up and put it onto the bunk
bed, tucking in the sides, ready for her mam. Dashing out of
the shelter, up the steps that were steeper and far more in
number than they should have been, her heart was pounding.
If she could just reach the house, help her father and sister
bring Mam and Bobby out to safety, then everything would
be fine. But as Flo took a step towards the house, time seemed
to slow, and she watched in horror as it crumpled in on itself
and she was thrown backwards by the blast. She screamed.*

'Flo, wake up!' A voice broke through, a hand gently shaking
her shoulder.

Struggling up from the deep depths of sleep, Flo slowly opened her eyes, her heart beating hard in her chest. Evie stood beside Flo's bed, her face lit by the pale silvery moonlight flooding the room where the blackout curtain had been pulled to the side.

'You screamed out,' Evie said softly. 'Were you having a nightmare?'

Flo frowned as memories of the sights and sounds she'd been experiencing moments before flooded back making her gasp. Tears filled her eyes and a great sob bubbled up and burst out. She began to weep, her shoulders heaving with each gut-wrenching sob.

Evie sat down on the side of the bed and gently pulled Flo into her arms. 'It's all right, you're safe.' Her voice was gentle.

When Flo's sobs had subsided, she pulled away and wiped her face with the sleeve of her nightdress. 'I'm sorry I woke you.'

'Don't worry about that. You sounded terrified.' Evie's face was full of concern.

Flo sniffed and nodded.

'Do you want to talk about it? It might help.'

Flo chewed on her bottom lip. Part of her longed to speak about it. To unburden the heavy weight that she carried inside her. Hiding it away hadn't diminished the pain. But she couldn't. She shook her head. 'I can't.'

Evie looked at her, searching Flo's face as if looking for clues. 'I had nightmares when I first came to live here,' she said, her voice soft. 'I used to live in London and one night after I'd finished my shift at the hospital, I caught the bus home, hoping to get back before the bombers arrived. Only the air-raid siren sounded halfway there and everyone had to get off the bus and hurry to a shelter. I'd been talking to a young woman who was sat beside me and she showed me a short-cut down an alley. Only I realised I'd left my bag on the bus and dashed back to get it while the woman headed to the shelter. But...' She paused for a moment and took a deep breath before going on. 'A bomb fell in the alleyway and there was nothing left of the woman except for her handbag, which had been blown out into the street. She was gone just like that! There was nothing left for her family to bury.' Evie's eyes glittered with tears. 'If I'd been with her, then I would have been gone too. It shook me up. Made me think about my life and what I was doing. That's when I decided to change things, to leave London. I was sent to work at Great Plumstead Hospital and was fortunate to be billeted here.'

Flo stared at Evie, who she'd never have imagined going through such a shocking experience. With her plummy voice and clearly coming from a wealthy family, Flo had thought Evie had lived a protected life, with only her work as a nurse exposing her to the more unpleasant things.

'That must have been terrible.' Flo put her hand on Evie's arm. 'There, but for the grace of God go I.'

'Exactly! It made me re-evaluate my life and make changes for the better. Before that, I...' Evie looked down at her hands for a moment before returning her gaze to meet Flo's. 'Let's just say I wasn't living a life that brought me joy, so I decided to change it and here I am now. I'm much happier, doing a job I love and living here in a lovely home.'

Flo turned to look out of the window where the garden was lit up in the silvery light of the full moon. That night back in December had changed her life, sending her off on a different track too. But unlike Evie, it wasn't one for the better as she had lost her family. Flo might enjoy her work as a Land Girl, but she would swap it in an instant to have them all back again, alive and well.

'My family were killed in Manchester's Christmas Blitz.'

The words spilled out of Flo's mouth before her mind had a chance to halt them. She turned to look at Evie. 'That was what I was dreaming about.' She let out a heavy sigh and hung her head.

'I'm so sorry.' Evie put her arm around Flo's shoulders. 'Is that what brought you here?'

Flo nodded. 'Eventually.' She took a deep breath and told Evie about what had happened that night and how she'd just relived in it in her nightmare. 'If only I'd been quicker in the shelter and gone back to help get everyone out.' Her voice wavered. 'Maybe then they would have got out before the bomb fell.'

'Or you would have been caught in there with them. They were probably going as fast as they could. You being in there with them wouldn't have made any difference,' Evie reasoned. 'If only the bomb had been released a few seconds before or later, then it would have landed elsewhere. It was the same with the young woman in London. It was pure chance, that's all,' Evie said, her voice sympathetic. 'It wasn't your fault, Flo. Your parents would have been glad that you weren't caught in it too.'

Flo nodded. 'I know, but it doesn't make it any easier to accept that I survived, and they *didn't*.'

'I understand. I felt that with the young woman and we'd only just met. Your situation is far worse as it was your family.' Evie gave her a sideways hug. 'I think you've shown great strength to carry on and start afresh in a new job and in a new place.'

'I wanted to do a job I loved. Seeing how easily life could be lost, I knew I could never go back and do what I did before, working in an office,' Flo explained. 'Joining the Land Army was a chance to do that.'

'And you do it so well.' Evie gave her a warm smile. 'But

you've kept your pain to yourself until now.' Her eyes met Flo's.

Flo nodded. 'I couldn't... You're the first person I've told. Please don't say anything to the others.'

'I won't. I promise you that your secret is safe with me. I am extremely good at keeping secrets when I need to.' Evie gave a wry smile. 'Perhaps I'll tell you more about that one day, but not now.'

'Thank you.' Flo instinctively knew she could trust Evie.

'We'd better get some sleep. It's another busy day tomorrow and Matron Reed has some spring cleaning on the agenda for tomorrow's shift *on top* of our usual routines.' Evie stood up. 'I'm always here to talk to anytime you want to.'

'I appreciate that, thank you,' Flo said again as Evie closed the blackout curtain plunging the room into darkness. Flo snuggled down under her covers and lay staring up into the pitch black, listening as Evie got back into bed and her breathing gradually slowed as she fell asleep.

Sleep didn't come so quickly for Flo, although she felt strangely lighter than she had for a long time. Sharing her secret had helped ease the burden slightly and for that she was grateful. Closing her eyes, she turned onto her side and in her mind took herself out into the garden and became engrossed with a task she loved, placing small seeds full of possibility into the soil, until her thoughts slowed and sleep claimed her once more.

CHAPTER 23

Sunday 13th April

Prue stared at her reflection in the mirror above her dressing table and smiled. Wearing the clothes Thea had loaned her had transformed Prue, she didn't look like her usual self at all. It was unlikely that Victor would give her a second glance if he saw her, as she'd switched from the more traditional-looking clothes she usually wore – the skirts and blouses in muted colours. He had no idea what she was doing in here as they had separate bedrooms and had done for many years.

Turning first to one side and then the other, Prue liked the way the navy slacks fitted. They flattered her slim figure and the cherry red cardigan over the white blouse was bright and cheerful. Her outfit was finished off with a red and white spotted scarf tied over her head and knotted under her chin to hide her ash-blonde hair.

Prue picked up the pair of sunglasses that would complete her disguise and put them on. She put a hand on her hip, watching herself in the mirror, making a bubble of laughter well up, and she couldn't help laughing out loud. What a difference a few clothes made. They didn't just make her look different, but she *felt* different, too. Bolder, confident and braver... and she needed some of that today. Was she crazy to do this? Did she *need* to do it? Prue had spent several sleepless hours last night thinking the same thing, but always the answer was the same. Yes, she did!

She heard the front door close and glanced at her watch. Victor was as punctual as ever, leaving to catch the train into Norwich as he always did on Sunday mornings. They'd been to the early church service and now he was off to one of his so-called meetings. Fortunately, he was someone who always allowed himself plenty of time, which would give Prue a chance to follow him to the station unseen, and still be in time to get on the same train.

With a last glance in the mirror, Prue picked up a bag that Thea had given her, into which she'd transferred the contents of her own handbag. Then she headed downstairs and out into the warm April sunshine to carry out some detective work.

'Prue!' A hushed voice called.

Prue started at the sound of her name and then laughed as her sister stepped out from beside the bicycle shelter near the entrance to Great Plumstead station.

'There you are!' Prue put a hand to her chest. 'Has he gone in?'

'Yes, and I've already bought our tickets. Thought I'd get them before Victor arrived and so no one in the ticket office could comment on your outfit and wonder what you're up to.'

Thea looked Prue up and down. 'You do look lovely. Those clothes suit you and you have the figure for slacks.'

Prue gave her sister a beaming smile. 'I must say I do like them and I feel so different in these clothes, too.' She took in Thea's outfit, a pretty dark green dress that she'd borrowed from Marianne. 'You look unlike your usual self, too.'

Thea spread her hands out wide and laughed. 'It's not really me though, is it? It is a lovely dress, but I'm much more comfortable in my slacks. Needs must today as we're in disguise.' Thea's face became serious. 'Are you *sure* you want to do this? You don't have to. It's fine to change your mind.'

'Yes, absolutely!' Prue said vehemently. 'I *want* to do this. I need to see her for myself, I'm not sure why…' She lifted a shoulder. 'But I do. And today is as good as any and, so far, I am enjoying it.'

Thea nodded. 'Let's go then.' She linked her arm through Prue's and together they walked towards the station entrance. 'Walk tall, look confident.'

They passed through the booking hall, which was busy with other passengers, and out onto the platform. Prue glanced to the right where she could see Victor seated on a bench, reading a newspaper which he must have bought at the station kiosk. Thea steered them to the left, towards the end of the platform furthest away from Victor where Prue positioned herself with her back to him in case he looked up.

'My heart's beating fast with all this undercover business,' Prue said in a hushed voice. 'What's he doing now?'

Thea glanced over Prue's shoulder. 'The same. He hasn't stirred and is still engrossed in the newspaper.' She put her hand on Prue's arm. 'Once we're on the train, you can relax. This is the trickiest bit. Once he's in Norwich, he won't even consider you could be around and it will be much busier there.'

'I...' Prue began but halted at the sound of the train coming.

As it pulled into the station, she risked a glance towards the other end of the platform, past the other passengers who were gathered, waiting to get on. She saw that Victor had got up and was now waiting with his newspaper tucked under his arm. Without a glance in their direction, he climbed aboard a carriage near the engine.

'Come on, we'll get in here.' Thea opened the door of an empty compartment and got in.

Prue followed her sister and moments later they were on their way to Norwich. Leaning back against the springy seat, Prue looked out of the window at the passing countryside, which was cloaked in fresh greens as the trees and hedgerows had burst into leaf with the warmer days. Beautiful white blossom was plentiful on the blackthorn bushes, making some hedges look like they were covered in snow.

'How are you feeling?' Thea asked from her seat opposite, sitting by the window with her back to the engine.

'A bit nervous,' Prue admitted. 'But I'm calming myself down by admiring the view, enjoying the spring. It's beautiful, isn't it?'

'It is,' Thea agreed. 'I love spring with everything so green and growing. It always brings me joy after the long, cold winter.'

They fell into silence for a few minutes, both looking out of the window, lost in their own thoughts.

'Do you remember the last time we went to Norwich together?' Prue asked. 'Back in December to celebrate Lizzie's new job at the Women's Land Army?'

Thea's face clouded. 'That's not a journey I'm likely to forget. The train getting shot at by an enemy plane and everyone having to flee to the woods for safety. Let's hope this trip is less eventful than that one.'

Prue shivered. She'd had dreams about that day for a while afterwards, replaying the feeling of terror and how her legs had turned to jelly as she'd run towards the wood with the little girl in her arms. The sound of the enemy plane as it came roaring in, its machine guns peppering the train and ground. If Prue could survive that, then she could cope with a bit of spying on her husband today.

'I hope so, too. Thanks for coming with me.' Prue gave her sister a grateful smile.

'I'm glad to help. I must admit, I am curious to see this woman who's charmed Victor. Have you imagined what she's like?'

'I've pictured her as some young glamorous woman, but then common sense tells me would such a person be interested in a fifty-five-year-old man like Victor? He's no rich movie star, is he?'

Thea burst out laughing. 'No, he's not! But there must be *something* that has attracted her.'

'Well, it's not because he has two little boys that need a mother,' Prue blurted out and then slapped her hand over her mouth. Her cheeks grew warm and she looked down into her lap. Why had she said that? It was true, but she didn't need to confess it out loud to her sister.

'I thought that might be why you married him,' Thea said in a gentle voice.

Prue slowly nodded. She'd never admitted as much to her sister, even when Thea had questioned Prue's decision to marry Victor all those years ago. He'd been a widower, fifteen years older than her, with two small boys who'd lost their mother the year before. With so many men of her own age being killed in the Great War, Prue had known her chances of ever getting married were tiny, and she *so desperately* wanted to be a mother. Prue had decided it was worth marrying Victor for, even if in normal times, she would never have dreamed of tying herself to a man like him. 'I longed to be a mother so much.'

Thea reached across and took Prue's hands in hers. 'And you have been the most wonderful mother to Jack and Edwin, and then to Alice. They are lucky to have you. Although Victor definitely didn't deserve you.' Thea's blue eyes held Prue's. 'But I understand why you did it, although you would never admit it.'

'When we were arguing over Edwin being a conscientious objector, Victor told me that the only reason he married me was so I could look after the children. He even said that maybe it might have been better to have had a nanny to care for the boys instead...' Prue blinked back sudden tears. 'But that would have cost him money in wages! Whereas I didn't need to be paid.'

Thea gasped, her eyes wide in horror. 'He's a pompous fool. I'm sorry you've been treated so unkindly by him.'

Prue lifted a shoulder. 'I knew what I was getting into, that there was no love there. It was a marriage of convenience, I suppose. I had the chance to be a mother and he had someone to care for his children. I did have a child of my own too. Being married to Victor hasn't been easy, but I have loved being a mother. I made my choice and would do it again...' She paused for a moment and looked out of the window, before returning her gaze to Thea. 'But now they've all grown up and don't need me as they used to. The only tie between Victor and myself is a legal one. He clearly feels no loyalty to me and our marriage. I don't care that he has a fancy woman, in fact I'm *glad* he spends time with her as it means I see even less of him!'

'Isn't it about time you called a halt to your marriage, then?' Thea asked. 'Free both of you to live your lives away from each other.'

Prue drummed her fingers on the arm of her seat. 'Victor would never condone a divorce. He is a *respectable* business owner, chairman of committees and councils, upstanding member of the community... unfaithful husband!' She raised an eyebrow. 'Imagine the scandal if we got divorced? The best I can hope for is that we remain legally married but to all intents and purposes lead separate lives. We do that pretty much now, anyway. Although he still tries to boss me about. I'd like to put a stop to that!'

'Maybe you can.' Thea smiled wryly. 'Armed with information and evidence from today, I'd say you would have a strong case to put to him. You could use it to persuade him to improve things at home. Maybe not divorce but stop his domineering ways.'

Prue smiled. 'I could, couldn't I? Knowledge is power, as they say.'

'What about if you fall in love with someone else and want to marry them?' Thea asked.

Prue burst out laughing. 'I think that highly unlikely. I've experience of one marriage and that is quite enough.'

Arriving at Norwich's City Station, Prue's heart began to beat faster as the train slowed and came to a halt alongside the platform. What if Victor saw her? How would she explain what she was doing in Norwich when she'd told him she planned to spend the day working at the WI's allotment? He would be furious if he thought she was spying on him. But if he was with his fancy woman, he would be in the wrong and caught red-handed, she reasoned. Squaring her shoulders, Prue took a deep breath. She *could* do this and owed it to herself to see what was going on with her own eyes and not just go by what her sister Lizzie had told her.

'Can you see him?' Prue asked as Thea opened the carriage door and peered out. 'We mustn't lose him.'

'He's out and walking towards the exit. Come on.' Thea stepped down onto the platform and Prue hurried after her.

Keeping Victor in sight, but staying well back from him in case he should turn around, they went through the station building and were watching him cross the road when they were joined by another conspirator.

'Hello fellow spies,' their sister Lizzie said in a hushed tone, grinning broadly as she stepped out from behind a parked lorry.

'Lizzie! I'm glad you're here,' Prue said. 'If we lose him — *you* know where he's going.'

'You're both so different!' Lizzie looked them up and down. 'Those slacks are fabulous on you, Prue, but I'm not so sure about your outfit Thea.' She grinned. 'At first glance, though, I didn't recognise either of you!'

'Good!' Thea laughed. 'That's the whole point. Come on, we mustn't lose sight of our target.'

They crossed over the road and followed Victor, who seemed unaware that he was being watched as he strode purposefully along.

'We were talking about what Victor's fancy woman is like on the way,' Thea said. 'Whether or not she's glamorous.'

Lizzie threw her a sideways look. 'I'm not saying anything. I'll let you see for yourself.'

'You're intriguing us even more now!' Thea said.

Lizzie gave a snort of laughter. 'Victor and intrigue were never words I thought I'd hear together.'

'He's certainly been up to something he shouldn't,' Prue said as they waited at the kerbside to cross over another road, her eyes firmly fixed on Victor, who'd already crossed and was making his way along the street.

After they'd followed Victor for another couple of minutes, Lizzie grabbed hold of their arms, bringing them to a halt.

'We should stop here. Her house is halfway along this street, so if we wait by this shop we can seem like we're looking in the window and not raise any suspicion in case he looks round.'

Prue positioned herself so that anyone glancing at them would think she was perusing the shop's display of tins and packets and not in fact watching her husband going to his fancy woman's house.

'He's there,' Lizzie hissed as they watched Victor stop and knock on the door of a house that opened straight onto the street.

Prue stared, thinking that he didn't look like a man who was committing adultery. He wasn't looking around furtively. In fact, he looked positively pleased with himself. The door opened, and he went in, but there was no sign of the woman.

'Is that it?' Prue said in a deflated voice. 'I wanted to see them together.'

'You will,' Lizzie reassured her. 'They'll be out again in a few minutes.'

Prue tapped her foot on the pavement. 'What if they don't come out? What shall we do then?'

Thea put a hand on Prue's arm. 'Be patient.'

Now Prue was here, doubts about the wisdom of doing this flooded through her. Had she done the right thing coming to see her husband with the woman he was betraying his wedding vows to Prue with? But then their marriage was a hollow, empty one, there just in name and legal attachment. There was no love and never had been. It was a sham.

'Here they come!' Lizzie hissed, bringing Prue's attention back to the present.

Prue watched as Victor stepped out of the house, followed by a woman who was a similar age to herself, in her early forties at the most. She was ordinary looking, dressed neatly in a dark green skirt and jacket and matching hat. Victor waited patiently while she locked the door and then he linked his arm through the woman's and they headed off towards the city centre, fortunately walking away from where Prue, Thea and Lizzie stood.

'She looks... normal,' Prue said, breaking the silence that had fallen over them as they'd watched. 'Not a glamorous dolly bird at all!'

'Have you seen enough?' Thea asked gently.

'No, I'm curious.' Prue started to follow Victor and the woman and her sisters soon drew alongside her, linking their arms through hers.

All the while, Prue kept her eyes on the couple ahead, who were unaware they were being tailed. Again, Victor showed no signs of sneaking around or trying to hide his affair, but then he'd been carrying on like this for some time and, as far as he knew, Prue was none the wiser.

'Look at that!' Prue hissed, noticing how he dipped his head towards the woman, moving closer and even throwing back his head and laughing. Victor had *never* behaved like that with her. He'd never linked arms with her in public, parading her around, showing they were a couple. 'He's different with her!' She halted, a heavy, sickening lump settling in her stomach. 'I've seen enough. Let them go off and do whatever they do.' She flapped a hand in their direction, watching as they turned off the street and headed up one of the side alleys that led to the city centre.

'Are you sure?' Thea asked.

Prue nodded. 'Yes, I honestly don't like Victor or want anything more from him but seeing him like that...' She shuddered. 'He was never attentive to me in that way. I thought that was just how he was, but clearly not. He *is* capable of it if he wants to be. I don't want to see any more; it makes me feel...' She hesitated, searching for the words to explain the horrible hollow emptiness inside her. It wasn't jealously, more like a profound sadness that she'd wasted so much of her life, time and energy on Victor. 'Sad!'

'Don't be sad, be *mad* at him!' Lizzie protested, throwing her hands up in the air. 'The man's a fool and you shouldn't waste precious energy on him. You've been a far better wife than he deserves, Prue. It's time for you to put *yourself* first. He always has.'

Prue looked at Lizzie, who had always grabbed life with both hands and squeezed every drop of enjoyment out of it. She had never shackled herself to any man. 'You're right. I've seen enough. Victor and his lady friend are welcome to each other. There are plenty of other people in my life who I value and things I do that make a difference.' Prue managed a smile and raised her chin. 'So come on, let's not waste any more time. Shall we go and get something to eat, make the most of being in Norwich?'

Lizzie grinned. 'Come on, I know just the place.'

CHAPTER 24

Saturday 19th April

'Can I see them?' George whispered, peering into the open door of the hutch where Flopsy, the doe rabbit, had made her nest. 'Please.' His eyes shone with excitement.

'Just a quick peep. We don't want to upset their mother.' Flo glanced at Flopsy who'd gone out into the run and was feasting on the pile of plants that Flo and George had gathered a short while ago after he'd come home from school.

Flo gently teased the hay nest apart, which was lined with soft fur that Flopsy had pulled from her body to make her babies a warm bed. 'Can you see them?'

George's face was alight with delight. 'They ain't got no fur!' he whispered. 'And their eyes are shut.'

'They'll soon grow some and will open their eyes,' Flo reassured him.

'How many are there?' Betty asked as she peered in the hutch.

'I'm not sure yet. I've seen at least four, but there could be more. I've only just had a quick peep.' Flo checked that Flopsy was still busy eating. The doe's enormous appetite would ensure she could produce enough milk for her babies.

'Can we hold one?' Betty asked.

'No, they need to stay in the warm and we don't want to upset Flopsy. She'd be able to tell if you had by the smell from your hands,' Flo explained. 'Once the babies are old enough to venture out of their nest, then you can.' She gently closed the nest over again and shut the hutch door.

Betty, satisfied that there was no chance of holding a baby rabbit right now, stood up from where she'd been kneeling next to the hutch and headed off to the house while George remained, watching Flopsy eat.

'She ain't got a big tummy now her babies are born,' he said.

'No, but it's not surprising it was round with at least four babies in there. I wonder what colour the babies' fur will be when it grows?' Flo mused. 'Some might look like Flopsy or like Benjamin.'

'I don't mind what their fur looks like,' George said. 'They'll all be lovely.'

Flo looked at the little boy and smiled. 'Yes, they will be. Are you going to stay here and watch Flopsy?'

He nodded. 'I promise I won't look at the babies again. I don't want to upset Flopsy. I just like watching her eat. Shall I give her some more from the sack if she finishes that lot?' He pointed at the pile of plants, which had already gone down since they'd put it in the run for Flopsy to tuck into.

'Yes, she needs to eat plenty. And I trust you not to look at the babies, George.' Flo patted his shoulder. 'I know how much you care for the rabbits.'

He nodded and gave her a beaming smile and then

returned his attention to watching Flopsy, who was now chewing a long piece of hogweed. It was disappearing into her mouth at a rapid rate, her jaws moving from side to side, her whiskers twitching.

Flo stood up and went to the greenhouse, where she had some pricking out of seedlings to attend to. She admired George's devotion to the rabbits. The little boy hadn't once missed going with her to forage for food for them and always helped to clean out the hutches. He spent a lot of time sitting watching the rabbits when he was home from school, his thoughtful, kind nature shining through. Flo had to admit that she enjoyed being with George too. Her plan to keep her distance from him because he reminded her so much of Bobby was crumbling, though she wasn't yet sure if that was a good thing, or not.

CHAPTER 25

Monday 28th April

'Good morning!' Thea pulled the blackout curtain back from the window, letting the bright sunshine flood into the children's bedroom. 'Time to get up.'

She went over to the bed where Betty lay wide awake, while George was still fast asleep beside her, his cheeks flushed. Thea's stomach lurched as something was clearly wrong. Usually, George woke up first and was eager to get up when Thea came in to open the curtains.

'George is 'ot but he keeps shivering,' Betty informed her. 'What's the matter with him?'

Thea sat down on the side of the bed and put her hand on the little boy's forehead. He definitely had a fever.

'It looks like he's unwell. Let's get you up, but George needs to stay in bed to rest.'

As Betty clambered out of the bed, her brother stirred and he opened his eyes.

144

'How are you feeling?' Thea took hold of his hot hand in hers.

'Sore throat,' George croaked. 'It 'urts when I swallow.'

'Don't worry, I'll ask Evie to come and have a look at you. It's her day off today.' Thea stood up. 'I'll be back soon.'

With Betty following close behind, Thea hurried down to the kitchen where she was glad to see Evie was up and eating her breakfast, along with Flo, Ada, Marianne and Emily.

'Evie, can you come and see George?' Thea asked. 'He's not well.'

'Of course.' Evie stood up from the table.

'Come and have some breakfast, Betty.' Hettie came over and took hold of the little girl's hand, her eyes meeting Thea's, who gave her a nod of thanks.

'But I want to...' Betty began turning back to follow Thea.

'No, you need to have your breakfast first, so you're not late for school.' Hettie put her arm around Betty's shoulder and steered her towards the table where Flo was ladling some porridge into a bowl for the little girl.

'What's the matter with George?' Evie asked as they walked up the stairs.

'He's feverish and has a sore throat,' Thea explained. 'Says it hurts to swallow.'

'I'll just get my things from my room and will have a look at him.' Evie put her hand on Thea's arm as they reached the landing. 'Try not to worry.'

As Evie examined George a short while later, Thea felt grateful that they had a nurse living with them. It was an anxious time for any parent when their child was ill. Thea wasn't George's mother but she was looking after him for his parents who were in London, and that was a big responsibility. She felt it even more so now he was poorly.

'Open your mouth as wide as you can for me, like this, and

stick out your tongue.' Evie demonstrated to George what she wanted him to do. 'I'm going to shine my torch inside to see what's making your throat so sore.'

George did as she asked and Evie had a careful look inside.

'Your tonsils are swollen. No wonder it's hard to swallow. You can close your mouth now.' George obeyed and she switched off her torch. 'Now I'm going to feel around your neck.' Evie gently felt either side of his jaw and the top of his neck. Then she took his pulse, using the watch she usually had pinned on her nurse's uniform.

'I think this young man has tonsillitis,' Evie said, looking up at Thea from where she sat on the edge of the bed. 'He needs lots of rest, cold fluids and we must bathe him with tepid water to get his temperature down. No school for you until you're well enough.' She took hold of the little boy's hand and gave it a gentle squeeze. 'You'll soon feel better.'

'Can I get up to feed Flopsy and Benjamin?' George asked, struggling to sit up.

'No.' Thea gently stroked his hair. 'You must rest. Don't worry, Flo will make sure the rabbits are well looked after.'

He looked relieved as he sank back against the pillow.

'I'll bring up some of Hettie's elderberry rob and honey, as that's good for sore throats,' Thea said. 'And some tepid water and a cloth.'

Evie nodded. 'I'll stay here.' She turned to George. 'Perhaps we should read a story?'

'That one.' He pointed to a book on the chest of drawers.

'I won't be long.' Thea patted George's shoulder, mouthed thank you to Evie and then headed downstairs.

In the kitchen, while Thea busied herself making a drink from the elderflower rob Hettie made every autumn to help with colds and soothe sore throats, Marianne was organising Betty ready for school.

'I want to stay here with George,' Betty declared. 'I don't want to go to school without him.'

'He's too poorly to go today,' Thea explained. 'He has to stay in bed and rest, but you're well, so you must go.'

'George will spend a lot of today asleep and we'll all have to be quiet so as not to disturb him,' Hettie added. 'You'll have more fun at school playing with your friends.'

Betty looked thoughtful and finally nodded. 'Will George be awake when I get home?'

'Probably if he's had plenty of sleep,' Thea said. 'Then you can tell him what you've been up to all day. He'll like that.'

'Come on, let's go and wash your hands and face.' Marianne, who had Emily balanced on one hip, held out her hand to Betty. The little girl took it and they headed off to the bathroom.

'George was worried about not being able to help feed the rabbits,' Thea told Flo, who was clearing the used bowls off the table and stacking them by the sink.

'Tell him I'll take good care of them. Perhaps I can go and see him later and let him know how they are?' Flo suggested.

Thea smiled. 'I'm sure he'd like that.' She put the cup of elderflower rob and honey on a tray, along with a jug of water and a glass, and a bowl of tepid water and a clean cloth, and headed upstairs to help look after George. What Thea had planned to do this morning could wait. Looking after the little boy was far more important.

CHAPTER 26

Wednesday 30th April

'Their eyes were open this morning when I peeped in the nest.' Flo watched as George's pale face broke into a wide smile. 'And their fur is growing. It won't be long before the baby bunnies start to explore outside their nest.'

'I need to get well enough to go and see them,' George said.

'You'll soon be able to get outside again,' Flo reassured him. After two days confined to his bed and with plenty of rest and care from Thea, Hettie and Evie, the little boy had improved enough to come downstairs to lie on the sofa in the sitting room where a flickering fire in the hearth threw out a gentle warmth.

Each day since George had become ill, Flo had spent some time with him, bringing him up to date with the latest developments with Flopsy, Benjamin and their babies, as well as reading to him.

Flo had missed George's company when she'd been out

foraging for food for the rabbits. Without him, it had been so quiet – just her and the surrounding sounds of the countryside. She'd grown used to the little boy's keen observations about the things they saw and the joy it gave him. Despite her intention to keep her distance from him, there was no doubt that he'd become important to her. She'd been worried about him and it was a relief to see George looking better. Although he was still pale, he was much improved from the feverish child who'd found it hard to swallow.

When Flo fed the rabbits she was sure they'd noticed his absence too. Normally, George would spend ages with the rabbits, stroking and talking to them as they ate. He was a quiet little boy who didn't waste words, but when he did speak he was always worth listening to.

'What story would you like today?' Flo asked.

'Peter Rabbit.' George selected the book from the pile of Beatrix Potter books which had been brought down for him from his and Betty's bedroom. He held it out to her.

Flo laughed as she accepted it. 'I think we could probably recite it off by heart now.' She had read it to him several times over the past few days, along with *The Tale of Benjamin Bunny*. George never tired of it and she had to admit she loved the books too, enjoying their beautiful illustrations.

'Sit here.' George shuffled over and motioned for Flo to sit at the end of the sofa.

She did as he asked, and once she was sitting down, the little boy leaned back against her. Flo's breath caught in her throat. She recalled her brother Bobby doing the same thing so that he could see the pages of the book she was reading to him. Flo missed her brother so much. But George wasn't Bobby, Flo firmly reminded herself. She had been wrong to think she should keep her distance from George. It hadn't been fair to him or to herself if she was honest. Just because she'd suffered the terrible loss of her family, it shouldn't mean that she must never let others become close and important to her. George had no idea that he had broken down Flo's resolve, but she was grateful that he had.

'Are you comfy?' she asked, tucking the soft woollen blanket around him.

He turned and looked up at her. 'Yes, are you?'

'I am.' Flo gave him a wide smile, opened the front cover of the book and began to read.

CHAPTER 27

Wednesday 7th May

'Wake up!'

The urgent voice was accompanied by a firm shaking of Flo's shoulder and she slowly dragged herself from the depths of a deep, comfortable sleep.

'Come on, you must get up. *Now!*'

Flo squinted her eyes open, blinking in the cowled torchlight illuminating Evie, who stood beside Flo's bed.

'What's the matter?' Flo mumbled.

'There's an air-raid warning. We need to get to the shelter,' Evie said, tying the cord of her blue woollen dressing gown around her waist.

Flo frowned. She couldn't hear anything, apart from barking coming from downstairs. Reuben's dog, Bess, was staying here tonight while Rueben was out on duty with the Home Guard. Flo had heard enough air-raid sirens wailing above the rooftops of Manchester to know exactly what an air-raid warning sounded like, and it wasn't anything like this.

'It's nothing… Go back to sleep.' Flo turned on her side, pulling the covers up around her shoulders.

'Wait! Listen.' Evie strode over to the window, pushed the blackout curtain to the side and heaved up the bottom sash. Cool night air spilled into the room along with the faint up and down wail of a siren.

Hairs stood up on the back of Flo's neck and her heart rate accelerated rapidly. 'It's a raid! We need to get out!' She leapt out of bed, stuffed her feet into her slippers, grabbed her dressing gown from the end of her bed and put it on.

'Why's the siren so quiet? We can hardly hear it,' Flo asked as she followed Evie out onto the landing.

'It's in Wykeham. That's four miles from here. Luckily the dog has better hearing and alerts us.'

'Good, you're both awake,' Thea said, coming out of the children's bedroom with a drowsy Betty in her arms. 'Evie, can you get George and carry him out? He's very sleepy too. Flo, could you go down and help Hettie take the baskets out to the Anderson. She's already gone downstairs to the kitchen. We'll be along shortly.'

Fear flared in the pit of Flo's stomach. 'No!' she snapped. She wasn't going to let history repeat itself, leaving anyone in the house in an air raid while she headed to the shelter. 'We need to get *everybody* out first! I'll fetch George.'

Before anyone could protest, Flo dashed to the children's bedroom and scooped the still sleeping little boy up into her arms. Fully recovered from his recent illness, he barely stirred as Flo covered him in a blanket from the bed and then headed out onto the landing. All the while, her heart hammered hard in her chest and her ears strained to pick up the sound of approaching bombers.

Flo was relieved to see Marianne was ahead of her, carrying a still sleeping Emily. She carefully followed them down the stairs with her precious load in her arms, fighting the urge to run for fear of dropping George.

When they reached the kitchen, it was empty, the others having gone out to the Anderson.

'We need to hurry!' Flo urged Marianne. 'The bombers could be here at any moment.'

'It's usually a false alarm. We've never been bombed here, I don't think Great Plumstead is likely to be a target,' Marianne said. 'It's probably just them passing over on the way to somewhere else that triggers the alarm.'

'*Yet!* You haven't been bombed *yet*,' Flo chided. Her home hadn't either until that night back in December and they'd never seriously thought it would be. But it had happened, and it could happen here too. 'You don't want to risk it.'

Outside, Marianne used the light from her cowled torch to guide their way across the grass, while overhead thousands of pinpricks of stars stood out against the inky blackness.

The yards to the Anderson shelter seemed to take an age to cover and Flo's nerves were tightly strung as she strained for any sound of approaching engines above in the night sky. There was nothing. The air-raid siren had fallen silent and only the sound of tawny owls could be heard calling to each other from the orchard.

Flo paused at the entrance and gestured for Marianne to go in first and then followed her down the short flight of steps to the safety of the shelter. Once they were inside, Thea closed the door behind her and pulled the blackout curtain across as Flo laid George down on the bed at the end beside his sister, who was asleep. Tucking the blanket around him, Flo closed her eyes and let out a silent sigh of relief. It had only been a matter of a few minutes since she'd been woken by Evie, but they had shaken her and stirred up feelings and memories which she'd tried so hard to bury. However they were clearly still there, just below the surface waiting to re-emerge given the right conditions.

'Come and sit down, Flo.' Hettie called. 'Have a cup of tea.'

Flo turned and smiled at the older woman and did as she was asked, taking a seat beside her on one of the long benches that lined each side of the shelter. Opposite her sat Thea, Evie and Marianne, who held her sleeping daughter in her arms. Bess lay by the doorway, head on her paws, eyes closed but with her ears twitching, listening out.

Hettie was pouring out cups of tea from a flask when it suddenly dawned on Flo that someone was missing.

'Where's Ada?'

'In her bed,' Hettie tutted. 'She's not coming out, not for no German bombers, so she said!'

'But she can't stay in the house!' Flo leapt to her feet. Bess sprang up and stared at her with her amber eyes. Flo grabbed a torch to take with her. 'I'm going to get her.'

'But…' Hettie began, but Flo didn't wait to hear.

She pushed the blackout curtain to the side, opened the door and headed back out into the darkness with Bess following at her heels. A surge of anger was flooding through Flo. How could Ada be so foolish as to stay in bed when the house could be bombed? Did she think she was invincible? That it couldn't happen to her? It could happen to *anyone*, anywhere. Just because they weren't in the middle of a city didn't mean that a bomber wouldn't drop its bombs on them.

Hurrying indoors, Flo ordered Bess to wait in the kitchen before running up the stairs to the front bedroom that Hettie and Ada shared. Without stopping to knock, she barged in.

'Ada! You need to get to the shelter. *Now*!' Flo advanced

across the room, her torch lighting the way. 'Come on Ada, get up!'

The hump in the bed stirred. 'Go away! I'm staying put.'

Fuelled with anger, Flo grabbed a dressing gown hanging on the door and then, with one swift movement, pulled the covers back, leaving Ada lying there in her long, voluminous white nightgown. 'I don't want any nonsense from you, not now. You either come with me of your own accord or I will pick you up and carry you over my shoulder like a sack of spuds.'

'I...' Ada began but fell silent as Flo held out the dressing gown to her.

'Put this on and then you've got to the count of three. One way or another, you're going to the Anderson shelter. How you do it is up to you Ada, but I'm not leaving you in here.' Flo stood, hands on her hips, watching as the older woman hesitated for a moment. 'One...' she began to count.

'You should show respect to your elders,' Ada said huffily as she got to her feet and put on her dressing gown, then stepped into her slippers. 'There's no need to go to the shelter. They aren't going to bomb here.'

'Two...'

'All right, I'm on my way, but I won't forget this, young woman!'

'After you then.' Flo gestured for Ada to go first. 'I'm risking my neck coming back in here for you.'

'I didn't ask you to,' Ada threw back over her shoulder.

'Move it!' Flo hissed.

'I shall be having words with Thea about your lack of respect,' Ada muttered as she made her way down the stairs.

'Go right ahead. And if any bombs fall on the house while we're in the shelter, you can thank me later for coming back to get you!'

155

Flo wasn't sure why she'd bothered to fetch the ungrateful woman, but her conscience wouldn't have allowed her to leave anyone in here while there was the potential, the possibility, of a bomb falling on it.

Hurrying across the garden, with Bess following, Flo scanned the sky for any sign of enemy planes, but there was nothing... yet.

Thea must have been listening out for them as she opened the door as soon as they descended the steps into the shelter and let them in.

'She made me come out!' Ada moaned as she stepped inside. 'And was rude and disrespectful. You need to have words with her, Thea.'

Ada sat down next to her sister, folding her arms across her thin body. 'I *told* you I was fine where I was.' She directed this to Hettie.

'You did, but Flo was worried about you, Ada. You should be grateful that she came back for you and risked her safety to return to the house.' Hettie's voice was firm.

'*Humph!*' Ada pressed her lips into a line. 'I neither asked for it nor wanted it. It's cold in here.' She gave an exaggerated shiver.

'Wrap this around you.' Thea took a folded blanket from one of the baskets stowed under the bench where she sat. 'You'll soon warm up.'

'And drink this.' Hettie held out a cup of tea she'd just poured from a flask. 'It will help warm you up from the inside.'

Ada took the blanket and cup without a word of thanks.

Flo sat down on the other side of Hettie, opposite Thea where she'd been earlier.

'This is for you.' Thea held out a blanket to Flo.

'Thank you.' Flo wrapped it around her shoulders like a cloak.

'And your tea.' Hettie pressed a filled cup into Flo's hands. 'You dashed off before you had any.'

'Thank you.' The warmth from the cup felt good in her hands. As she took a sip, she noticed Thea was looking at her across the width of the shelter, with a quizzical look on her face.

Flo looked away, her gaze settling on the cup in her hands, watching the spirals of steam rising from it into the cool air of the shelter. What must Thea and the others think of her behaviour tonight? No one else had reacted in the way she had. Nobody had panicked or been overly worried about Ada staying in the house. But then they hadn't experienced what she had, seen what an unexpected bomb could do. She desperately hoped they never would. That no bomb would ever land anywhere near Rookery House, but there was always the chance one could. Flo was not prepared to take a risk that people she'd grown fond of could be injured or worse. Even Ada, who she didn't hold in the same esteem as the others. But Ada was Hettie's sister, and Hettie would be devastated if anything happened to her and so that made her important, too.

Flo closed her eyes and leaned against the corrugated steel wall of the shelter, listening to the low voices talking around her, all the while waiting for the sound of bombers' engines overhead. She wouldn't rest until the all-clear had gone and they were back in their beds again.

CHAPTER 28

Prue arranged the lettuces into a pleasing display, their fresh green crispness looking inviting. Along with the bunches of pink and white radishes, this was the first crop to come from the WI's allotment and be ready for sale here on the Great Plumstead WI's stall at Wykeham's weekly market.

'You're as proud of them as a mother clucking over her babies.'

Prue turned to see Hettie giving her a knowing look.

She laughed. 'Though I wouldn't have sold my babies. But yes, you're right, Hettie. I *am* proud of these. A lot of time and effort has gone into getting them here to market and I hope our customers will snap them up. This is just the start of what our allotment will be providing over the coming months.'

'So I hear from Flo.' Hettie added some more jars of WI-made blackberry and apple jam to the display on the stall. 'She's enjoying helping there and I'm pleased that she's getting to meet more people in the village. Though where Flo finds the energy from, I don't know. She works all week for Thea and then spends her time off working at the WI allotment.'

'We're glad to have her helping us. Flo's taught us such a lot already and is making friends. Perhaps Ada might come along too,' Prue said. 'It would give her a chance to meet people. I suggested it to her before when I met her in Barker's grocers, but she said she's not one for joining in.'

Hettie tutted. 'She isn't! More's the pity. It would do her good to do something for the community but, sadly, there's little hope of that.' She sighed heavily, her usual happy-looking face wearing a weary expression which matched the bruised shadows under the older woman's eyes.

'Are you all right, Hettie?' Prue asked. 'Only you look tired.'

'We were up in the night with the air-raid siren going off,' Hettie said. 'But I was awake before that, to be honest, because Ada's snoring had woken me up again. I haven't had a good night's sleep since she moved in. It's not her fault she snores. I keep telling myself it won't be for long as we'll find her a new place to live, eventually.'

'She told me she wants a cottage to herself, but there's precious few of those available because we've had so many evacuees arrive. Now with the aerodrome being built, there's been more demand than ever, but we've got less housing.' Prue adjusted the position of a bunch of radishes. 'All there is available now are rooms to lodge in houses. I've been keeping an eye out, but there hasn't been anything suitable so far. Has she found anything?'

'No, nothing suitable, not if Ada wants to stay around here. She could go further afield, I suppose, but wants to live on familiar ground, which I can appreciate.' Hettie sighed. 'Ada's lost her home and the thought of having to start again somewhere completely unknown is too much for her.'

'And in the meantime, she's at Rookery House and you have to live with her.' Prue reached out and patted Hettie's arm.

'Well, she *is* family and there's no one else to help her. Our brothers are abroad — so it's up to me. I couldn't see her turned out of her house with nowhere to go and Thea kindly said she could stay at Rookery House, although,' Hettie raised her eyebrows behind her round glasses, 'she might have regretted that decision by now, as Ada's such a prickly character.'

'Has Thea said as much?' Prue asked.

'Of course not. But I know she's concerned. Rookery House has always been such a happy place, no matter who's come to live there, and we've had a few different people over recent years. But none of them have been like Ada. And she's *family* — that's what makes it worse!'

Prue let out a laugh. 'Family can be more difficult to live with than strangers. You only have to look at my husband to prove that. Perhaps if we put Ada and Victor together in the same house…?'

'Can you imagine that?' Hettie chuckled. 'I don't think it would last very long.' She paused. 'I shall keep that in mind when Ada's being difficult. It will cheer me up.'

The noise of someone clearing their throat caught Prue's attention and she turned to face the woman standing in front of the stall.

'Are those fresh?' She pointed at the lettuces.

'Absolutely, I picked them myself first thing this morning from our WI allotment,' Prue told her. 'The same goes for the radishes.'

'Then I'll have a lettuce and a bunch of radishes, please,' the woman said.

'Certainly.' Prue beamed at her, delighted that the results of her plan for the village WI to Dig for Victory was coming to fruition with their first customer. The first of many, she hoped.

CHAPTER 29

Thursday 15th May

'You need to move over so I can do my work!' Flo gently pushed one of the pigs out of the way of where she was trying to clean out the soiled straw.

The pair of them treated the regular cleaning of their pigsty as a chance to play, tugging at the legs of Flo's dungarees with their teeth. She bent down and scratched the pig's head for a moment and the other pig nudged at her free hand for some scratching too, not wanting to be left out. Flo always enjoyed spending time with them since their arrival six weeks ago.

Before the piglets came to Rookery House, Flo had had no experience with the animals, had no idea what characters they were and how clean their habits. They were particular about how they kept their indoor quarters, using a corner as their toilet, well away from the area which they used for their bed.

'Come on, I need to clean this out. I've got other jobs to get on with after this, you know.' Flo gave the piglet a final scratch and then took the fork from the wheelbarrow and began to load soiled straw into the barrow. She'd just finished clearing out the toilet area and replaced the soiled straw with bedding from where they slept, when a voice called from outside.

'How are you getting on?' Thea asked.

'Good, I'm nearly done.' Flo wheeled the full barrow out of the pig's indoor quarters to the walled yard of their sty. 'I just need to add the fresh straw and then they can sort their clean bed out.'

Thea leaned over the wall and scratched the heads of both piglets who'd followed Flo out and had gone to her for more attention. 'They've grown so much since we got them.'

'How long will they stay?' Flo asked. She didn't like to think about what would happen when it was time to say goodbye to them.

'Another three or four months at least.' Thea bit her lip. 'It will be hard when that time comes, but we need to remember that's the reason they're here. In the meantime, they're having a good life with us and are well cared for.'

Flo nodded. 'I try not to think about that and just enjoy being with them for now.'

Thea gave her a smile. 'Very wise. How are you feeling? Not too tired after last night? Did you manage to get back to sleep again?'

'A little.' Flo had struggled to sleep once they'd returned to their beds after an hour waiting in the shelter during the early hours of the morning. Her body had been tired, but her mind wouldn't rest, going over and over the air raid that had robbed her of her family and home. She'd only fallen asleep for what seemed like minutes before Evie's alarm clock had gone off a little after six, startling her awake again.

'We don't get as many raids as places like London do, but

we *always* take them seriously and go to the Anderson.' Thea's voice was serious.

'Are you going to give me a ticking off about making Ada go to the shelter? I didn't take any nonsense from her and wasn't respectful,' Flo admitted. 'But if I hadn't been, she wouldn't have budged.'

The corners of Thea's mouth twitched. 'I understand. Ada's not the easiest of people to deal with. But you seemed in a bit of a panic, even before that, with how you dashed off to fetch George. Was that the first air raid you've experienced?'

Flo shook her head. 'I wish it was,' she said softly. 'I've been through them before...' She hesitated for a moment, biting her bottom lip, and then the words poured out, as if they'd broken through a dam. 'I was in the Manchester Christmas Blitz last December. I lost... my family and my home.' She dropped her gaze to the ground, blinking back scalding tears that prickled her eyes.

Flo heard the wooden gate of the sty open and close, then felt Thea's arms wrap around her and hold her tightly. Sobs erupted out of her and she cried out from the pain that she'd been bottling up hoping that it would fade. But it hadn't.

When her sobs eventually subsided, Flo stepped back and pulled a clean handkerchief out of her dungarees' pocket and wiped it over her face. 'I'm sorry.'

'There's no need to apologise.' Thea's voice was gentle. 'I'm so sorry you've been through such a horrible time. I had no idea.'

Flo gave a half-smile. 'You weren't supposed to. I decided the best thing to do was hide it away, not mention it to anyone. I thought that way it couldn't hurt so much.' She frowned. 'Only it's never stopped hurting. I just got better at hiding it.'

'When you first came here you said you were from Lancaster?'

'Yes, it's where I was born and grew up. We only moved to Manchester when my … my father got a new job there. My grandparents, my mam's parents, are still in Lancaster and it's always been my proper home.'

'Did you have any brothers or sisters?'

'Yes, one of each. My sister, Joyce…' Flo's voice caught and she halted to compose herself. Swallowing hard, she went on, 'It's strange to say her name out loud again, but good. She was two years older than me, and we had a little brother, Bobby. He was six, a similar age to George. There was my mam and dad too. All of them were killed when next door took a direct hit and it blasted through and brought our home down on them. They were on the way to the Anderson. A few minutes more and they would have been in there safe.'

'Were you in the house?'

Flo shook her head. 'No.' She sighed heavily, blinking away tears. 'My dad sent me down to the shelter with the baskets to get it ready while he and Joyce went to fetch Mam and Bobby, who were ill in bed with the flu. I was about to go back in to help when the house blew up in front of me.' She squeezed her hands into tight fists as images of her home imploding on itself flashed through her mind.

Thea put her arm around Flo again. 'I'm so sorry.' She paused, looking thoughtful. 'When I asked you last night to take the baskets out to the shelter, it must have opened up your wounds. No wonder you said no and wanted to get everyone out.'

Flo sniffed. 'I'm never going to make that mistake again.'

Thea turned so that she was looking Flo straight in the eye. 'It wasn't *your* fault that your family was killed. It was pure chance that the bomb fell before they got out. You *mustn't* blame yourself.'

'I know. Logic says that, but I still wonder if I'd gone to help them as well, instead of taking the baskets out, then they might have been quicker.'

'It sounds like your mother and brother both had help. It wasn't as if they were left alone to struggle out,' Thea reasoned. 'You did what your father asked you to do.'

Flo nodded. 'But I want to have a reason *why* and who caused it to happen. Having someone to blame helps.'

'Well *you* certainly aren't to blame. *You* didn't drop the bomb.' Thea's tone was gentle.

'The blame lies firmly with the enemy bomber who dropped that bomb.' Flo took a deep breath. 'I wonder if they ever think about the devastation they're causing to innocent people, about how they wreck lives and homes?'

Thea frowned. 'Probably not, otherwise how could they live with themselves? It's war and a target, that's all.' She shook her head. 'War is *wrong*. Leaders might start wars, but they are seldom at the sharp end where people get hurt.'

Flo took another deep breath. 'I'm glad you know now. I didn't like not telling you because you've been so kind and welcoming to me. All of you have.'

'It's fine. It was your story to tell when the time was right. You weren't in the Land Army when it happened?'

'No, I had a job in an office. It was the most boring job typing letters, taking shorthand. Didn't suit me at all.' Flo grimaced. 'I lost it the night of the Blitz too, as the building where I worked was destroyed. After I went to my grandparents in Lancaster, I promised myself I would do something that I loved. Work that made me happy and that's gardening and growing things. Losing my family so suddenly showed me how easily life can be snatched away. I didn't want to waste any more of mine doing a job I hated. So I volunteered for the Land Army working in horticulture and here I am. I love my work here at Rookery House.' She managed a smile. 'It gives me joy.'

Thea touched Flo's arm. 'I'm glad you came here. We all love having you living with us. And you're right about doing what you love in life, what makes you happy. We all must work, so we might as well do something we enjoy. I don't suppose your horticulture training included looking after pigs, though.' Thea scratched the back of one of the pigs, who was leaning against her.

'No, but I think it's a bonus to look after them. I like it and they make me laugh.' Flo smiled as one of the pigs tugged at one of the legs of her dungarees again. 'I'd better get this finished.'

'I'm glad you told me about your family, Flo. If there's anything I can do or if you need to talk about them, then I am always ready to listen.' Thea's blue eyes held Flo's.

'Thank you. Evie already knows about it after I had a nightmare. Would you tell Hettie and the others for me? I don't mind them knowing, but I'd rather not have to go through explaining it to them all.'

'Of course, I understand. I've got to take the vegetable order down to Barker's grocery, so I'll see you later.' Thea gave the nearest pig a final pat and let herself out of the sty yard.

Left on her own with the two piglets, Flo finished off the job, shaking out clean straw for them in their indoor quarters. She laughed as she watched them skittering around, leaping with delight as they charged through the fresh straw. Flo knew this game would go on for a while before they began the serious business of moving it and organising it into a new bed. Their happiness in such a simple thing reminded her to take joy from her everyday life, things that she did which made her smile, laugh, or just gave her a sense of satisfaction. She was alive and must appreciate that she had been spared when her family hadn't been so fortunate.

With a final smile at the pigs' antics with the straw, Flo went out to the sty yard, opened the gate and pushed the full wheelbarrow through it. Making sure she closed the gate securely behind her, she headed for the muck heap to deposit this load of manure to rot down, then she had some seeds to sow in the greenhouse. Flo felt so much lighter now she had shared her secret. Keeping what had happened from Thea hadn't felt right and had become harder with every day that passed as her love for living here at Rookery House with this wonderful group of people had grown.

CHAPTER 30

Friday 16th May

Thea loved the lighter evenings that grew steadily longer every day. Coming out to the sun-warmed greenhouse to check on the seedlings and water them each night after tea was always a pleasure.

She checked on the progress of the sunflowers, which were shooting upwards, developing more pairs of leaves, and would soon be ready to plant out. This was the first year of growing them here and she'd wanted to give them as good a start as possible, especially as the young plants made a tasty morsel for slugs and snails. At least if the sunflowers were well established and larger by the time they were planted out, then they stood a better chance of surviving to flower and go on to produce seeds which would be used to feed the chickens.

Thea was watering some delicate seedlings, keeping the flow of droplets from the spout of the watering can steady, when she heard the door of the greenhouse open behind her. She turned and saw Marianne standing in the doorway.

'Can I speak to you about something?' Marianne's expression was apprehensive.

'Of course. Are you all right, and Emily?' Thea put the watering can down.

'Emily's fine. I've just taken her up to bed. She was asleep as soon as I tucked her in. It's been a busy day with The Mother's Day Club this morning and then going into Wykeham this afternoon.' Marianne looked down at the floor briefly before returning her gaze to meet Thea's. 'I need to ask you if you'd be willing to have another lodger at Rookery House?'

Thea was startled by the question, but something told her not to jump to any conclusions. 'It would depend on who they are and how long they'd be thinking of staying, but only because we don't have an extra room to spare now.'

'They wouldn't take up much space and would share mine and Emily's bedroom.' Marianne's face broke into a smile and she placed her hand on her belly. 'I'm expecting!'

Thea gasped. 'That's marvellous news! Congratulations!' She hurried over to Marianne and gave her a hug. 'When did you find out?'

'This afternoon. I saw the doctor while I was in Wykeham. The baby's due around Christmas time!'

Thea smiled. 'A Christmas baby, how wonderful! And yes, of course he or she would be most welcome here. You didn't think I would say otherwise, did you?'

'Not really, but the house is full and a young baby with all its noise might not be appreciated,' Marianne said. 'I hoped you would let us stay, though. This is my home while Alex is in the RAF and I'd hate to leave and go elsewhere.'

'There's absolutely no need. This is yours, Emily's and your new baby's home for however long you want it to be. Have you told anyone else?'

'Only Alex. I managed to telephone his mess and spoke to him. He's delighted.'

'I'm sure he is. With him now being stationed in Lincolnshire, he'll hopefully be able to come and see you more often than he did while he was so far away training.'

'I hope so. He's missed so much of Emily's life already.'

'How are you feeling?' Thea asked.

'Fine. Luckily, I was never sick with Emily. I feel well apart from being more tired than usual, but that happened before. I should probably have an afternoon nap while Emily has hers.'

'Definitely. This time you have a small child to look after, so you should rest while you can. Hettie's going to be delighted, you know. She'll be knitting more baby clothes for you.'

'I'm going to tell her now. I wanted to check with you first. Thank you so much for letting us stay.' Marianne gave Thea a hug, squeezing her tightly.

'Rookery House wouldn't be the same without you and Emily here.' Thea returned the young woman's smile. Since Marianne had arrived as an expectant mother, she had settled in so well and now felt like family. 'I'm looking forward to the new addition too.'

After Marianne had gone back to the house to tell Hettie her wonderful news, Thea returned to the watering, thinking how once again things were changing at Rookery House. News of Marianne's baby was a lovely surprise, and it would be welcomed by everyone. Well, maybe not *everyone*, Thea suddenly realised. Ada might not be so happy to have a small baby in the house, but perhaps she would have moved to live somewhere else by the time Christmas came. The thought of a new baby arriving might spur Ada on to find a home more suited to her.

CHAPTER 31

Sunday 18th May

Flo undid Primrose's halter and then rubbed behind the cow's ears.

'There you go, my lovely.'

Primrose tilted her head towards Flo enjoying the attention for a short while, before lowering it and starting to graze. Flo gave the cow a final pat on her shoulder and then headed back to the open gate, thinking how much she'd grown to enjoy milking Primrose and spending time with her. There was something about being around the gentle animal that was calming. She loved listening to the soft rhythm of Primrose tearing the grass off with her lips and chewing it, repeating the process over and over.

Closing the wooden gate behind her, Flo leaned on it, looking over the field at Primrose, who'd wandered further in, grazing as she went. Flo took a deep breath, enjoying the scent of the May early evening. Spring was in full show now, the trees in the hedgerow surrounding the field coming out in fresh green leaves, the snowy white hawthorn blossom in the hedge bursting into flower. Swallows were darting back and forth over the grass, catching insects.

Something wet nudged at her hand and she looked down to find Bess staring up at her with her amber coloured eyes, her tail wagging from side to side.

'Hello Bess.' Flo stroked the dog's head and looked around to see Reuben walking towards her. 'Good evening Reuben.'

'Evening. Primrose all right?' he asked, coming to stand beside her leaning on the gate and looking across the meadow at the cow.

'Yes, she's fine. I like to watch her for a bit after I bring her back here for the night,' Flo told him.

Reuben nodded. 'I know what you mean. It's peaceful.'

They stood in comfortable silence for a few minutes, gazing out across the meadow, while a blackbird sang its clear flutey song from its perch on top of the barn. Flo thought about how Reuben reminded her of her grandad in that he was a man of few words. He didn't say anything unless it needed saying, and he had a calmness about him that she liked.

'Thea told me about your family,' he said, breaking the silence. He turned to face her. 'I'm sorry for your loss.'

Flo gave a quick nod. 'Thank you.'

'It's hard to lose family at the best of times, but in war it's…' he paused. 'Especially how it happened to them at home, and so sudden. I lost my brother, William, in the Great War. We enlisted together and were in the same platoon. He was shot by a sniper while we were on a scouting party in no-man's-land. He died in my arms.' Reuben took off his flat cap and ran his hand through his silver-threaded brown hair, before replacing it again. 'I stayed with him sheltering in a shell hole and then carried him back to our trench after dark so he could have a proper burial. I couldn't leave him out there to be...' He shuddered. His blue eyes, which were the same colour as Thea's, met Flo's. 'I don't usually talk about what happened, but I wanted to tell you that I understand and to also say that time will help you. You'll never forget, but eventually it won't hurt as much.'

Tears prickled behind Flo's eyes and she nodded quickly before looking away, focusing on Bess who was leaning against her legs as if to provide her with comfort. 'I'm sorry you lost your brother.'

They fell into silence again. Flo's mind was awash with memories of that awful night back in Manchester.

'But I feel so guilty sometimes!' The words burst out of her, and she looked at Reuben through tear-filled eyes. 'That I lived, and they didn't!' Her voice was hoarse.

He nodded, his expression sympathetic. 'I did too. I kept asking myself why had *he* died and not me? The sniper's bullet could so easily have hit me instead of William.'

'I could have been the one in the house helping bring my brother downstairs, instead of my sister, not out in the air-raid shelter getting it ready. I was on my way back indoors when it... blew up!'

'In wartime, the difference between life and death can be a matter of moments or the shortest of distances,' Reuben said sagely. 'What helped me was when someone asked me if William would have wanted me to feel guilty that he died while I lived.'

'What did you say?'

'I said he wouldn't. He'd have been horrified that I felt like that and would have urged me to live. To enjoy my life, make the most of it...' He paused. 'To live it well for him.'

'And have you done that?'

Reuben nodded. 'I've done my best to. It's not always been easy, especially at first. But I remind myself what my brother would have said and that keeps me on the right track. Would your family have wanted you to feel guilty that you survived when they didn't?' he asked gently.

'No! Definitely not. They would be *glad* that I survived.' Flo bit her bottom lip. 'They'd want me to be happy in my life. It's just…'

Reuben gave her an understanding look. 'It is hard to shrug off that feeling of guilt, but you will. Just keep asking yourself if that's what they would want and if you're living a good life for them.' He looked out across the field, watching the swallows for a few moments before turning back to face her. 'Keep going. Don't give up and let sadness and guilt pull you down.' He patted her shoulder. 'Right, I promised Hettie I'd check the chain on her bicycle. It keeps coming off.'

'Thank you.' Flo gave him a grateful smile. 'I appreciate what you've told me and I'll ask myself that question.'

He tipped his head in acknowledgement and headed off towards the house, whistling to Bess, who followed him after one last rub of the ear from Flo.

Returning her gaze to Primrose, Flo thought about what Reuben had revealed. She guessed it wasn't something that he had shared with many people over the years but had kindly told her because he knew it would help. Nothing would ever fill the hole that her family had left. They were irreplaceable. But looking at it from the viewpoint of what they would have wanted for her was enlightening. They would have hated for her to feel guilty that she'd been spared that night and would have wished for her to embrace life. It had only been a matter of a few moments and a short distance that had made all the difference between her getting caught in the bomb blast and not. It was nothing that she had done or not done. It was *not* her fault! She had nothing to feel guilty for.

Tears trickled down Flo's cheeks and she wiped them away with the back of her hand. She still had the precious gift of life and must use it. Enjoy each day, continue to do the work she loved and be thankful that she had the chance. Flo took a deep breath and looked upwards into the clear blue sky. I'm going to live the best life I can for you all, she promised.

CHAPTER 32

Tuesday 20th May

'Thank you, Hettie, that was delicious and most welcome.' Evie placed her knife and fork neatly together on her empty plate.

'I'm glad you enjoyed it.' Hettie gave the young woman, who'd recently returned from her shift at Great Plumstead Hall Hospital and was still dressed in her nurse's uniform, a warm smile. Evie's long hours meant that she didn't get home until after the rest of them had eaten their evening meal. Hettie always saved food for her, keeping it hot and ready for when she came home. Tonight, Evie had made short work of stew and dumplings.

'I always do. You're such a wonderful cook. We're so lucky to have you here. Where is everyone?' Evie asked.

'In the sitting room, listening to the wireless. There's an apple pie in the pantry if you'd like some for pudding.'

'Yes, please.'

Hettie put down her knitting and started to get up from her seat on the opposite side of the table.

'You stay there. I'll help myself to a piece.' Evie got up, collected a bowl and spoon from one of the dressers and went into the pantry, returning to her chair moments later with a slice of apple pie.

'How are things at the hospital?' Hettie asked, working on the sock she was knitting.

'Good, all the patients are doing well. We've got new ones arriving tomorrow, so have been getting everything ready for them. They will take us up to full capacity. I don't mind though as I like to be busy. Although I'm not so sure that Lady Campbell-Gryce is so happy about it being such a busy place right now.' Evie popped a spoonful of apple pie in her mouth and chewed slowly.

'Why's that?' Hettie asked. 'Surely that's what the hospital is there for.'

Evie swallowed her mouthful before replying, 'I think she'd be glad to have the hospital full ordinarily, but she's in a bit of a flap at the moment because her housekeeper has handed in her notice. She was talking to Mrs Platten, our Quartermaster, about it this afternoon in the staffroom while I was in there on my break.'

Hettie frowned. 'You mean Mrs Bartlett?'

'Yes. Her sister is ill and Mrs Bartlett's going to care for her in Suffolk. She's leaving in three weeks' time. Her Ladyship is in a panic about finding someone else to replace her. Apparently, getting new staff is harder than ever and she hasn't got much time to devote to it. Hardly anyone wants to work in service now and Lady Campbell-Gryce is adamant that she needs someone *good* to oversee her household.'

'Her Ladyship wasn't happy when I handed my notice in to retire, but I gave her plenty of warning and I'm glad to say she found another good cook in Dorothy Shepherd.' Hettie had been uncertain about the new Cook's abilities but, since meeting her at the village Christmas party held at the Hall back in 1939, she'd been most impressed by her replacement's cooking skills. Now she always enjoyed a chat with Dorothy whenever their paths crossed.

'But I left before the war started, which made things easier for them to find a replacement for me,' Hettie. 'Everything's different now with so many women working in other jobs which didn't exist then. Finding a housekeeper at short notice will be more difficult, although it's not as if it is the *whole* house to oversee the way it once was. The Campbell-Gryces only living in one wing is a lot less work for a housekeeper to manage than what they had to do before it became a hospital.'

'Well, if you know of anybody who might be interested in the job, do tell them about it,' Evie said.

'I'm not sure I do. All the housekeepers I knew are now retired except for Mrs Bartlett. I...' Hettie halted as the door from the hall opened and Ada walked in.

'Are you making any cocoa?' Ada asked.

'Not at the moment, but if *you* want some, you know where the milk and cocoa powder is in the pantry,' Hettie said sweetly. 'And if you're making some for yourself, you might as well make enough for everyone else too. I wouldn't say no to a cup.'

'Nor me. Thank you.' Evie stifled a yawn. 'I won't be long before I go to bed tonight. I'm tired after such a busy day.'

Ada pressed her lips into a thin line, looking like she wished she hadn't asked. 'Very well then.' She stalked into the pantry to collect the ingredients for cocoa.

Hettie looked down at her knitting as she suppressed a smile. If Ada could get away with being waited on, she would, but Hettie was much wiser to it now and it really was for Ada's own good that she pulled her weight more around the house.

'I forgot to say that accommodation goes with the job as well,' Evie said, before popping the last spoonful of her apple pie into her mouth.

'What are you talking about?' Ada asked, coming back into the kitchen with a jug of milk and a tin of cocoa. 'What job?'

'Working as housekeeper for the Campbell-Gryces up at the Hall, but only looking after the west wing of the house where they now live,' Evie explained. 'The rest of the Hall is used for the hospital and is under the care of the hospital staff. I was just telling Hettie that Lady Campbell-Gryce's housekeeper is leaving and her Ladyship is desperate to find a replacement.' Evie watched as Ada poured milk into a saucepan and put it on the hot plate of the range to heat up. 'Apparently there's a nice little set of rooms that goes with the job in the wing where the Campbell-Gryces live.'

Ada didn't say anything, just gave a nod and turned her attention to watching the milk so that it didn't boil over.

Hettie met Evie's gaze, and she raised her eyebrows. Both of them had become accustomed to Ada's ways since she'd arrived here at Rookery House. Although Hettie wished that sometimes Ada would at least *try* to be more friendly and willingly contribute towards the family feeling this home had. If only Ada could, Hettie was sure her sister would benefit from it and everyone else too. The place hadn't felt quite the same since her sister's arrival. Somehow Ada's dourness had cast a shadow over the home and Hettie felt responsible for the change.

~

'Are you awake?' Ada's voice came out of the darkness, jolting Hettie out of the sleep she'd just fallen into.

'I am now!' Hettie mumbled. 'What's the matter?'

'I've been thinking about that job at the Hall and the accommodation that goes with it. I could apply.'

Hettie rolled onto her side, facing her sister's bed, although she couldn't see her in the pitch blackness of the room. 'Are you serious?'

'Yes. Completely serious.'

Hettie pulled herself up into a sitting position and felt for the matches that she kept on the bedside cabinet beside her bed. Hettie took one out and struck it, the sudden bright orange flare of the flame making her squint as she used the match to light the candle in its holder by her bed. Carefully blowing out the match flame, she put the spent match on the saucer bottom of the candle holder and looked across to her sister's bed. Ada was sitting up in bed, her arms folded across her chest.

Ada stared back at her. 'I mean what I said. I could apply for it.'

'But you're not a housekeeper, Ada. What chance have you got of getting the job?' Hettie asked, keeping her voice low as she didn't want to wake the others asleep in the house.

'I know I've never been a housekeeper in a Hall, but I have kept a house of my own for forty-six years, and from before that when I took over after Ma died, as you well know.' She gave Hettie an odd look. 'I gave up my apprenticeship at the milliners to do that and then I never stopped running a household, first Dad's, then mine and Walter's. And I've worked cleaning rich people's homes back in Geswick too. I *know* how to take care of a house, big and small.'

Hettie was speechless for a few moments. This was the first time that Ada had ever mentioned giving up her apprenticeship after their mother died. Hettie had long suspected that it had been a thorn of resentment in Ada's side. Although her sister had never said as much, Hettie had felt it was there, festering away over the years.

'That's true but being a housekeeper for people like the Campbell-Gryces isn't quite the same. They aren't like ordinary folk. They have different expectations. I know what they're like after working for them for so many years.'

'Exactly. You *know what they're like* and so you could teach me. You worked closely with housekeepers as Cook, didn't you?'

Hettie nodded. 'But working with someone isn't the same as doing their job.'

'No, but if you tell me everything you know, it will help me prepare. I could offer to work alongside the current housekeeper for a bit before she leaves,' Ada said enthusiastically. 'If I got the job, I could move out of here and live at the Hall. Imagine that, me living at Great Plumstead Hall!'

Hettie stared at Ada in the flickering candlelight. She was astonished at her sister's eagerness. She hadn't seen her like this for… well, she couldn't remember the last time she'd seen Ada enthusiastically fired up about something. The reality, of course, was that Lady Campbell-Gryce was highly unlikely to give Ada the job, but Hettie didn't want to spoil her sister's keenness.

'Maybe you should apply. I can tell you everything I know about the job. I worked with several housekeepers over the years I was there. They each had their own ways of doing things. Some were better than others. If you're serious about applying, you need to get in quick,' Hettie advised.

'I'll write to Lady Campbell-Gryce tomorrow and can deliver the letter by hand. If I tell her that I'm your sister, it's bound to help.' Ada gave Hettie a thin smile. 'So, can you start my training tomorrow?'

'All right. I'll tell you everything I know. Now we'd better get some sleep. Good night.'

Hettie blew out the candle and settled in her bed once more, her mind going over what had just happened. Was Ada foolish to raise her hopes about this housekeeping job? Would Lady Campbell-Gryce seriously consider employing someone with no proper experience, other than Ada running her own home and cleaning wealthier folks' houses? There was more to a housekeeper's job than Ada imagined. A good part of it was managing staff and her sister wasn't someone who was good at dealing with other people, but sometimes needs must, as they say. Hettie would do what she could to help Ada and, if by some miracle her sister became housekeeper at the Hall, that meant she would move out of here and Hettie would get her bedroom back to herself. As Ada began to snore, Hettie thought that would be no bad thing. A quiet night's sleep would be a blessing!

CHAPTER 33

Saturday 24th May

In the eight weeks since Flo had first come along to help on the WI allotment the difference in the plot was striking. Through many hours of hard work by members of The Mother's Day Club and Women's Institute, it had been transformed. Where brambles, nettles and docks had once sunk their roots deep into the soil, there now grew neat rows of vegetables – each plant growing bigger by the day in the warmth of late spring.

Flo glanced over from where she was carefully hoeing between pea plants, to where Prue and Gloria were planting out the tomato plants which Flo had brought with her from Rookery House. They'd grown more than they needed so Thea had donated them to the WI allotment.

Flo loved how the women of the community came together on this plot, and it had given her a chance to get to know people in the village. It wasn't something she'd imagined when she had first joined the Land Army and pictured herself living in a hostel with other Land Girls. Her billeting at Rookery House had been a surprise, and not one she would have chosen to start with, but it had given her so many unexpected things – working here being one of them, and for that Flo was grateful.

'Flo… You're off with the fairies!' Gloria's voice broke into Flo's thoughts.

'Sorry, I was miles away.' She smiled at the joyful East Ender who stood with her hands on the hips of her purple, flower-patterned dungarees.

Gloria's red lipsticked lips curved into a smile. 'I could see that. I was just saying to Prue that I've been thinking about starting a singing group 'ere in the village. I wondered if you'd like to join? You've got a lovely voice.'

Prue stood up and dusted down her hands on the legs of her own, less vibrant, navy-blue dungarees. 'It's a wonderful idea. Singing makes people happy to take part in and to hear it. With you leading it Gloria, and your professional singing experience, it's bound to be good, so you can count me in.'

Gloria gave a throaty laugh. 'I know how to get the best out of a singer's voice. We'll be doing the important warm-up exercises for sure.'

'When would it be?' Flo asked.

'One evening a week. We could hold it in the village 'all.' Gloria looked at Prue. 'Could you see if there's a night that's free?'

Prue nodded. 'Of course. I'll check in the village hall diary when I get home. There must be something even if it's just for an hour after the Girl Guides meet.'

'Are you interested then, Flo?' Gloria prompted her.

The last time Flo had been in a singing group, it was with some other women from where she worked in Manchester.

They used to practise in their dinner time and had been planning to go out carol singing on the 23rd of December last year, only it had never happened.

A memory of how she had been singing her favourite carol, *The Holly and the Ivy*, while washing up, came back to her. The kitchen had been filled with the scent of newly baked mince pies. Her father had come in, hoping to try one, but she'd refused, telling him he would have to wait till Christmas Eve. A short while later, he'd been killed. Oh, how she wished that she had let him have a mince pie that night.

Flo felt someone grab hold of her arm.

'Come and sit down. You've gone right pale.' Gloria led her over to the bank under the hedge where the women often sat on their tea breaks. 'Are you feeling all right?' she asked as Flo sat down.

Flo gazed up at Gloria, who stood in front of her, and managed a smile. 'I'm fine, I just remembered something, that's all.'

'Have some tea,' Prue said, arriving with a flask, from which she poured out a cup and handed it to Flo.

'Thank you.' Flo took it and sipped the hot drink. Its familiar taste was most welcome.

'I hope I didn't upset you.' Gloria sat down next to Flo, her face full of concern. 'If you'd rather not join the singing group, that's fine. You've got enough on your plate with working at Rookery House and 'elping out 'ere.'

'It's not that. I would like to join. I love singing. It's just...' Flo hesitated. 'It reminded me of the last singing group I was in. We were due to go carol singing last December, but it never happened because...' Flo told them what had happened that terrible night. The two women stared at her, lost for words for a few moments.

'I'm so sorry, ducks.' Gloria grabbed Flo's free hand and held it tightly in hers.

'I had no idea,' Prue said. 'I'm sorry, Flo. To lose your family like that is dreadful.'

Flo gazed down at the ground and poked at the soil with the toe of her boot. 'Sadly, it's not uncommon these days with so many cities getting bombed.' She looked up, raising her chin. 'But we have to go on and yes, I would like to join the singing group.'

Gloria beamed at her. 'Good. You'll create some new, 'appier memories of singing again. We'll sing songs that make us 'appy. We all need that in our lives I think. Doing things that bring us joy is especially important these days.' Gloria looked thoughtful. 'Are we going to 'ave any more village dances, Prue? Only they went down so well. We 'aven't 'ad anything since the Valentine's one.'

'We've been pretty busy getting this into shape.' Prue gestured at the allotment. 'But now things are under control here, maybe we *should* think of something to put on this summer for all the village. Leave it with me.'

CHAPTER 34

Prue sat at the kitchen table twirling a pencil around with her fingers as she stared at the blank piece of paper in front of her.

'You look thoughtful.'

At the sound of the voice, Prue looked up to see Nancy standing in the open back door, a wicker basket of newly dried laundry, fresh off the washing line, in her arms.

'I'm trying to come up with an idea for a village event with something for everyone, but not another dance.'

Nancy came into the kitchen, put down the basket, pulled out a chair from the table and sat down opposite Prue. 'How about a fete? With stalls and attractions?'

Prue nodded. 'That's a good idea! We could hold it on the village green. There could be sports too. Races for the children, like the egg and spoon, sack race and three-legged race.'

'When were you thinking of holding it?' Nancy asked. 'Only something like that will take a bit of organising.'

Prue tapped her pencil on the paper, considering. 'How about towards the end of July, after the school has finished for the summer? Hopefully, we'd have lovely weather for it then as well.'

'What's brought this on?' Nancy asked. 'I thought you already had more than enough on your plate, to be honest. What with taking on the WI allotment, The Mother's Day Club, WVS canteen, WI, salvage collections…' She frowned. 'How on earth do you plan on fitting in organising a village fete on top of all that?'

Prue leaned back in her chair. 'To be honest, I wasn't intending to. But at the allotment yesterday, Gloria was asking about what social event we were having next in the village. It got me thinking that it has been a while since we had something for *everyone* to join in. The last was the Valentine's dance in February.' Prue smiled at the memory. 'It was popular and we all had a marvellous time.'

'That was before you took on the allotment, though,' Nancy pointed out.

'I know, but that's under control now and doing well. If we held an event in late July, it gives us plenty of time for organising it and would be much more manageable,' Prue said. 'And I wouldn't be doing it all on my own. I'm sure others will help.'

'I'll 'elp of course. But even so, you'll oversee and organise everything even if you do have people 'elping out. It's still a lot of extra work on your plate,' Nancy warned her.

Prue nodded. 'I realise that, but I thrive on being busy, you know me! I think a fete's an excellent idea. We could even include a garden show with competitions for the best fruits and vegetables, and baking!'

Nancy laughed. 'This event is getting bigger by the moment. It's just as well there's a couple of months to organise it then.'

'The sooner we get started, the better.' Prue began to write down the ideas they'd come up with. 'I'll ask at The Mother's Day Club, see who's willing to help, and at the next WI meeting. The village summer fete will be something to look forward to, Nancy!'

CHAPTER 35

Monday 26th May

Hettie and Ada pedalled their bicycles along, side by side, past the gate houses that stood at the end of the long drive leading to Great Plumstead Hall.

'Are you all right?' Hettie glanced at her sister, who was quiet, her face pensive.

'A bit nervous,' Ada admitted. 'I haven't done anything like this since Ma took me into Norwich to see about getting the apprenticeship at the milliners. I was scared then and so desperate to get it.'

'I remember being the same when I came here to have my interview to be a scullery maid,' Hettie recalled. 'But you are older and wiser than I was then, plus a lot more experienced now. Remember that, Ada. And you're as ready as you can be.'

Since Ada had been asked to come to the Hall for an interview, Hettie had spent many hours explaining to her sister how housekeepers did their job. To her credit, Ada had taken it seriously, asking thoughtful questions, helping Hettie to give her a comprehensive knowledge of the workings of the Hall and how the housekeeper ran it. Nothing could replace the actual experience of doing the job but, in the absence of that, Ada was as prepared as they could make her.

'I hope I'm ready,' Ada said quietly.

They fell into silence, Hettie taking the opportunity to admire the magnificent beech trees that lined the driveway which were cloaked in fresh lime-green leaves. She loved this long drive and had travelled along it countless times during her time working at the Hall.

Reaching the end of the trees, the drive opened up into a wide sweep of gravel in front of the magnificent building, whose bricks glowed a warm honey colour in the sunshine.

'We need to go around to the back entrance.' Hettie pointed to the side of the hall and steered her bicycle in that direction. 'Round to the servants' entrance.'

Bumping over the cobbled courtyard at the rear of the Hall, Hettie brought her bicycle to a halt and jumped off. Returning here always gave her a sense of homecoming, as this had been her home for so many years. She loved living at Rookery House, but the Hall would for ever hold a special place in her heart. It may have been where she worked, but she'd enjoyed her time here, living with all the other servants. They were like a sort of family to each other, away from their own families.

'We'll leave our bicycles here.' Hettie leaned hers against the wall near the back door and Ada followed suit . 'You all set?' Hettie caught her sister's eye.

'As I'll ever be.' Ada's face was creased with anxiety. 'Now it's come to it, I can't help wondering if I was crazy to apply. What chance have I got?'

Hettie briefly placed her hand on her sister's arm. 'There is a chance. I don't think her Ladyship would have wasted time seeing you if she wasn't going to consider you. Just do your best. If the answer is no, then you'll be no different to how you are now.'

Ada gave a quick nod and Hettie led her inside.

~

'This is delicious,' Hettie said after swallowing a mouthful of light buttery scone.

Dorothy Shepherd smiled. 'That is praise indeed. Thank you.'

The pair of them were sitting in the servants' dining room, enjoying some afternoon tea while Ada was having her interview.

'It seems odd being in this wing of the house.' Hettie looked around her at the room, which was much smaller than the old servants' dining room in the east wing, where she'd eaten many meals during her time at the Hall. That was now in the part of the house used by the hospital and where the mobile patients ate, so Evie had told her.

'Being in the west wing everything is on a smaller scale and we have a reduced staff looking after the Campbell-Gryces. Though I must admit, I rather like it.' Dorothy took a sip of tea. 'The war has changed so many things.'

Hettie nodded. 'And it keeps on changing them. I don't think Ada ever imagined she'd be forced to leave her home to make way for an aerodrome to be built. So how much interest has there been in the housekeeper's job?'

'Not a lot. I know that her Ladyship has been in a flap about finding a replacement for Mrs Bartlett, and at such short notice. It's bad timing with Lady Campbell-Gryce being so involved with the hospital. She spends a lot of time working there helping to keep the place running smoothly.'

'Will she be desperate enough to give my sister the job? Before the war Ada wouldn't have stood a chance of getting it but perhaps now...' Hettie gestured with her hand. 'We'll just have to wait and see. Tell me about Cecilia Campbell-Gryce? I heard a rumour that she was going to join the Wrens. Is that true?'

By the time Ada appeared in the doorway of the servants' dining room, Hettie and Dorothy had drunk several cups of tea and enjoyed a catch-up of the latest happenings with the Campbell-Gryce family.

'How did you get on?' Hettie asked, scanning her sister's face for any sign.

Ada's face broke into a smile. 'Her Ladyship has offered me the job! On a three-month trial. I'm to start on the 11th of June and can move in the day before.'

Hettie gasped and put her hand to her mouth. 'That's marvellous!'

'Come and sit down and have some tea and a scone to celebrate,' Dorothy said.

Ada pulled out a chair at the table and sat down opposite Hettie. 'Lady Campbell-Gryce said that because I'm your sister, she's willing to give me a chance even though I've never worked as a housekeeper proper before.' Her eyes met Hettie's and she gave a grateful smile. 'That and the fact that I knew so much about a housekeeper's work, all the things you taught me. Thank you.'

Hettie's eyes filled with tears. For Ada to thank her so

nicely was a rarity. 'I'm glad I could help. I honestly hope you'll enjoy the job. You are very capable of doing it well.'

'I hope so. Her Ladyship was impressed that I suggested working with Mrs Bartlett for a week before she leaves to learn all the routines.' Ada added some milk to the cup of tea which Dorothy had just poured for her.

'It showed willingness and that's important.' Dorothy smiled at Ada. 'I'm sure you'll do well. I look forward to working alongside you.'

Ada's cheeks grew pink. 'Thank you. I never thought I stood a chance...'

Hettie lifted her cup in a toast. 'Here's to your job as the new housekeeper.'

Ada and Dorothy raised their cups and gently clinked them against Hettie's. 'To the new housekeeper!'

CHAPTER 36

Sunday 1st June

Spending a warm sunny summer's afternoon earthing up potatoes was a pleasant thing to be doing, Prue thought, as she used her spade to draw earth up around the green potato plant. It was methodical, useful and exactly what she needed after a busy few days. It was a chance to gather herself ready for the coming week ahead when, if the June weather held fine and warm, they would be haymaking at Rookery House. She'd promised Thea that she would help. Not that she had experience of haymaking, but she was sure she could learn.

'Have you heard the news?' A woman's voice called out.

Prue stopped what she was doing and turned to see Nancy and her two daughters hurrying towards them along the rutted pathway through the allotments.

'Aye, aye, somethin's up by the look of it,' Gloria said, standing up straight from where she'd been bending down, doing some weeding between lettuce plants. She rubbed her back. 'Do you think Hitler's surrendered?'

'Unlikely, but I wish he would,' Sylvia, who Gloria was billeted with, said, leaning on her hoe. 'But it must be something worth shouting about.'

'What's the matter?' Gloria called out as Nancy and her girls arrived at the WI allotment.

'It's been announced on the wireless that the Board of Trade is going to ration clothes and footwear and it starts *today*, the first of June!' Nancy declared in a breathless voice.

Prue looked at Gloria and Sylvia, who, from the expression on their faces, were as surprised as her.

'There's been no warning that was coming! Not like with food rationing,' Prue said. 'What else did they say?'

'That rationing clothes would make it fair for all. I suppose if they'd 'ave warned us, then those that could afford it would 'ave bought up everything they could to last them for years.' Nancy frowned. 'But 'ow are mothers supposed to clothe their children if we can only 'ave so much clothes? They keep growing out of things!' Her voice rose in frustration.

'Don't panic, Nancy. We've got the clothes exchange at The Mother's Day Club. There are always items coming in and out as children grow out of their clothes and need bigger sizes,' Prue reassured her. 'We'll keep that going and add to it as much as possible.'

'Everyone's in the same boat,' Gloria added.

'I'm sure there are things we can do to stretch what we've got and make the best of the resources we have. We will use our ingenuity to get around this latest restriction,' Prue said, injecting a note of optimism into her voice.

Nancy nodded. 'It was a shock. Made me wonder what they'll put on the ration next... fresh air?' she joked. 'I don't like the suddenness of these announcements either. It makes me feel our lives are out of our control with the government saying what we can and can't do and 'ave.'

'I know what you mean,' Gloria agreed. 'But we ain't got no choice in the matter, Nancy. We've just got to do what we are told because we're at war. When the country's fighting for its survival, new clothes ain't a priority. Uniforms for our servicemen and women are. My sister works in a clothes factory sewing uniforms, but before the war she used to sew dresses and blouses.'

'Gloria's right,' Prue said. 'We need to look on clothes rationing as another way of doing our bit for the war effort. If you're interested in staying here for a bit and helping out, perhaps you and the girls would like to sow some lettuces?'

Nancy smiled. ''Course we will.' She looked down at Marie and Joan, who nodded in agreement.

Once everyone was busy tending to the growing allotment, Prue let her mind dwell on the latest problem of clothes rationing as she worked on earthing up the potatoes again. Nancy had a valid point about how fast children grew out of their clothes. The clothing exchange at The Mother's Day Club worked well, but their stock wasn't huge. It would come under even more pressure now that the ability of mothers to buy new clothes and shoes was limited. The new rationing didn't just apply to children – adults' clothes were limited too. This extra rationing was going to call for new ways of doing things to make the most of what they did have. An idea popped into Prue's head, making her smile. It could work. It could make a difference. If they worked together on it, their combined skills and efforts would be worthwhile. She needed time to think it over and tomorrow's Mother's Day Club would be a good place to test out the idea.

~

Prue wasn't surprised that all anyone wanted to talk about when they arrived at The Mother's Day Club the next morning was clothes rationing.

Nancy came in with a newspaper that she'd bought from Barker's shop on her way, and proceeded to spread it out on one of the tables and read through the detailed information printed about the new rationing rules.

'From now on, if I want to buy a new overcoat, it'll cost me fourteen coupons!' Nancy pored over the list of items of clothing and the number of coupons required for each. 'And it will be eleven for a child's coat.'

'A frock would cost me eleven,' Gloria said, leaning over Nancy and running a red painted fingernail down the newspaper's list. 'If we're only getting sixty-six coupons for the whole year, I ain't going to be buying many new dresses. The ones I've got will 'ave to last me.' She stood up straight and smoothed down the skirt of her emerald-green dress.

'I heard that even knitting wool will need coupons.' Hettie sat down next to Nancy, checking through the list. 'One coupon per two ounces of wool.' She frowned, her eyes concerned behind her round glasses. 'It's going to alter how we do things.'

'I've been thinking about what we can do to help ourselves,' Prue announced. 'I have an idea. Ladies, if you'd like to listen a moment, please.' She raised her voice so she could be heard over the babble of conversations going on around the hall and then waited as the women fell silent and looked at her.

Prue gave a smile of thanks and continued, 'I'm sure you were all as surprised as I was to find that our clothes and shoes are now being rationed. Seeing how many coupons are needed for various items, our annual allowance of sixty-six each isn't going to go very far. We need to adjust. Make the best of what we have and use our skills to keep the clothes we do have in good order by mending them to make them last longer.'

'I ain't no good at mending things. I make a right mess of darning socks or sewing patches on,' one of the mothers called out.

'That's a fair point and why we need to do something about it. I suggest that we apply ourselves to learning to look after our clothes better and making more of them from things we already have and don't want. Coats from wool blankets, dresses from unwanted curtains or tablecloths. We will help each other. Those that have the skills can teach others at Make and Mend parties.'

'I'll help with teaching the sewing,' Marianne called from where she was overseeing a group of infants playing with toys on a blanket in the corner.

'I was hoping you would. Thank you, Marianne,' Prue said. 'What do you all think?'

'Making and mending ourselves is going to be a necessity,' Gloria answered. 'It's a good idea, Prue. The more I can learn to keep me and my little one clothed, the better.'

'Same for me,' Annie agreed.

Gloria and Annie's enthusiasm was echoed by the other mothers around the hall.

'Good, thank you, everyone,' Prue nodded. 'I'll get a Make and Mend party organised. I thought if I put up some posters around the village asking if anyone's got any blankets, curtains etc that they don't want, then we can build up a stock of material to use for making clothes with too.'

'Ask for knitted garments as well,' Hettie said. 'We can

unpick them and pull the wool out, give it a wash and then re-use it to knit new things.'

Prue clapped her hands together and beamed. 'I hadn't thought of that. Thank you for your support. The Board of Trade might have brought in clothes rationing, but it's not going to stop us from looking our best or from keeping our children warm and clothed.'

''Ear, 'ear!' Gloria shouted.

The Mother's Day Club had finished a quarter of an hour ago. Prue was doing a final check of the village hall, making sure that everything had been put away and tables and chairs returned to where they should be. Hettie was doing the same in the kitchen, the pair of them being the two volunteers on duty this morning.

Prue heard the door of the hall open from the outside and turned around, thinking it must be one of the mothers come back because they'd forgotten something. The sight of who stood in the doorway made her gasp, putting her hand to her mouth. It was her youngest son, Edwin.

'Hello, Ma!' He smiled broadly as he put down his suitcase and strode across the hall to where she stood, stock-still with shock.

'Edwin!' she managed to say as he wrapped his arms around her, picked her up and spun her around.

Prue laughed happily and beamed up at him as he put her down. 'I didn't know you were coming.' She looked him up and down. 'It's so wonderful to see you.' She hugged him tightly, loving the feel of her son in her embrace again.

Releasing him, she grabbed hold of both of his hands in hers. 'How long are you home for?'

'Two weeks. It's good to be back. I…' he began but halted at the sound of his name.

'Edwin!' Hettie shrieked, standing in the doorway that led into the kitchen. She hurried across the hall, her blue eyes dancing with delight behind her round glasses, her arms held out wide.

'Hello, Hettie.' Edwin folded her in his arms, his tall frame towering over her.

Prue smiled at the pair of them who had a close bond. Hettie wasn't a blood relation but had been Prue's mother's best friend and like an aunt to Prue and her siblings, growing up. Hettie had then taken on a grandmotherly role to Prue's children.

'This is a wonderful surprise,' Hettie said when she finally let him go. 'Did you know Edwin was coming home, Prue?'

'No, it's a complete surprise.' Prue beamed at her son.

Edwin laughed. 'It was meant to be.'

'Where are you staying?' Hettie asked. 'Are you coming to stay at Rookery House?'

Edwin's eyes met Prue's. 'I don't think it's a good idea to stop at Ma's. I'd like to but…' He sighed.

Prue bit her bottom lip, fighting back the tears that prickled behind her eyes. 'I wish you could, but Victor…' A dart of hatred for her husband and the way he'd treated Edwin for being a conscientious objector sliced through her. Prue knew it was the right thing for Edwin to stay at Rookery House where he'd fled to after his father had thrown him out. But it hurt that he couldn't come home where she'd be able to look after him while he was on leave. 'It's not because I don't want you there…'

Edwin nodded, his face full of understanding. 'I know Ma, and I wish I could stay there with *you*, but not him. We'll still see a lot of each other while I'm home, I promise.' He turned to Hettie. 'I'd love to stay at Rookery House if that's all right with you and Thea?'

'Of course it is, though I must warn you we're bursting at the seams since you last stayed. We've got Flo, our Land Girl and my sister Ada living there now. You'll be sleeping on a camp bed in the dining room,' Hettie warned him.

'That's fine. As long as I've got somewhere to sleep, I'm happy,' Edwin reassured her.

'Good, well, I'd best get home and let Thea know that you'll be arriving. She'll be delighted.' Hettie grabbed Edwin's hand and squeezed it. 'I'm so pleased to see you.'

After Hettie had gone Prue gathered her coat and bag and prepared to lock up the village hall. 'Will you come home with me for something to eat before you go to Rookery House? Your father won't be there.'

'I'd like that Ma, thanks. I need to tell you something first though.' Edwin hesitated, his expression anxious. 'I'm on embarkation leave.'

Prue stared at him, the words slowly sinking in. She'd been here before with Jack, Edwin's older brother. He'd come home on embarkation leave before he'd been sent to France early last year. That had ended with him being rescued off the beach at Dunkirk. Jack had been lucky to escape the enemy alive and uninjured. Too many of his fellow soldiers hadn't been so fortunate.

'Ma, say something?' Edwin's face was full of concern.

'But… but you are with the Friends Ambulance Unit. You're not a soldier.' Prue frowned, shaking her head. She had never expected to hear this from Edwin. 'What about your work in the East End?'

'There hasn't been any bombing since the last big raid in May and the FAU were looking for volunteers to drive ambulances abroad, so I said I'd go. I've done some more driving training and I'm ready.' Edwin put his hand on Prue's shoulder. 'I want to do something more to help and this is a chance and I'll see some of the world as well. I hope you understand.'

Prue sighed. 'It's a just shock. I know the bombing has stopped for now but it could start again anytime. I thought you were happy helping in the hospital.'

'I was, but there's a need for ambulance drivers overseas too.'

'Where are you going?' Prue asked.

Edwin gave a rueful smile. 'I can't tell you that. I'm sorry.'

Prue nodded. She had an urge to argue with Edwin, beg him not to go, but he was a grown man. He'd been through the thick of the Blitz, seen things that no one would have wanted to see. Now he was going to do more. He had never used his conscientious objector status to keep himself out of harm's way. He was about to put himself in even more danger as she presumed he was heading to where the fighting was if it was somewhere they needed ambulances. She was proud of his bravery and commitment.

'Ma?' Edwin said. 'What do you think?'

Prue forced herself to smile. 'I think you are a brave young man. You could have stayed where you were for the duration. They always need help in hospitals.'

'I'm not going to take risks. Don't worry. I will be helping the wounded *behind* the battle lines, getting them safely to hospital.'

Prue nodded, not daring herself to say what she was thinking. That battle lines moved. Stray bombs fell where they shouldn't. In a war zone, *nowhere* was completely safe. Whatever her thoughts, she would keep them to herself as she didn't want to spoil what precious time she had with her son arguing. His mind was made up. He was trained and ready to leave. Prue doubted she could stop him, even if she tried.

'You must ask Thea about driving ambulances,' Prue said, forcing her voice to sound normal. 'She will give you some good advice, I'm sure.' She smiled at Edwin, linking her arm through his. 'Come on, let's go home and have something to eat and you can tell me about your training.'

CHAPTER 37

Thea flicked the section of cut grass over with her pitchfork, turning it upside down and fluffing it up, then stepped to the side and repeated the process again with another forkful. She breathed in deeply, enjoying the sweet smell of grass drying into hay that filled the air. With another day of warm sunshine, it wouldn't be long before the hay would be dry and ready to go into the barn, providing the wonderful weather held.

She glanced across the field where Edwin, Flo, Alice, Prue and Marianne were all doing the same as her, working their way along the rows of cut grass, turning and fluffing up the cut stems with their pitchforks. The six of them had already turned the hay once today and were doing the same a second time, which was helping to make the most of the sunshine and speed up the drying process.

Thea was glad that Edwin had returned a few days ago and had willingly volunteered to help with the haymaking. As well as the hay to turn, there was still all the other regular work to be done, so Flo, Alice and Thea were already busy. His leave had come at a most opportune time, Thea thought.

Nearing the end of her row, she spotted Hettie pushing Emily's pram towards the gate of Five Acres. The older woman had said she'd bring out a drink for them all as haymaking was hot, thirsty work.

'Time for a break!' Thea called out to the others, who stopped what they were doing and stuck their pitchforks into the ground to mark their place.

Hettie took a basket out from under the pram. While she handed each of them a cup and then poured elderflower cordial into it from a bottle, Marianne checked on her daughter who lay fast asleep in the pram.

'How are you getting on?' Hettie asked,

'It's going well.' Thea took a long drink, enjoying the sensation of the cool, tangy liquid as it soothed her parched throat. 'The hay's nearly dry, a few more hours of sunshine and it'll be ready to bring in.' She glanced up at the clear blue sky above. 'I'm not sure how much longer this weather will hold. There's bound to be a storm sooner or later.'

'Reuben was saying the same this morning,' Hettie said. 'They're busy haymaking on the estate too, racing to get it dry and stored while the sun shines.'

'Do you think it might rain tonight?' Edwin asked.

'Maybe, though I hope not. But these hot summer days often end with a thunderstorm.' Thea drained the rest of her cordial and handed the cup to Hettie. 'Thank you. I needed that. Come on, we'd best get back to work to finish this turning. If we can do one more this afternoon, it will hopefully be enough.'

~

Thea rubbed a handful of dried hay between her fingers and then, in cupped hands, lifted it to her face and sniffed it. It was ready. They'd turned the hay again mid-afternoon and the hot sun had done its work, turning the grass into precious hay, which would help keep Primrose and the rabbits well fed throughout the winter months.

Thea had been keenly observing the weather and was aware of a change in the atmosphere. The air was growing close and sticky and had the feeling of a storm brewing. The sky was still clear overhead, but there were signs of clouds building in the far distance. A storm might not hit for a few hours yet, but it was highly likely that rain was coming. The hay needed to be brought in or they would lose it.

The plan had been for Reuben to bring a horse and cart from the estate to transport the hay from the field to the barn. Only now Thea didn't want to risk waiting for that to happen. As Hettie had said, Thea's brother and other workers were busy haymaking on the estate land and couldn't spare a horse or cart now, as they'd all be in use. No doubt they would be racing to get their own hay in before the weather broke.

'Is it ready?' a voice called.

Thea turned to see Flo striding towards her through the gateway.

'Yes, and it needs to be brought in. I think there's rain on the way. We're in for a storm later.' She gestured at the clouds on the far horizon.

Flo nodded. 'It feels like it. What are we going to do? Will Reuben be here in time?'

'I doubt it. They're in the same boat on the estate and will be hurrying to get their hay crop in too. We can't wait.' Thea gazed around at the rows of hay, which they'd all put so much time and effort into making over the past few days. 'We've got to do it ourselves.'

'We haven't got a horse and cart.'

'I know, so we'll have to improvise. Use what we have!' Thea gave Flo a smile. 'Come on, we need to get the others to help.'

~

'I knew these would come in useful.' Thea spread out one of the large tarpaulins that she'd found in a shed when she had first moved to Rookery House. 'If we pile them up with hay, then we can drag them to the barn in pairs. Don't overfill them as you'll need to be able to pull them. Edwin, if you pair up with Flo. Prue, you go with Marianne and keep your loads smaller, I don't want Marianne hurting herself or the baby. Alice and I will work together.'

'We'll get it done.' Edwin's tone was optimistic.

Thea gave him a grateful smile. 'We'll do our best because we can't just leave it here to get rained on.'

Working together with Alice, it didn't take long for them to gather hay from the rows and pile it on to the tarpaulin. Then with the two edges gathered together, Thea and Alice were hauling it towards the gate when Hettie, Betty and George appeared, the children carrying a blanket between them. Hettie was pushing Emily in the pram, who was sitting up looking around at what was going on.

'We're going to help!' George declared. 'We can use this old blanket to carry some hay in.'

'We all want to do our bit too,' Hettie said, who'd gone to fetch the children home from school. 'Ada is making the tea for us for when we finish.'

'Every bit of help adds up,' Flo said as she and Edwin hauled their full tarpaulin past on the way to the barn.

'It certainly does,' Thea agreed.

The time passed quickly, everyone working hard to harvest the precious crop. Using the large tarpaulins worked well and the nearby small barn filled up with the sweet-smelling hay. After discovering that their hay-filled blanket didn't slide along the ground as well as the tarpaulins did, Hettie and the children had switched to moving it balanced on top of the pram. With her pram being borrowed for transporting hay, little Emily toddled along beside them, her hand in Betty's and delighted to be part of it.

All the while Thea monitored the sky, which was growing a more ominous grey, bruised colour as the clouds built and spread. They didn't stop except for a brief break to refuel when Ada brought out some buns and more elderflower cordial. Thea kept a close eye on the children and seeing them flag after a couple of hours, she got Hettie to take them inside to have some tea and get ready for bed.

Working on, hot and sticky from the warm day and hard work, they brought in all the hay safely. The last load was dragged into the barn only a few minutes before the first spots of rain fell. It quickly turned into a heavy downpour, as lightning lit up the sky off in the distance, followed by thunder rolling overhead.

'Just in time!' Thea said, gazing out of the barn door, alongside Edwin, Flo, Alice, Prue and Marianne, their faces streaked with dirt. 'Thank you all for your hard work. I wasn't sure if we could manage it, but we did.' She peered into the dim barn interior where one end was piled high with the sweet-smelling hay. 'If we'd waited for the horse and cart, this lot would have been ruined.'

Edwin put his arm around Thea's shoulders. 'I thoroughly enjoyed myself. We were up against time and the elements and we did it!'

Alice laughed. 'So did I! I am hot and filthy, but there's

something about being challenged that's very satisfying. We had to try after all the work we put into it.'

Thea smiled at her niece. 'There's nothing we can do about the weather. Everything we grow here is at its mercy. I'm proud of what we've achieved today.'

'Even George, Betty and Emily did their bit,' Flo said. 'They worked so hard and will sleep well tonight.'

'I think we all will,' Thea said. Now her worries about getting the hay crop in safely were over, she knew she would rest easy.

CHAPTER 38

Tuesday 10th June

'It looks a lot bigger in here now.' Hettie surveyed her bedroom with a sense of gratitude and relief. After what had seemed like extra-long weeks since her sister had moved in, Hettie's room had been returned to normal once more. The last of Ada's belongings had been taken out and were on their way to Great Plumstead Hall in Alf Barker's van, along with her sister, ready to begin her new job.

'I'm not surprised with Ada's double bed gone. You did well to manage with both of you in here with all the extra furniture.' Thea gave a wry smile, her eyes meeting Hettie's.

'It wasn't easy, I must admit. There were times when I wanted to go down and sleep on the camp bed in the dining room for some peace and quiet,' Hettie confided. 'But I wasn't going to give in and do that because Ada would have suggested I moved down there permanently while she was here!'

'I'm sure she would have,' Thea agreed.

'We got through it, despite it being difficult at times. I know it was the right thing to do to have her here. We helped my sister when she was in dire need of it.' Hettie straightened the blue eiderdown on her bed which she and Thea had moved back into its normal position in the middle of the room. 'Now, I wish her well for her new job and hope she'll be happy up at the Hall.'

'It gave Ada some breathing space and a chance to come to terms with losing her home. To have it taken from her with no choice was hard. If Rookery House was taken away from me, I'd be devastated.' Thea looked thoughtful. 'For Ada it was worse as she'd been there for so long. I hope she settles in well in her new home.'

Hettie glanced at her watch. 'I'd better be off if I'm going to help Ada unpack at the other end. I want to be sure that she's settled and make it homely for her. She'll be busy enough when she starts her housekeeping job tomorrow.' She put her hand on Thea's arm. 'Thank you for letting Ada stay here. I know she isn't the easiest person to live with. I appreciate you welcoming her here.'

'I'm glad we could help. It was the right thing to do. She's your sister and that makes her part of our Rookery House family too,' Thea said in a gentle voice. 'We look after each other in good times and bad.'

Hettie nodded. 'Indeed we do, and that's one of the reasons I love living here with everyone. This house and the people in it are special!'

～

As Hettie bicycled along the beech tree lined driveway towards the Hall, she thought back over the past couple of weeks since Ada had been given the job by Lady Campbell-Gryce. Her sister had done her best to prepare herself for her new role and had spent the last week shadowing Mrs Bartlett, the outgoing housekeeper, to learn the job she'd be stepping into. To Hettie's delight, Ada had returned home each night full of enthusiasm for what she was learning, which boded well.

Hettie had almost reached the end of the drive when Alf Barker's van came heading towards her. He slowed to a stop, winding down the window of the driver's door as Hettie braked and halted beside the cab.

'Ada's all moved in,' Alf said. 'Her Ladyship organising those three lads who work on the estate to assist with the move has been very helpful. We've done it a lot quicker than when we moved Ada into Rookery House.'

'Thank you for your help once more Alf. Will you at least let me pay you for your petrol today?' Hettie asked.

'There's no need. Her Ladyship has given me some money for that.' Alf tapped the top pocket of his jacket. 'She was most insistent and I wasn't going to argue with her. The Hall's a good customer at the shop and don't they say the customer is always right?' He chuckled. 'Anyway they've got plenty of money. You keep yours Hettie.'

'Fair enough. Her Ladyship is desperate for a new housekeeper, so she's willing to do what's necessary and it's only fair that you're paid one way or another. I'd better go and help Ada unpack. See you soon and thanks again.' Hettie gave him a grateful smile and set off towards the Hall.

Reaching the end of the drive, she pedalled across the sweeping gravel at the front of the beautiful honey-coloured stone building and headed for the west wing where the Campbell-Gryces now resided. Ada, as part of their staff, would live there, too.

Hettie smiled to herself, thinking that her sister's new job was like a distorted mirror image of her own time here. She could recall as clear as anything the day she'd arrived to start work as a scullery maid at the tender age of fourteen. Over many years she'd worked her way up to becoming Cook. While Ada was arriving as a much older, experienced woman and starting with the top woman's role on the staff! Something that would never have happened in normal times but, with the country at war, things were not as they once had been. Even the Campbell-Gryces were having to let go of the rigid expectations of the past to keep themselves in staff. It was fortunate for Ada that they were.

'Where would you like this?' Hettie asked, holding up a china figurine she'd just taken out of a box and unwrapped from the newspaper it had been stored in. She recognised it as the one which had once stood on the mantlepiece in Ada's sitting room back in her old cottage.

'I think on the mantlepiece in here.' Ada pointed at the fireplace in her sitting room which adjoined her bedroom in the servants' area of the west wing. It was a small but cosy room and would give Ada a chance to have some privacy when she needed it.

Hettie placed it where Ada had instructed and was delving in the box to unpack something else when there was a gentle tapping on the half-open door and Dorothy, the Cook, stepped into the room carrying a tray with cups and a plate on it.

'I was wondering if you were ready for a break? Only I've made some tea and there are some freshly baked biscuits too.' Dorothy gave a warm smile as she held out the tray.

'Shall we take a break?' Hettie looked at her sister, who'd been putting things away in the dresser that had come from her cottage.

'I could do with a cup of tea, thank you.' Ada moved a box from the table and gestured for Dorothy to put the tray down on it.

'How are you getting on?' Dorothy asked, gazing around the room. 'It looks much better in here with your furniture. Mrs Bartlett didn't have any of her own, so it was quite basic. You've made it look lovely and homely.'

'I'm glad you think so.' Ada picked up a cup, took a sip of tea and sighed appreciatively. 'I needed that. There's not that much more to do, is there Hettie?'

'Just this box I'm emptying and that's it.' Hettie took the remaining cup of tea and helped herself to a biscuit from the plate. 'It's good that you can finally have all your things around you again. There wasn't room at Rookery House so they've been packed away in boxes out of sight.'

'It will make you feel more at home.' Dorothy looked at the framed photograph that Ada had placed on the little table by the armchair. 'Is that your husband?'

Ada nodded. 'That's my Walter.' Her face was wistful. 'He would never have believed I'd end up working as a housekeeper at Great Plumstead Hall. Not that he wouldn't believe I was capable, but...' she made a gesture with one hand. 'Well, he'd never have imagined I would have had to leave our cottage. But there we are.' She raised her chin. 'What's done is done. There was nothing I could do to stop it so I must make the best of things. I think I'm going to enjoy living and working here.' Ada cast her gaze around the room. 'At least I've got my things which I had when Walter was alive. That's a great comfort.'

The backs of Hettie's eyes prickled and she blinked away

tears. She'd never heard Ada speak like this before, as her sister always kept her thoughts to herself. But today was a new beginning for Ada, a chance to start again. To hear Ada sounding positive and optimistic was something that Hettie would never have imagined possible a few weeks back. The new job and move to the Hall were clearly a turning point for Ada, and Hettie hoped it worked out well for her.

CHAPTER 39

Thursday 12th June

One of the things that Flo loved about living here at Rookery House was how much more aware of nature she was than she had ever been before. She'd always been conscious of the passing of the seasons through working on the family allotments, first in Lancaster and then in Manchester, but she had never lived in the countryside before. Here, she was surrounded by the goings-on of the natural world and had taken to enjoying a walk after the evening meal had been cleared away and the evenings were light. Flo enjoyed seeing what was going on in the grounds of Rookery House or further afield.

Tonight, she was walking around the boundary perimeter of the large five-acre field in the hope of spotting the barn owls hunting. Reuben had told her that the pair of owls had a nest in the old oak tree in the far corner and going by the amount of hunting they were doing now, they must have chicks to feed.

Flo sat herself down on the bank under the hedge. While she waited for the owls to appear, she contented herself with watching the swallows and house martins darting and swooping over the area where the hay had been cut. She loved their lively chattering to each other.

'You look miles away.'

The voice startled Flo and she turned to see Edwin heading towards her.

'I'm waiting for the barn owls. No sign of them yet.'

'They shouldn't be long. They're hunting earlier than normal these days. I saw them the other night. Do you mind if I join you to watch?'

Flo shook her head and gestured for him to take a seat on the bank near her.

Edwin sat down. 'I am going to miss being here.'

'Even though you've been put to work helping out with the haymaking and other jobs?' Flo glanced at him, a smile on her lips.

He gave a laugh. 'I have enjoyed it – honestly! I've spent most of the past nine months in London and I missed the countryside so much. It was a shock being surrounded by so many people and in such a built-up area. I never got used to it. Some days, I yearned to be out in the green countryside. It's been good to be back again.'

'I'm the opposite, coming from a city to the country, but I love it here,' Flo told him. 'Although Lancaster is nothing like as big as London. Did you enjoy your work there? It was with the Friends Ambulance Unit. Is that right?'

'Yes, I worked in the London Hospital on Mile End Road in the East End, or I was sent out doing first aid in the Blitz.

You know I'm a conscientious objector?' Edwin asked, turning to face her, his eyes meeting hers.

'Yes, Alice told me. I think you're brave to stand up for your beliefs. It can't have been easy.'

Edwin's face clouded. 'No, it wasn't, but my conscience wouldn't have let me do otherwise. It was purely because I could never kill another person. I knew if I joined up I'd be expected to, if necessary,' Edwin explained. 'But I did want to help others and joining the FAU has allowed me to do that.' He fell silent for a few moments. 'When men of my age group were called to register for military service I registered as a CO; that got me thrown out by my father. That's how I ended up living here and working for Thea.'

'I'm sorry. That must have been hard,' Flo said, sympathetically.

Edwin nodded. 'Yes, but I knew it would happen. My father is... well... let's just say he has his ways and couldn't stand the idea of one of his sons not doing their duty.'

Flo frowned. 'I'd say you are doing your duty but in another way which is just as important. You were out in the thick of the Blitz and that can't have been easy, and you'll soon be off abroad to drive ambulances carrying wounded soldiers to hospital. You're hardly shirking responsibility and have put yourself in danger as much as any soldier.'

Edwin gave her an appreciative smile. 'It's good of you to say so. I must admit it was difficult being out in air raids and I saw some dreadful things.' He stared out across the field, his expression pained. 'The Blitz hurt and killed so many innocent people. Women, children, the elderly, right there in their homes. War isn't just about soldiers fighting on the battlefield.' He sighed and leaned forward, his elbows on his knees. 'What man can do to man is terrible, and for what?'

A burning question sprang into Flo's head. She wasn't sure

if she should ask it or not, but the words burst out before she could stop them. 'Didn't seeing all that make you change your mind? Make you want to fight back?'

Edwin sat up and looked at her. 'No, never!' His voice was firm.

'But what if had been *your* family killed in the Blitz? Would you change your opinion then?'

He shook his head. 'I don't believe so.'

Flo stared down at the ground, poking at a stone with the toe of her boot, her thoughts whirring around. 'What do you think about us bombing them back then, an eye for an eye?' She raised her head to face him.

He ran a hand through his brown hair. 'I know that some believe that's the right thing to do, and it's what's being done. Only I can't help thinking there are *no winners* in this – just innocent people losing their families, lives and homes. The leaders who make the decisions sit back in safety and let others do the dirty work and face the consequences. What do you think?' He glanced at Flo.

She blinked away tears and raised her chin. 'That we must fight back! I'm *glad* they're building the aerodrome to do just that. I…' She waved her arm in the direction of where the new aerodrome was under construction. 'Because I lost my family in the Manchester Christmas Blitz last December.'

Edwin's eyes widened and he took hold of Flo's hand in his. 'I'm so sorry. I had no idea. No one has said anything to me about it.'

'It's not a secret any more, but I don't go around shouting about it either.' Flo frowned. 'But I do *know* what it feels like to lose your family in an air raid. My parents, sister and brother were innocent people who'd never harmed a soul, but they died in their home a few days before Christmas.' She pulled her hand out of Edwin's and folded her arms across her body.

'And that makes me want our country to do the same to the enemy as they're doing to us.'

'I understand how you would feel that way,' Edwin said in a gentle voice. 'And perhaps if the same had happened to me, then I might think differently. We can only do what feels right for ourselves.'

Flo nodded and met his eyes, which were sympathetic. 'I'm not sure I would have said the same before my family was killed. I'd not really thought about it, if I'm truthful. But now it's directly affected me and I've lost my family for ever... well, it's not something that's easy to forgive or to not want retribution for, is it?'

Edwin shook his head. 'War changes people, makes them do and think things they would never have considered before.'

Flo mulled over what he'd said. Amidst her turmoil after her family had died, she'd often wondered if the men flying the bombers over Manchester that night had ever stopped to contemplate what devastation their actions would unleash. Did they think about the innocent people who'd be killed by the bombs they dropped?

'I keep wondering if they ever consider what their bombs do to people. What do you think?' she asked.

'I'm not sure. Perhaps if they did, then they wouldn't be able to do it. Up there they're very removed from it.' Edwin glanced up at the sky as if imagining flying in a plane. 'They don't see the damage inflicted on the ground apart from the fires. They don't witness the people killed and injured. They're acting on orders. It's what men must do in the army or air force or whatever.'

Flo sighed. 'It's...' She halted as she spotted a movement out of the corner of her eye and turned to see a ghostly pale barn owl, with some prey dangling from its claws. 'The owl!' she said in a hushed voice.

'It's beautiful,' Edwin whispered, watching as it flew silently past them and up to land on a high branch in the oak before disappearing into its nest hole.

Flo turned to Edwin and smiled. 'Let's not talk any more about the war and what it's done. It's too horrible a thing to spoil a lovely evening. We should just enjoy being here now.'

He nodded. 'I'm fine with that.'

They fell into silence and watched as the owl reappeared and flew off to begin hunting along the thick, tussocky area running by the hedgerow at the far end of the field. It flew low, quartering up and down, listening out for prey.

'Tell me how you first got interested in gardening?' Edwin asked. 'Aunt Thea is full of praise for your skills and knowledge. She's told me she has learned a lot working with you.'

'I was taught by the best – my grandad. I worked on his allotment with him for as long as I can remember,' Flo told him.

Edwin asked about Flo's grandad and what he'd taught her and by the time the light was fading, they'd walked further around the field and talked about many topics, avoiding mention of the war again. Although thoughts of their earlier discussion still simmered away in Flo's mind. What had happened to her *had* made her think in a different way, and she wasn't wholly comfortable with it. But how else could she cope with the consequences of that terrible night?

CHAPTER 40

Monday 16th June

Prue felt sick. Seeing either of her sons off at the station never got any easier and today's farewell to Edwin was the worst yet. She had no idea when she would see him again. With Edwin being sent overseas, it could be years, or even... No! Prue wasn't going to go down that avenue of thought. Edwin had come through the Blitz and was a sensible young man. She had to keep the faith and believe that he *would* return, however long it took, otherwise what Prue was about to do would be impossible.

Her eyes met Edwin's over Alice's head as he hugged his sister tightly. The seconds were ticking down before he had to board the Norwich-bound train, which had steamed into Great Plumstead station moments before, filling the air with the tang of coal smoke. Edwin smiled at her and Prue's chest tightened. Summoning all her strength, she bit down the urge to weep and forced herself to return his smile.

Letting Alice go, Edwin stepped towards Prue and looked down at her face, studying it carefully as if imprinting it on his mind. 'I promise to write often, Ma. But if you don't get letters regularly, do not worry. It will be because they'll be coming from a lot further away than London. It won't be that I'm not writing them.' He smiled, his blue eyes holding hers.

Prue nodded. 'And I'll write back, keeping you up to date with what's happening here.' She forced another smile, aware that precious seconds left with her son were slipping away like sand through a glass timer. 'You will be careful won't you?'

'Always. And you look after yourself, Ma.' Edwin stepped forwards and wrapped her in a warm, loving embrace.

Prue rested her head against his chest and closed her eyes, encircling him in her arms, wanting to keep him there safe.

'All aboard!' the guard's loud voice shouted from further down the platform.

After a final squeeze, Edwin loosened his hold and still holding onto Prue's arms, he looked at her, their eyes meeting once more. 'This is just farewell for a while.'

Prue nodded, not daring to speak as a lump lodged in her throat and tears were only a moment away.

Edwin kissed her cheek and let go, then picked up his suitcase and with a final smile, climbed into the carriage and closed the door behind him. He pulled the window down and leaned out.

Prue reached out towards him and he grabbed her hand. 'Take care.' Her voice was hoarse as she struggled to keep her emotions in check.

'And both of you too,' Edwin called as the carriage began to move.

Prue walked along for a few yards but had to let go as the train picked up speed. Her eyes were fixed on his face as he looked back at them, waving. She returned his wave and kept on waving until the train disappeared around the bend in the track.

Dropping her arm to her side, Prue stood staring in the direction the train had gone, carrying away her son.

'Ma?' Alice's voice was croaky.

Prue turned to her daughter, whose face was tear streaked, her eyes brimming over. 'It's all right, Edwin will be back.' She pulled Alice into her arms and hugged her tightly, this time allowing her own tears to fall.

'I hate saying goodbye,' Alice said when they pulled apart.

'So do I.' Prue took two clean handkerchiefs out of her pocket and handed one to Alice, then used the other to dab the tears from her own face. 'And it doesn't get any easier the more you do it, either.'

'Do you really think he'll come back?' Alice asked, her blue eyes wide, her voice uncertain.

Prue took a deep breath. 'I hope he will, Alice. I really do. And that's what I'm going to hold on to because thinking anything else won't help me or you…' She looked pointedly into Alice's eyes. 'We've got to carry on doing our work and not get weighed down with worrying. It won't do us any good and Edwin wouldn't want us to do that.'

Alice sniffed and nodded. 'I'll try.'

'Good. Now you need to get to Rookery House and I'm due at The Mother's Day Club this morning.' Prue linked her arm through Alice's and they headed for the station exit. Prue *did* mean the words she'd just spoken to her daughter, but meaning them and actually *doing* them herself were two different things. Prue knew in her heart that she wouldn't be able to stop worrying about Edwin until he was safely home again and this whole, destructive war was done.

CHAPTER 41

Thursday 19th June

Flo hadn't managed to get to the first two meetings of Gloria's new singing group. The first week haymaking had been in full swing at Rookery House and Flo had worked well into the evening. Last Thursday she'd been exhausted after a long, hot day working outside and needed to rest rather than go out in the evening. But tonight, Flo was determined to give the group a try, although her stomach was aflutter with butterflies as she bicycled into the village on the warm June evening.

The thought of singing in a group again was both exciting and yet nerve-wracking at the same time. It wasn't that she'd never sung with others since last December, as she'd happily joined in with the singing at the WI meetings and while working on the WI allotment. But those occasions had felt different, as the singing was just an accompaniment to the work or meeting. Tonight was more serious, more focused. Gloria had said they'd be singing fun, joyful songs, but the whole ethos was focusing on the singing, rather than it just being an add-on.

Flo bit her bottom lip as she pedalled along, telling herself that she was overthinking things. Tonight was really about a group of women who loved singing just enjoying making music, that was all. Only, deep down, Flo was scared what it might trigger in her, reminding her of the last time she'd been in a singing group, with friends from her work. And how their planned Christmas carolling had been prevented. Singing and what had happened that fateful night last December had somehow become inextricably linked for Flo. She desperately hoped that she could break that bond, free herself to sing once more and enjoy the pleasure it gave her.

Arriving at the village hall, she left the bicycle she'd borrowed from Hettie leaning against the wall and went in. Flo saw that she wasn't the first to arrive. There were several other women already sitting in the semi-circle of chairs that had been set out in the middle of the hall, including Prue and Alice.

Gloria, who was setting out some cups on a table near the doorway into the kitchen, spotted her and came over, her arms held out wide.

'Welcome!' She wrapped Flo in a warm, perfumed embrace. 'I'm so glad you're here.' Gloria took a step back still holding on to Flo's arms. 'It will be good for you to sing again and it will bring you joy.' Their eyes met, a look of understanding passing between them.

Flo nodded, not daring to speak for a few moments as a wave of emotion swelled inside her.

'Go and sit down and we'll be making a start in a few minutes,' Gloria added.

Flo headed over and sat in the empty seat between Alice and Prue, which Alice had saved for her. It was Alice's encouragement earlier today that had convinced Flo to come tonight and she didn't want to let her friend down, or Gloria who'd been so kind to her.

By the time seven o'clock came round, more women had arrived, extra seats had needed to be set out, and a buzz of expectant chatter filled the hall.

Gloria made her way to the front so that she was standing facing the semi-circle of women.

'Welcome everyone! It's lovely to see more new faces here tonight.' She looked around and when her gaze fell on Flo, Gloria's smile widened even more. 'Clearly, news of the wonderful time we have here has spread and the more singers we have, the better. When I sing with others, it fills my heart with joy,' she pressed her hands to her heart, 'and I hope you will feel that too. Now if you'd like to stand up, we'll begin by warming up our voices.' Gloria raised her hands, encouraging them to rise to their feet.

For the next five minutes Gloria led them through a series of vocal exercises, sending their voices soaring from low to high notes and back down again. They were encouraged to stretch their lips and take in deep lungfuls of air to fuel their notes. As she followed the warm-up exercises, Flo began to lose herself in the sounds she was making and she realised how taut she'd been holding herself as her shoulders dropped and she started to relax.

'Let's begin with our first song, our old favourite, *Daisy Bell*.' Gloria gave a nod to Sylvia, who was seated at the piano. As Sylvia played the introductory notes, Gloria counted them in ready to start singing by waving three beats with her hand.

As Flo sang along with the other women, she found her spirits soaring. There was a special alchemy in singing as a group like this. They were all completely focused on the song, not just doing some singing while they did something else.

She loved how their voices melded and complemented each other, and it made Flo smile. Glancing round at the others, she could see similar looks of happiness on their faces too.

When eight o'clock came around, Flo felt that time had somehow sped up as the hour had passed so quickly. She had truly lost herself in the joy of singing as Gloria had taken them through song after song. As Flo helped clear the chairs away, she realised that her hesitancy about joining the group had been proven wrong. The memory of her previous singing group had been overwritten, replaced with something joyous and one which could be repeated each week.

'Did you enjoy it?' Gloria asked, adding a chair to a stack by the wall.

Flo nodded. 'I did, *very much*. It was wonderful, singing like that just carries you away.'

Gloria beamed, her eyes shining with delight. 'It certainly does. Singing never fails to raise my spirits. I hope you'll come back next week.'

Flo returned Gloria's smile. 'Yes, I definitely will.'

CHAPTER 42

Thursday 24th June

'Welcome to our first Make and Mend party!' Prue surveyed the women seated at the various workstations that had been set up around the village hall, a wide smile on her face.

'I hope you'll all enjoy this afternoon and will leave here having learned new skills that you can use to keep yourself and your family well dressed now that we're faced with clothes rationing. Do take the opportunity to try out different things and share your skills with others. This is a chance for us to help each other and be better prepared to cope with what limited resources we have. This afternoon you can learn how to use old worn-out garments to make something new or if you've struggled with darning, then Nancy will help you master the art!'

'I'll do my very best,' Nancy said.

'I need all the help I can get with the number of holes my

husband manages to get in his socks,' a stalwart member of the WI said, making the women laugh.

'There's rag rug making, how to turn a worn collar or cuffs on a shirt, how to create a dressing gown from a blanket,' Prue pointed to the tables they had set out with these different activities on. 'And unravelling knitted items. We plan to have more of these parties so we can make other things too. This is just a start! Before we begin, I'd like to announce that a village fete with sports day races is being planned for July. We're looking for volunteers to help. If you'd like to be involved, please add your name to this.' Prue held up a sheet of paper and then placed it on the table which had been set out with teacups ready for the tea break. 'Without further ado, let's get making do and mending!'

''Ear, 'ear!' Gloria called out, which was met by a round of laughter and applause from the women.

Within a short time the village hall was abuzz with activity and good-hearted chatter. Over the past few weeks, after posters had been put up appealing for unwanted clothes, old blankets and curtains, the women of The Mother's Day Club had been sorting through donations and now there was a good stockpile to use at parties like this afternoon.

After popping into the kitchen to switch the hot water urn on to make some tea, Prue stood in the doorway back into the hall watching what was going on.

At a table nearby, Marianne was holding up a pair of men's brown corduroy trousers that had been donated.

'You can see here that the material's worn thin on the seat and again on each knee.' Marianne pointed out the difference in the thickness of the material, the light showing through the worn parts. 'But here,' she rubbed her finger and thumb on the lower legs, 'the fabric is still good and perfect to re-use. There's enough in these trousers to make a skirt or a child's garment. The same applies to all these items.' She gestured to the pile of folded clothes that had been placed on the table, ready to be processed. 'All we need to do is unpick the seams, then the material can be washed and the good parts used to sew something new at another Make and Mend party.'

It would be very satisfying to see what garments could be made from the worn-out clothes, Prue thought. Having restrictions placed on them because of the war was making women become resourceful with what they already had.

A burst of laughter drew Prue's attention to where Hettie and Gloria were unravelling unwanted knitted jumpers, chatting as they wound the freed wool around the backs of chairs to make hanks. Like the unpicked fabric, the hanks would be washed ready to be knitted into new items. Hettie had offered to do that after today's session and said she'd be weighing down each hank as it dried on the washing line to stretch out kinks in the wool.

Returning to the kitchen to make the tea, Prue felt happy. They had only just begun, but already she had a good feeling about this. Making and mending wasn't only about making sure people were suitably clothed, it was about community and friendship, too.

CHAPTER 43

Monday 30th June

Planting out leeks was a job that Thea always enjoyed. There was a sense of satisfaction seeing the plants that they'd been nurturing in the greenhouse since they first poked their spindly green stalks above the soil, set in place where they were to grow and mature, ready to be harvested through the winter months.

She made another hole with the wooden dibber to finish the row, gently placed a small leek plant in it and then went back and poured water into every hole from the watering can to settle each plant's roots in safely.

'The afternoon post has arrived!'

Thea put down the can and looked over to the gate of Five Acres to see Hettie waving a white envelope in the air as she headed towards her.

Leaving the watering can by the row to mark where she'd got to, Thea walked to meet Hettie.

'There was one each for Evie and Flo, as well. Evie can get hers when she comes home from the hospital tonight and I gave Flo hers on the way here,' the older woman explained.

Flo and Alice were doing some hoeing in the large vegetable plots nearer the house to keep a check on the weeds, which were growing fast in the warm June weather. It was a necessary and frequent job to give their precious crops space and light to grow well.

'It's from Jess,' Hettie said, handing over the envelope.

Thea looked down at the familiar handwriting and frowned. There was nothing unusual in the children's mother sending letters to Rookery House. She'd written each week since George and Betty had come to live here, though always addressed the envelope to the children. But this one was sent to Thea alone. It sent an uncomfortable shiver down Thea's spine. Why write it just to her? Was it about something Jess didn't want her children to know?

From the look on Hettie's face Thea could tell she was thinking the same thing.

'You'd best open it to see what it says,' Hettie advised her.

'It's probably nothing to worry about.' Thea opened the envelope, took out two sheets of paper and unfolded them. One was written to George and Betty and was their regular weekly letter from their mother. The other was for Thea. She began to read the letter addressed to her.

Dear Thea,

I hope all is well with you and everyone at Rookery House. I'm writing to ask if I may take up your kind invitation, which you've often added to the bottom of George and Betty's letters to me. I'd like to come and visit you all for a few days. Now the bombing has stopped, it's a good time to get away and see the children again. I hope this would be convenient for you. I haven't mentioned it to George and Betty in their letter as I don't want to get their hopes up until I know you agree to me visiting.

If you're willing, then I'd like to visit from the 20th to the 27th of July.

I look forward to hearing from you if that would be acceptable.

With my best regards,

Jess

'She wants to come and stay.' Thea handed the letter to Hettie to read for herself.

'That's all right, isn't it?' Hettie asked, scanning through it. 'The children will be delighted to see their mother. They haven't seen her since they came to live here last autumn.'

'Yes, of course, though she'll have to sleep in the dining room, or we could move the camp bed up into the children's room so she could be with them. I can ask Jess what she'd prefer when I write back.' Thea bit her bottom lip. 'But why does she want to visit *now*? She says it's because the bombing's stopped. Does that mean she's coming to take them home again? I've read in the paper about how some evacuee children are returning to London now the Blitz is over. Would she really want to take George and Betty back when there's the risk that the bombers could return at any time? Just because they haven't been for a while after the last big raid in May, it doesn't mean it's over. London is still a target.'

Hettie laid her hand on Thea's arm. 'I hope that's not why she's coming.' Her blue eyes were concerned behind her glasses. 'But she is George and Betty's mother and if she decides to take them home again, you can't stop her.'

Thea's stomach twisted at the thought of George and Betty going back into potential danger, along with the fact that she would miss them dearly. She had become very fond of the two children who had unexpectedly come into her life. Saying goodbye to them would be hard.

She nodded. 'I know. But I would challenge her on the wisdom of it. In my opinion, it would be madness! While we're still at war, London could be attacked again at any time. It's not safe for children there until we have peace once more.'

'It might not come to that. Jess is a sensible woman. Remember, she left George and Betty here when she went back to look after her husband. Not all mothers did that when they returned home,' Hettie reminded her. 'I don't think Jess would do anything rash to put her children in danger. Until you know otherwise, don't go worrying yourself about what might or might not happen and what is out of your control. You've enough to do with running this place and your WVS work.'

Thea managed a smile. 'You're right, Hettie. I know I shouldn't worry about the what ifs because they might not come true. It's just...'

'Stop right there!' Hettie held up her hand. 'Worrying is a complete waste of time and energy.' Her eyes held Thea's. 'Take it from one who's done enough worrying over the years and when I look back, it was a total waste, so don't go spending your precious time brooding.'

'I'll try.' Thea handed Hettie the letter. 'Will you take it indoors, so it doesn't get dirty? We can tell George and Betty later that their mother's planning a visit. They'll be delighted.'

CHAPTER 44

Sunday 20th July

'Here it comes!' Betty shouted, running back from the far end of the platform where she'd been watching for the first sign of the approaching Norwich train.

Thea, who was waiting with George, his hand tightly holding on to hers, smiled at the little girl who was brimming over with excitement at the prospect of seeing her mother again. George, on the other hand, was anxious. He was looking forward to seeing his mother but had been clinging on to Thea all the way here from Rookery House and hadn't left her side.

'Not long to wait now,' Thea said cheerfully, gazing down at the little boy.

He returned her gaze, his eyes uncertain.

'Mam's nearly here!' Betty, who now stood waiting with them, hopped from foot to foot in delight.

'Watch out for which carriage she's in as the train slows down. See if you can spot her,' Thea suggested.

Despite Hettie's advice, Thea had not been able to stop worrying about the reason for Jess Collins's visit. Was she just coming to see her children or to take them back to London with her at the end of her stay? Thea knew what she hoped would happen, but whether it would was completely out of her control.

'There she is!' Betty shrieked, pointing at the carriage that had just slid past where they stood as the train came to a halt. She ran to the carriage door and reached for the handle as her mother pushed it open from the inside. 'Mam!'

Jess stepped out of the train, dropped her suitcase to the ground and hugged her daughter tightly, her eyes meeting Thea's over Betty's head.

Jess smiled. 'Hello, Thea.' Her gaze then fell on George, who still held on tightly to Thea's hand. 'Hello George.' Releasing Betty, she crouched down in front of him and held her arms out wide to her son.

'Go on,' Thea said softly, letting go of his hand and encouraging him forwards.

The little boy did as he was bid and stood quietly as his mother hugged him tightly, closing her tear-filled eyes for a moment.

Loosening her hold on her son, Jess stood up and stared at her children. 'I can't believe how much you've both grown. Must be all that good country food and clean, fresh air.' She gave Thea a grateful smile. 'I can see how well cared for they are. Thank you for all you've done for them.'

Thea nodded. 'It's a pleasure. We love having them at Rookery House with us. Can I carry your suitcase for you? Then you'll have two free hands.'

'Thank you.' Jess picked up her suitcase and handed it to

Thea. 'Now I can hold hands with both of you.' She reached out and Betty and George each took hold of one of their mother's hands.

'You must see the baby rabbits and the piglets,' Betty said excitedly.

'There are six baby rabbits. Two white with brown splodges and the other four are brown,' George added, his shyness forgotten as he talked about the animals he was so passionate about.

'I look forward to seeing them.' Jess smiled at her son. 'I liked the pictures you drew of them in your letters.'

With the children still talking about the animals, they set off to walk back to Rookery House. Thea walked alongside them listening to the chatter, glad that Betty, and now even George, were happy to be with their mother again. Jess was clearly delighted to be reunited with them.

Thea couldn't help wondering if this was the start of them being a proper family once more. If Jess had decided to take the children back with her next week, Thea knew there wasn't much she could do to stop it. The best thing she could do was show Jess how well George and Betty were looked after at Rookery House. Prove to their mother that it would be in the children's best interests to stay here even if the bombing had now stopped in London. Thea had a week to prove how much and how well she cared for George and Betty and she was determined to do just that.

The children had taken Jess up to their bedroom to show her where she was going to sleep. They were so excited that their mother had opted to have the camp bed put in their room so she could be with them, rather than sleeping down in the dining room.

Thea could hear laughter from upstairs as she cut slices of the cake which Hettie had baked that morning.

'Are you all right?' Hettie asked, her shrewd eyes fixed on Thea.

'Yes.' Thea managed a smile. 'The children are pleased to be with their mother again.'

Hettie nodded. 'That's good. Did Jess say anything about taking them back?'

'No, nothing yet. But it wasn't the time or place. I'm going to be on tenterhooks waiting to see if she does.' Thea sighed. 'I...' She halted at the sound of the telephone ringing and hurried out into the hallway to answer it.

'Hello, Great Plumstead 377,' Thea said into the receiver.

'Good afternoon, can I speak to Miss Thornton?' a woman's voice came down the line.

'Speaking.'

'I'm calling from WVS headquarters in Norwich to ask you to take part in a four-day invasion exercise on duty with a canteen. I know that you and your partner...' There was a pause and rustling of paper. 'Mrs Wilson are both experienced and extremely capable. You've been part of similar exercises before, I believe.'

'Yes, we have, but only for one day at a time,' Thea said. 'When will it take place?'

'It starts tomorrow. You'll need to be ready to leave Wykeham with your canteen at seven a.m. Exact instructions on where to go will be provided in the morning. I take it that this is acceptable and that you'll continue your excellent work and keep up the high WVS standard supporting the troops and civil defence?'

Thea grimaced. This couldn't have come at a worse time

with Jess here. If Thea was off working with the canteen for *four* long days, it wasn't going to give a good impression of how well she cared for the children. But an invasion exercise was important because if an invasion happened for real, then they needed to have practised and be prepared.

'Miss Thornton? Are you there?' the woman's voice broke into Thea's thoughts.

'Yes, I'm sorry.'

'Will be able to man the canteen or not?'

Thea had no choice in the matter. 'Yes of course. Have you contacted Prue, Mrs Wilson? She's my sister?'

'I'm about to telephone her next. I'll tell her you're on board too. So be ready to leave with the canteen at seven a.m. sharp in the morning. Good luck. I'm sure you'll do the WVS proud.' Not waiting for a reply, she rang off.

Thea slowly put the receiver down and let out a heavy sigh.

'What's up?' Hettie called through the kitchen doorway. 'Bad news?'

'No, but extremely badly timed.' Thea headed back into the kitchen and closed the door behind her. 'I've been asked to go out with the WVS canteen to help cater for the troops taking part in an exercise.'

'You've done that before, so you know what to do, don't you?' Hettie said.

'Yes, but this time it's for *four days*, starting tomorrow! With Jess here...' She frowned and lowered her voice. 'I was hoping to show her how well I care for George and Betty, but now I won't even be here for more than half of Jess's visit! How's that going to look?' Thea pulled out a chair and sat down, leaning her elbows on the table and rubbing at her temples with her fingers. 'She'll definitely want to take them back with her now.'

Hettie put a hand on Thea's shoulder. 'The children won't

be abandoned. I'm here, so are Marianne, Flo and Alice. We *all* help to look after them. Remember, we work as a *team* here, working around our various commitments. George and Betty always have someone looking after them. It's never only been on your shoulders.'

Thea glanced up at Hettie, who stood beside her. 'You're right, I know. Any other time it wouldn't have mattered, but it might be enough to make Jess doubt the wisdom of her children staying on here. If she hasn't already.'

'Or she might see that George and Betty have many people who look after them. Plus, not only do *you* care for them, but you also do your bit for the *war effort* too!' Hettie said firmly.

Thea forced a smile. 'You always look on the bright side.'

Hettie raised her eyebrows. 'I try to. We will carry on pulling together as a team. Jess can enjoy time with her children here and what comes to pass next week,' she gestured with her hand, 'we'll just have to wait and see.'

They heard voices and footsteps coming down the stairs.

'Chin up,' Hettie instructed her. 'After we've had something to eat, you need to get yourself organised for tomorrow and beyond.'

Thea nodded. 'Thank you.'

'You're welcome.' Hettie patted Thea's shoulder. 'Here they come, just in time for some tea and cake,' she said as the door opened and Betty came in first, followed by George holding his mother's hand.

CHAPTER 45

'It couldn't have come at a worse time!' Prue tapped the pencil she was holding against the long list of things to do spread out before her on the kitchen table. 'How can I go off running the canteen for *four* days when there's so much to do here organising the village fete?'

'If there ever is an invasion, they're going to come when it suits them, not us. It might not be convenient if we've got a Make and Mend party planned or a salvage drive...' Nancy, who was sitting opposite her, quirked an eyebrow. 'Treat this exercise as a trial run like it's supposed to be, Prue. And as for the fete preparations, you ain't the only person who can do them.'

Prue sighed and shook her head. 'I'm sorry. I do tend to...' she gestured with her hand, 'always think I must do it all myself, which is silly. Now that's been taken out of my hands.'

'You have plenty of people who you can delegate tasks to. Me, for a start. Lots of the women at The Mother's Day Club 'ave already said they're willing to 'elp. There are others at the WI too.' Nancy turned the list around on the table so that they could both read it. 'Why don't we look through this, divide up the jobs and write the names of who would be best at doing them. Tomorrow I'll go to The Mother's Day Club and assign people with their different tasks? I can visit the WI members' 'omes as well. We've got four days to finish getting everything sorted.'

Prue nodded. 'If only the exercise wasn't for so long, then I could help too.'

'You can still be involved on the day of the fete. There'll be lots to do then setting up the stalls.' Nancy's mouth curved into a smile. 'Don't worry, Prue, you won't be allowed to do nothing. Although to be 'onest,' she tapped the list with her finger, 'you've already put a lot of time and effort into organising the fete. And it's not as if you're off on 'oliday or anything. Running a canteen is 'ard work, and it's going to be busier than ever for you, with goodness knows 'ow many soldiers wanting their cups of tea or soup and a sandwich.'

'You're right.' Prue managed a smile. 'I just don't want to let anyone down.'

Nancy barked out a laugh. 'Honesty, Prue, you do more in this village for other people than any other person.'

'I like to be busy and with the war on – there's always plenty to do.' Prue added silently that keeping herself occupied had become a distraction from her unhappy marriage and helped fill the gap left by the children growing up. If she didn't keep busy, then...?

'Prue?' Nancy's voice cut into her thoughts. 'Is Thea 'appy about the four-day exercise?'

'Not really. She's agreed to run the canteen, same as me, but it's come at a bad time for her too,' Prue explained, her sister having telephoned a short while ago, after the woman from the WVS had rung. 'Jess Collins arrived today to stay for a week and Thea's worried that she might take George and Betty back to London with her.'

'What!' Nancy's eyes grew wide. 'Has Jess said she's going to do that?'

'Not yet, but now the bombing appears to have stopped, she might want to.'

'I remember the day she turned up 'ere to leave the children before she returned to London,' Nancy recalled, her face serious. 'At least she 'ad the sense to do that. She'd be mad to take them back there. The bombing might start again any time.' Nancy frowned. 'If she sees 'ow well George and Betty are getting on 'ere, then maybe she won't be tempted to take them home with 'er.'

'Let's hope so. Jess has come at a good time with the fete coming up. She'll be able to see how we have fun in the village.' Prue picked up her pencil. 'We need to think who'll be best doing each job.'

Nancy ran her finger down the list. 'Gloria's already got the singing group organised and well practised.' She pointed to where the singing group was written. 'Shall I ask Flo and Alice to be in charge of the sports, sorting out the bats and balls, skipping ropes and running the races?'

'Good idea.' Prue added the names against the tasks. Sometimes, she thought, it was best to let go of things, give other people an opportunity to take the lead. She had every faith in them. But then Prue didn't have any other choice, did she?

CHAPTER 46

Wednesday 23rd July

Thea had lost count of the number of cups of tea she'd served up over the past few days. Today, the third day of the invasion exercise, had been just as busy as the two previous ones. Their WVS canteen was a magnet for those taking part, to get themselves a hot drink and something to eat. They'd served soldiers, members of the Home Guard, policemen, ambulance crew, firemen, first aiders, nurses and ARP wardens. Any service that was part of the Civil Defence of the country was involved in the manoeuvres and being put to the test.

'Can I have some soup and a sandwich, please?' a soldier with a mud-streaked face asked, stepping forward to the front of the queue.

'It's tomato,' Thea said, handing him a cup of red soup she'd ladled out of the urn for him. 'Help yourself to one of the rolls.' She pointed towards the prepared bread rolls that were set out on a tray on the canteen hatch. 'There's spam or fish paste.'

'Thank you. Fish paste will do me.' The soldier handed over his money and took a filled bread roll. He bit into it and chewed, a smile spreading across his face.

Thea handed him his change. 'You look like you needed that.'

He grinned. 'I certainly do.' He wandered off to sit on the grassy bank nearby, where other soldiers had gathered to eat and drink what they'd bought from the canteen.

'We're running low on hot water again,' Prue said. 'I'll need to fetch another top-up from the rectory.'

Thea glanced at her sister, who was keeping things going in the back of the canteen while Thea served at the hatch. 'That will be the fourth time we've needed it today and it's only two o'clock! You'd better go now so we can get it on to heat up again.'

While Prue hurried off to collect more water for the urn from the rectory which was the nearest house, Thea continued to serve. She was surprised to see a familiar face when the last person in the queue stepped forward. It was her brother Reuben whose usually smart khaki uniform was streaked with dirt. He was taking part with his Home Guard unit, but until now Thea hadn't seen him.

'Hello, how are you getting on?' he asked, looking up at her.

Thea gave him a wide smile. 'This is a nice surprise. It's been busy. We've hardly stopped. How about yourself?'

'We're being put to the test, that's for sure.' Reuben rubbed the back of his neck with his hand. 'But we caught some of the so-called enemy paratroopers early this morning, ambushed them in a wood.'

Thea had heard that parachutists had been dropped in last

night under cover of darkness, mimicking what could happen if the enemy decided to invade. The invasion exercise hadn't stopped overnight but carried on twenty-four hours a day. At least she and Prue had been relieved after their twelve-hour shifts, when another fully stocked WVS canteen had arrived to take over for the night shift, and they'd been able to go home to rest.

'I hope an invasion never comes; this has been hard enough. You look tired.'

Reuben lifted a shoulder. 'I'm all right. I'll catch up on some sleep when I can. At least this exercise has an end to it. If the real thing happens, it will be much longer and who knows what would happen. The good thing is this is showing what we *can* do and what we need to get better at.' He looked at the food on offer displayed on trays. 'Can I have a pie and a cup of tea, please? I'm starving.'

After Thea had served her brother and he'd gone to join the others eating nearby, she started on some more washing up. It was a never-ending job keeping a supply of clean cups for the many teas and soups. As she worked, Thea's thoughts drifted to what was going on at Rookery House. She wondered how George and Betty were getting on with their mother. For the past two nights Thea hadn't got back to Rookery House until after nine o'clock by which time the children were in bed and fast asleep. Jess had still been up and had seemed happy and to be enjoying herself.

'You look miles away!'

Prue's voice startled Thea. 'Just thinking about what's going on at home.' Thea wiped her hands dry on a tea towel. 'Hand one to me.' She took one of the large jugs that Prue had fetched water in, removed the lid from the almost empty metal tea urn and poured it in.

'Has everything been all right at home while you've been

away?' Prue asked, pouring her jug into the urn then replacing the lid.

'Yes, Hettie says it's all been fine. There's been no mention of the children going back to London so far. George and Betty seem happy spending time with their mother and she with them.'

'That's good, isn't it?'

Thea nodded. 'Of course, but this isn't how I planned to spend Jess's visit.'

'I should be working on the fete!' Prue threw up her hands. 'But we're here because we're needed. And I know that the fete won't fail because I've not personally organised each thing. Other people are quite capable of doing it.'

Thea couldn't help smiling. 'Hark at you! You've changed your tune, Prue. You never would have been willing to delegate like that before.'

'Needs must, and to be honest, I'm relieved to let others take more of the responsibility for once.' Prue looked thoughtful. 'The longer this war goes on, the more there is to be done. We're Digging for Victory, Making Do and Mending, salvaging scrap, knitting for the troops, taking in evacuees... the list is endless and keeps getting added to.' She sighed. 'Sometimes I just...' Prue hesitated. 'Well, I feel like escaping for a while and this,' she gestured her hand around the inside of the canteen, 'strangely feels like a sort of escape. It has been hard work, but it's a change and I'm glad about it. It's taken my mind off things for a bit.'

'You mean Edwin?' Thea's voice was gentle.

Prue nodded. 'I haven't heard anything from him since that last letter postmarked from Glasgow, from where he must have sailed off to who knows where.'

Thea took hold of her sister's hand, giving it a squeeze. 'He'll be all right. Edwin's a sensible young man.'

'He is, but that doesn't necessarily mean he won't be hurt or…' Prue's eyes were bright with unshed tears.

'I know, but you mustn't torture yourself by worrying over what might never happen. Although I know it's easier said than done!'

'Easier said than done…' Prue repeated knowingly, before a soldier knocked on the hatch to attract their attention.

'Can I have some tea, love?' he called into the canteen. 'I'm parched.'

Prue pasted a smile onto her face. 'Back to work,' she told her sister.

Thea nodded, thinking that she would need to keep an eye on Prue. For all her busyness and Keep Calm and Carry On attitude, she was hurting inside.

Stepping to the front of the serving hatch, Thea smiled down at the soldier. 'What would you like with your tea?'

CHAPTER 47

Thursday 24th July

'That Mrs Danvers made the hairs on my neck stand up!' Alice declared, pulling a scared face as she pedalled along. 'She gave me the creeps.'

Flo burst out laughing. 'She wasn't the sort of housekeeper you'd want to find in your new home. It was a good film though. I really enjoyed it.'

They'd been to see *Rebecca* starring Laurence Olivier and Joan Fontaine at the pictures in Wykeham and were now on their way home.

'I'm glad Hettie insisted we should go,' Alice said.

'She's a wise woman is Hettie.' After a busy couple of days, it had been good to get out, Flo thought. With Thea away working long hours on the WVS canteen as part of the invasion exercise, Flo and Alice had had to take on extra work. They were responsible for keeping everything outside in the gardens running smoothly. They had shared the milking duties between them and after Flo had milked Primrose late this afternoon, they'd set off to Wykeham in time to make the early evening showing of *Rebecca*.

'Do you think Ada is like Mrs Danvers now she's housekeeper at the Hall?' Alice asked.

Flo glanced across at her friend as she rode alongside her. 'No. I know Ada can be a bit prickly, but she's nowhere near as bad as Mrs Danvers.'

'I think I might read the book if I can get a copy from the Wykeham library.'

'Evie might have a copy; she's got loads of books. You should ask her,' Flo suggested. 'If she has, then I might read it too. I...' Flo halted as she became aware of the sound of roaring engines growing louder. 'What's that?' She braked and came to a stop looking around her, and then she spotted the source of the noise and her stomach lurched. 'Look!' she shouted at Alice who'd stopped just ahead of her, pointing to the low-flying plane heading in their direction.

'It's coming down!' Alice shrieked, her eyes wide in panic.

Flo watched in horror, her heart racing, as the plane, with smoke streaming out of one wing, came towards them, getting lower and lower. The whining noise of straining engines filled the air. They both instinctively ducked as it roared over them about a hundred feet up and losing height rapidly. It was soon lost from sight behind the hedge. It was only the sound of a mighty *whoomph!* and the silence that followed that told them it had hit the ground.

Alice looked at Flo, an expression of shock on her face. 'What do we do?'

What should they do? Flo's thoughts echoed Alice's words. They were out in the middle of the countryside, halfway between Wykeham and Great Plumstead with not a soul around except for them. 'We have to help, if we can.' Flo's voice came out braver than she felt. 'Come on!'

They left their bicycles in the nearby gateway, climbed over the five-bar wooden gate and ran towards the stricken plane. It had crashed at the far end of the field, leaving a scar of brown earth freshly ploughed through the grass, marking the path where it must have skidded along after hitting the ground.

As she ran, Flo's legs seemed to be made of jelly. How they were propelling her forwards she didn't know, but slowly the gap between her and the plane grew smaller.

'Do you think it might blow up?' Alice asked, breathlessly running beside Flo.

'I hope not!' Flo couldn't see any fire. The smoke that had been streaming out of the wing when the aeroplane had passed over them was gone. Perhaps it had been smothered by the earth ploughed up when it hit the ground. As for the crew inside, there was no sign. Had they been killed on impact?

They were about twenty yards away from the plane when Flo spotted the symbol on the tail. It brought her to an abrupt standstill.

Alice, who'd run on, realised she'd stopped and did the same, turning round to look at Flo. 'What's wrong?'

'It's...' Flo's breathing was ragged as she forced out the words. 'It's a German!' She pointed to the swastika on the tail fin, which had partly sheared in two. A wave of panic hit, her stomach knotting. Flo took several deep breaths as memories and feelings pummelled her. This was an *enemy* bomber and could even be the one that had dropped the bomb which had killed her family.

'What do we do?' Alice's voice was shrill. 'I can see someone moving inside the cockpit. They're still alive. They might be hurt. We must help them.' She took a few steps towards the plane and then stopped and turned back to face Flo. '*Come on!* We've got to help them.'

Flo stood still, her body rigid. How could she go to their aid after what they, or others like them, had done?

'What's the matter with you?' Alice marched towards her. 'Look, I know they are the *enemy* but think if the same happened to Marianne's husband if his plane came down over Germany. Wouldn't we all hope someone would help him?'

Alice's words hit home. Inside that plane were other women's husbands and sons. Other children's fathers. Was she now so full of bitterness about the loss of her family that she couldn't help fellow humans in need? Flo thought. She knew that her parents would have wanted her to help these stricken airmen despite what had happened to them.

Knowing in her heart that it was the right thing to do, Flo nodded to Alice and together they ran towards the plane once more. It lay belly down like a stranded bird. Its propellers were twisted out of shape and the Perspex canopies on the nose, cockpit and top were shattered into a network of cracks.

Approaching the wreck, Flo could see that Alice was right and at least some of the crew were alive and struggling to escape, pushing at a cracked canopy to get out.

'We must try to pull it loose from the outside,' Flo said, thinking quickly. She grabbed hold of where the canopy had partly sheared off. With her and Alice pulling from the outside and the crew pushing from inside, they managed to free it, leaving the way clear for the crew to escape.

Flo held out her hand to help a man who must be the pilot. His leather-gloved hand grabbed hold of hers and he climbed out.

'Zank you,' he said, his eyes meeting Flo's through his goggles as he stepped down on to the ground.

Flo gave him a nod and then led him clear of the plane, noticing how his legs were staggering.

'Sit there.' She pointed to the ground and was relieved when he did as she asked.

Leaving him, Flo went back to help another crew member. Together, Flo and Alice helped the three remaining men out. None of them appeared to have been injured beyond some scratches and bumps.

'What are we going to do now?' Alice asked in a hushed voice as she stood with her arms folded staring at the men.

Flo surveyed the four German airmen who sat in a group on the ground, talking in low voices to each other. They were all dressed in the same outfit, light-tan coloured leather helmets, with life jackets over their khaki flying suits. They looked wholly out of place in the Norfolk countryside.

'They'll be taken as Prisoners of War, I suppose,' Flo said. 'We need to get them to the police station or go and fetch the police. We can't leave them here. They might run off.'

'I'm not going to get the police if that means leaving you here with them, and I don't want to be left here while you go,' Alice said firmly.

Flo gave her friend a smile. 'Of course not. We'll have to take them together somehow. That's if they'll cooperate.'

'But they might not!' Alice hissed. 'There's four of them and only two of us. If they try to escape, we can't do much to stop them.'

'They don't look like they want to, so far. I think...' Flo paused as the airman who she'd helped out of the plane first stood up and approached them, limping slightly.

Alice went to take a step backwards, but Flo grabbed hold of her arm.

The airman must have seen Alice's reaction and held up

both his hands. 'Zere is no need to be afraid. We surrender. We are very happy to be here in England.'

Flo stared at him. 'You understand that you will be taken as Prisoners of War?'

He nodded and smiled, his blue eyes bright in his dirt-smudged face. 'Things are bad in Germany now and we are happy to be free of this flying.' He looked towards the plane, an expression of relief on his face. 'It is done. Over.'

'We need to take you to the police. Do you understand?' Flo asked.

'Yes. We walk?' he said.

Flo nodded. 'Are you all able to do that?'

'I zink so, maybe more slowly than normal. I tell my men.' With a bow of his head, he returned to the rest of the crew and spoke to them in German.

Flo looked at Alice. 'I don't think they're going to give us any trouble, not if they're glad to be here. We'll have to take them to Wykeham police station and hand them over.'

'I wasn't expecting this when Hettie suggested we go to the pictures.' Alice managed a smile. 'I'm shaking.' She held up her hand, which was indeed shaking from the shock of what had happened.

Flo took hold of Alice's hand and gave it a gentle squeeze. 'It will be all right. I honestly think they're relieved to be out of it. They were lucky to survive the crash and now they won't have to fly any more. They can spend the rest of the war here. Maybe they never wanted to do what they've been doing in the first place. Let's get moving. It will take the pilot a while to walk to Wykeham as he's limping.'

'It's this way.' Flo gestured with her arm to the men who were all now standing, waiting to go. None of them looked dangerous, just relieved to be alive.

'Zank you.' The pilot smiled politely and he motioned for

the crew to follow on as Flo and Alice led the way across the field.

'We need to slow down,' Alice said, looking back at the airmen after they'd gone a short way. 'They're not keeping up with us.'

Flo turned and saw that the pilot was now being helped with a crew member on each side of him, helping to support him as he limped along, obviously having hurt his leg in the crash.

'We'll wait for them at the gate.' Flo kept walking and as they reached the gateway was relieved to spot some familiar khaki-clad figures approaching down the road at a steady jog, their guns resting on their shoulders and pointing upwards. It was the Home Guard and Reuben was leading the way.

Flo waved to them and they quickened their pace.

'Did you see where the plane landed?' Reuben called breathlessly as he came within hailing distance. 'We saw it coming down.'

'It's in there.' Flo pointed through the gateway to where the airmen were still following them. 'The crew all survived. We helped them out and they've surrendered. We were on our way to the police station in Wykeham.'

Reuben stared at her, an incredulous expression on his face. 'Are you all right? They didn't hurt you?'

'Not at all. We're perfectly fine and they've been very polite,' Flo informed him, giving him a reassuring smile.

Reuben looked relieved. 'We'll take over from here.' He turned to the group of Home Guard with him and issued orders.

Flo stood by Alice and watched from the gateway as the Home Guard, with their guns now aimed, went into the field and advanced on the aircrew. At the sight of the Home Guard, the German airmen immediately halted, putting their hands up to clearly signal their surrender. There was no struggle, no trying to escape.

Reuben talked to the airmen then returned to where Flo and Alice were standing. He'd left most of the Home Guard watching over the Germans, who were now sitting down again, waiting.

'I'm going to send for some transport to come and pick them up. The pilot can't walk far on his leg, probably twisted his ankle,' Reuben informed them. 'They said they're glad to be here and aren't putting up a fight. Don't blame them. They're out of the war now.' He looked thoughtful. 'You did a brave thing helping them. It could have been a different outcome if the plane had blown up or they weren't pleased to be here. You'd best get home and have a sweet cup of tea or something.'

'Thanks Uncle Reuben,' Alice said. 'It was scary, but we had to do something.'

'And to be honest, we didn't realise it was a German plane at first, not till we got close to it,' Flo admitted. 'It was a shock to see.' Her eyes met his and a look of understanding passed between them. Reuben knew about what had happened to her family.

'I can imagine. You did the right thing to help them.' His face was serious for a moment, but then he smiled. 'All's well that ends well, as the saying goes. You two can go on home now, and I'll make sure they're looked after properly.'

Flo and Alice collected their bicycles from where they'd left them, while Reuben sent one of the youngest members of his Home Guard platoon to run back to Wykeham at a fast pace to call for transport.

'Will you tell us what happens to them?' Alice asked.

'Of course. Now you both get home, and mind how you go, you've had a shock,' Reuben advised them.

'I can't quite believe that just happened,' Alice said as they pedalled towards Great Plumstead once more.

Flo glanced at her friend. 'Well it did, and it wasn't a dream. We certainly didn't expect our evening out to see a film to turn out like this!'

∼

A gentle tapping on the bedroom door brought Flo away from Manderley and back to Rookery House.

'Come in,' she called, putting down the book she was reading, which Evie had given to her before leaving to go on her night shift at the hospital.

The door opened and Thea stepped inside, wearing her green WVS uniform, clearly just home from her day manning the canteen.

'Hettie told me what happened earlier. How are you feeling?' Thea's face was full of concern.

Flo pulled herself up into a sitting position in her bed. 'I'm fine. It was scary at the time and an awful shock when I saw it was a German plane, but it all turned out well. The pilot spoke English and was very polite. He said they were glad to be here in England.'

Thea sat down on the edge of Evie's bed, facing Flo. 'After what happened to your family, that can't have been easy.'

'It did make me hesitate,' Flo admitted. 'But Alice made me see sense. She helped me think of them as not just the enemy in a bomber, but *real* people who have families back home who love them and will be worrying about them. If Marianne's Alex crashed in his plane, we'd hope that someone would help him, wouldn't we?'

Thea nodded. 'That's true. Did the crew try to escape and run off?'

'Not at all. They weren't aggressive or arrogant. They seemed nice.' Flo bit her bottom lip. 'I never thought I would think like that about enemy airman, but inside those planes are ordinary people. I got the impression that the crew we saw today didn't want to be dropping bombs. Maybe they were forced into it. How many more are like that, being made to carry out the orders of those in charge?'

'That's what happens in war, unfortunately. It sounds as if it might have been cathartic for you.'

Flo looked down at the book lying on her lap for a moment before returning her gaze to meet Thea's. She gave a rueful smile. 'I think it was. It's made me view things differently and I feel...' She searched for the right words. 'That I can let go now. I will never, ever forget my family or stop missing them, but I couldn't carry on holding on to the bitterness about what happened and hating those who caused it. It wasn't doing me any good.'

Thea stood up and came over to Flo's bed and took hold of one of her hands. 'You're a brave young woman and yes, you're right, hanging on to bitterness doesn't help anyone in the long run. Your parents would be very proud of you, Flo. I am as well.' She bent down and kissed the top of Flo's head. 'I'll leave you in peace to rest and to read...' She looked at the title of the book. '*Rebecca*.' With a warm smile, she left the room, closing the door quietly behind her.

Flo leaned back against the feather pillows, let out a long sigh and smiled to herself. She hoped if her mam and dad were looking down on her now, that they would indeed be proud of what she'd done and how she was living her life.

CHAPTER 48

Saturday 26th July

Prue was relieved that the morning of the village fete had dawned bright and clear and was set to be a beautiful sunshine-filled July day. It was perfect for the outdoor events. After the past few days, Prue needed something different, something fun, she thought as she walked towards the green where the fete would be taking place.

Working in the WVS canteen for four days straight had been exhausting. That, combined with the news of Alice's brush with the crashed enemy bomber and its crew, had left Prue feeling strung out. Last night her dreams had been peppered with unsettling images of what could have happened if the plane had come down on Alice and Flo, or if the German airmen had put up a fight. The outcome could have been so different.

Prue took a deep breath, inhaling the fragrant scent of roses from one of the cottage gardens as she passed. It reminded her that there was still plenty of beauty in the world, despite the country being at war. She raised her chin, telling herself that it wouldn't do to dwell on what *could* have happened, because luckily it hadn't. Mulling over and prophesizing disasters would only serve to make her unhappy and she really had no time or energy for that. Today, she needed to focus on the fete and enjoy herself, as she hoped many others would do too.

Arriving at the village green, which was busy with a variety of stalls being set up by members of The Mother's Day Club, WI and Girl Guides, Prue spotted Nancy. Her friend had left the house earlier after reassuring Prue that everything was under control. Nancy had insisted that Prue shouldn't be in a rush, but must take the time to have a leisurely breakfast. After four days of being up at the crack of dawn, and then not home till late, she hadn't argued.

'How are you getting on?' Prue asked, approaching Nancy, who was checking through her list.

Nancy turned and gave Prue a reassuring smile. 'Everything's going to plan. As you can see, we've brought tables out of the village hall for the stalls and they're now all in place. Flo and Alice have got my girls helping to mark out where they're holding the races.' She pointed to where Marie and Joan were hammering poles, with strings of bunting attached, into the ground to create a sports area. 'Hettie and Marianne are arranging the WI stall. The Girl Guides are setting up their hoopla and fishing games.'

'It all looks wonderful, thank you.' Prue put her arm around Nancy. 'I appreciate you stepping in and everybody working hard to bring it together.'

'I appreciate you putting your trust in me.' Nancy put her arm around Prue and gave her a sideways hug. 'I'm enjoying myself. The only thing for you to do is go to the WI allotment and harvest some things to sell on the stall. We need to show the doubters that the WI isn't just about making jam!'

'It would be my pleasure! I'm looking forward to selling our produce when it's my turn to supervise the stall.' Prue loved the prospect of bringing together the different arms of what the women did in the village today, proving just what they were capable of despite the reservations of some of the community. The simple fact was that without the women of The Mother's Day Club or WI, it was unlikely that an event like today's fete would be taking place. It was testament to what they could achieve as a group. Prue was proud to be part of it.

'I hope you sell something to Percy Blake. He was moaning the other day about the slugs eating his lettuces.' Nancy gave a wry smile.' He may well be on the lookout to buy some.'

Prue lifted an eyebrow. 'That would indeed be a win for our allotment, don't you think?'

CHAPTER 49

Thea watched as Betty and George lined up at the start of the three-legged race with other pairs of similar age children. They had their arms around each other and their adjoining legs tied together with a scarf. Betty had a determined look on her face.

'I hope they do well.' Jess waved to George, who had spotted them watching, and he waved back, looking excited. 'Betty 'as 'ad them practising over and over for the past few days since they broke up from school for the summer holidays. They kept going until they got the 'ang of it.'

Jess's words made Thea's stomach knot – she hadn't been there to see this as she'd been taking part in the invasion exercise. Normally, she would have been there to watch and now it might prove to be one of the last things the pair did at Rookery House, even though Jess still hadn't said anything about taking them back to London with her.

Pushing down her worry, Thea returned George's wave from where she stood next to Jess. They were standing outside the race area which had been marked out with poles. 'I hope they do well. It certainly won't be from lack of determination.'

Flo, who was acting as the starter, called the children to attention before shouting, 'On your marks, get set... go!'

Thea watched as all the contenders surged forwards, some with more success than others. Several pairs tumbled to the ground as their uncoordinated movements tripped them up. Betty and George, their legs and arms pumping in synch, took the lead. As they sped past, Thea could hear Betty's voice barking out, 'One, two, one, two...' keeping them both in rhythm.

'Come on!' Thea encouraged them in a loud voice.

Beside her, Jess was cheering loudly, her eyes shining with pride as she watched her children.

None of the other runners could match Betty and George and they romped home in first place, a few yards ahead of their nearest rivals. Alice waved a red flag as the pair crossed the finishing line and they promptly lost their rhythm and tumbled over, laughing.

'They won!' Jess clapped with delight, beaming at Thea.

'They were wonderful!' Thea applauded too, watching as Betty and George got up and happily received their winner's prize – a certificate. Then the pair hobbled over to where Thea and Jess stood, their faces brimming over with happiness.

'We won!' they chorused, holding up the certificate.

'Well done.' Jess bent down and hugged them both. 'All that practice paid off. I'm so proud of you.'

'Did *you* watch, Aunt Thea?' George asked, looking up at her.

She smiled at him. 'I did, every moment, and you were both *amazing*!'

He nodded at her and grinned. 'Can we undo our legs now?'

Jess crouched down and undid the scarf. 'I daresay you could both do with somethin' to eat after that. Why don't you go over to see Hettie on the WI stall and buy one of them little cakes each?' She reached into her pocket and handed Betty a coin. 'I'll catch up with you in a minute. I want to speak to Thea.'

Thea's stomach lurched. She knew what was coming. As she watched the children make their way over to the WI stall, hand in hand, she realised with a lump in her throat that it was a sight she wouldn't be seeing for much longer.

'Thea?' Jess's voice cut into her thoughts.

'What do you want to talk to me about?' Thea asked, hoping that her face didn't betray the dread she was feeling inside.

'My time here is running out as I'm going back to London tomorrow. I've been wanting to speak to you about the children, only with you bein' away, I haven't had the chance till now.' Jess gazed steadily at Thea. 'I'm so 'appy with how well you've looked after them, you, Hettie, Marianne. Everyone at Rookery 'ouse. Betty and George 'ave thrived living here. I…'

'You want to take them back to London with you,' Thea interrupted, unable to hold it in any longer.

Jess's eyes grew wide with surprise. 'Why would you think that?'

'Because the bombing has stopped… at least for now!'

'It might 'ave, but I ain't foolish enough to think that's it! That London is safe now. Because it *ain't*! The bombers will be back sometime, and I don't want my children there when they do.' Jess glanced over to the WI stall where the children were buying their cakes, before returning her gaze to Thea. 'As much as I miss 'em it's the best and *safest* thing for them to stay 'ere with you. That's if you're still willin' for them to carry on livin' with you with the house being so full now.'

Tears welled in Thea's eyes. 'Of course. I... we all love having them with us at Rookery House. I've been so worried that you'd come to take them back because it's still not safe in London. My good friend, Violet, is station officer at Ambulance Station 75 off the Minories. She's told me how things have been there and says they're still on alert, ready for the next wave of bombing. They don't believe it's finished or that the danger's over. Not until the war is done.'

Jess put her hand on Thea's arm. 'I think that too,' she said wisely. 'I want to say thank you for givin' my children such a 'appy, caring 'ome, Thea. They couldn't wish to be in a lovelier place or with better people. Knowing that George and Betty are 'appy and looked after is a massive 'elp to me. I miss them dearly, but that is a small price to pay for their safety.'

'You could come and live at Rookery House, too. I mean that,' Thea offered.

'Thank you, I appreciate your kind offer. I really do. But I need to look after my 'usband. He's useless at caring for himself and I need to keep an eye on him!' Jess raised an eyebrow. 'I did try leaving 'im to his own devices when we first came 'ere but it didn't work out. I'll go back to London tomorrow, refreshed from seeing Betty and George again and content knowing they are 'appy.'

'My offer is *always* there if you change your mind.' Thea reached out and touched Jess's arm.

'Thank you. I appreciate that. Shall we see what the children have bought from the WI stall? They 'ad their eye on some nice little buns earlier and I think Hettie was going to put some by for them.' Jess linked her arm through Thea's.

As they headed towards the WI stall Thea realised that the

heavy weight of her worry about George and Betty's immediate future had slipped from her shoulders. Thea felt lighter than she had since Jess's letter had arrived. She was relieved to know that Jess's priority was her children's safety and that they were staying at Rookery House for now. That made Thea very happy indeed.

CHAPTER 50

Hettie watched as Thea, hand in hand with George, and Jess, hand in hand with Betty, all headed over to sit in the shade of the large beech tree to picnic on the buns they'd bought at the WI stall. Thea had given Hettie a nod, her face lit up with a beaming smile. It told Hettie that everything was all right. The worry that had haunted Thea about the children's immediate future had gone, which must mean they were staying. It was the most wonderful news, for George and Betty, Thea and Hettie and all who lived at Rookery House.

'Is there any chance of trying some jam before you buy it?' A familiar voice cut into Hettie's thoughts and she turned her gaze to the person standing in front of the stall.

'Hello, Ada.' Hettie gave her a welcoming smile. In the six weeks since her sister had moved into Great Plumstead Hall, Hettie hadn't seen Ada, although she'd heard news of her and how she was getting on from Dorothy Shepherd when she saw her at church. Thankfully, it had all been positive and from the look on Ada's face she seemed far happier now than when she'd left her cottage back in March. Her sister had the air of woman who was content with her lot. 'It's lovely to see you. How are you and how's the new job and home?' Hettie asked in an eager voice.

'All very good, I am pleased to say. I'm enjoying the work and living at the Hall.' Ada's face lit up. 'I'd never have thought it would suit me, but it does. Keeps me busy.'

'I'm glad to hear that,' Hettie said in a heartfelt tone.

Ada nodded. 'I…' she hesitated. 'Thank you for what you did for me, Hettie. I appreciate you giving me a home and helping me get my job. I know I wasn't the easiest person to live with while I was at Rookery House. Though I probably never was! But losing my cottage hit me hard.' Ada's eyes brightened with tears and she quickly blinked them away. 'Now I've found something new to do and I'm happy doing it.'

Hettie had the urge to rush round to the front of the stall and hug her sister but knew that wouldn't be welcome. Instead, she reached across and patted Ada's arm briefly. 'Life has a way of working out in ways we would never expect sometimes. When one door closes, another opens…'

'I remember our mother saying that.' Ada's expression softened at the memory.

'Ma was right,' Hettie agreed. 'And yes, as it's you, I'll let you have a taste of the jam, although I can assure you that it will be delicious. I made this batch myself. It's apple and blackberry.' She picked up a jar of the rich purple jam and was about to open it when Ada put up her hand to stop her.

'Since *you* made it, then I know it will be good. There's no need to taste it first. You are an excellent cook, Hettie.' Ada removed her purse from her handbag, took out the exact money shown on the price tag leaning against the stack of jars, and handed it over.

Hettie didn't know what to say. It was rare for Ada to praise her cooking. She passed her sister the jar. 'I hope you enjoy it. Though I'm sure Dorothy has made jam at the Hall that you can have there.'

'She has, but I like to support the WI. I'm thinking of coming along to the meetings now I've settled into the job,' Ada announced.

'Then you'd be most welcome!' Hettie gave her sister a beaming smile. 'The next meeting is this coming Wednesday evening, six o'clock in the village hall. I hope to see you there.'

Ada put the jar of jam in her basket and with a nod of her head, she wandered off to the bookstall nearby.

Hettie stood watching her go, amazed at her sister's transformation.

'Is everything all right?' Prue asked, putting a hand on Hettie's shoulder.

She turned her attention to Prue who was supervising the stall alongside her, and nodded. 'Everything is fine. Ada just surprised me, that's all, but in a *good* way.'

'I'm glad to hear that. And you'll be even more surprised to know that I've just sold a lettuce to Percy Blake! He said they were fine looking specimens.' Prue's eyes danced with glee as she gestured at the display of fresh produce from the WI allotment. It was proving popular with customers and at the rate it was selling would soon be sold out.

'Poetic justice, don't you think?' Hettie raised her eyebrows. 'Although I notice he didn't buy any of our jam.'

'Perhaps he now believes the WI isn't *only* about jam making!'

'We're changing people's perceptions and that is a good thing,' Hettie said, thinking that Percy Blake wasn't the only person to have his opinions altered in this village. Slowly but surely, the work of the women was making a difference in so many ways and Hettie loved doing her bit to help make that happen.

CHAPTER 51

The races had been a great success, Flo thought as she coiled and then knotted a skipping rope before putting it in the wicker basket of equipment borrowed from the village school. The egg and spoon and sack races were hilarious to watch and the mother's running race had seen a close contest between Nancy and Gloria. Gloria had taken off her high heels to run barefoot but Nancy had won, although only by the shortest of margins.

Now, with the sports over, Flo knew it was only a short while until the singing group would be called to do their performance.

'Are you all right?' Alice asked, folding a brown hessian sack and placing it on the pile of already folded sacks by her feet. 'You're very quiet.'

'I'm nervous about singing,' Flo admitted.

'Whatever for? You've got a lovely voice and you know all the words.' Alice put her head on one side. 'Is it because you'll be singing in front of an audience?'

'Nothing like that.' Flo bit her bottom lip. 'The last time I was planning to sing in public, it never happened because of the Christmas Blitz. I was supposed to go out carol singing with a group of girls from work, but...' She gestured with her hands. 'We didn't, for obvious reasons. Today reminds me of that.'

Alice reached out and touched Flo's arm. 'Think of today like putting that memory to rest. You'll be making a new much happier one instead. If you're able to cope with a crashed enemy bomber and its crew, then you can easily sing with our group.'

Flo nodded. 'You're right. I need to keep things in perspective.' Seeing the plane come down, their dash to rescue the airmen and then the shock of realising it was a German bomber had shaken Flo. It had stirred memories. Made her question herself but importantly had also freed her of what she'd been holding on to following her family's deaths. Flo had learned from Reuben that the crew were now being held in a local Prisoner of War camp where they would safely see out the rest of the war. She wished them well.

'Did you hear that?' Alice cut into Flo's thoughts. 'Gloria's ready for us.'

Flo glanced over to Gloria, who was standing on a wooden box, calling out for the singing group to assemble by her. Flo's mouth went dry. 'I don't know...' she began as panic gripped her.

'Come on, it will be fine. All you need to do is concentrate on the first few lines and then just let the song carry you away.' Alice tucked her arm through Flo's and led her over to where other members of their singing group were gathering around Gloria, taking up the positions they'd practised standing in according to their voices.

'Good luck,' Alice whispered as she pushed Flo towards where she had to stand and then headed to her own position.

Flo took some slow breaths, focusing her eyes on Gloria, who stood in front of them, a beaming smile on her face.

'Enjoy yourselves and *sing your hearts out!*' Gloria's gaze passed over them all, her eyes dancing with enthusiasm, and then she turned to the crowd of villagers who were gathering to watch them. 'Ladies and gentlemen, come and listen to some beautiful songs performed for you by the Great Plumstead Village Singing Group. Do feel free to join in if the urge takes you!'

Turning her back to the audience, Gloria faced the group once more and with three beats of her hand counted them in. As one, they began to sing *Daisy Bell*.

Flo concentrated hard, focusing on the words and the tune. She willed herself to sing as she had so many times in their practices in the village hall. Slowly, she began to relax and let the music carry her away. With the other women singing around her, she felt like a small part of a whole. Something much bigger than her alone. It made her heart swell along with her voice.

The words of *Daisy Bell* were proving infectious as Flo noticed several of the audience were already joining in. More picked up the song as they sang their way through it. She spotted Marianne, with Emily in her arms, Hettie and Thea who were all singing, their faces shining with happiness. It was only a few short months since she'd gone to live at Rookery House and they'd welcomed her into their home, and yet she now felt as comfortable with them as she had with her family. They would never replace her parents, sister or brother but they had become important to her and she had grown fond of them. They might not be related to her by blood, but Flo had learned that wasn't necessary.

Tears filled Flo's eyes, but not through sadness. These were tears of happiness and joy. After what had happened last

December, she'd never imagined she would feel so content and happy again, but she had found peace and understanding at Rookery House. It was where she wanted to stay, working in a job she loved with the amazing people who'd helped her heal her broken heart.

Flo took a deep breath and sang with all her heart.

Dear Reader,

I hope you enjoyed reading Flo's story and spending time with Thea, Hettie and Marianne at Rookery House, along with other residents of Great Plumstead. It's a joy to write about the characters again and I've heard from many readers how they've come to think of them as friends.

Look out for them all returning in the next book *A Christmas Baby at Rookery House.*

I love hearing from readers – it's one of the greatest joys of being a writer – so please do get in touch via:

Facebook: **Rosie Hendry Books** or join my private readers group - **Rosie Hendry's Reader Group**
Twitter: @hendry_rosie
Instagram: rosiehendryauthor
Website: **www.rosiehendry.com**

You can sign up to get my monthly newsletter delivered straight to your inbox, with all the latest on my writing life, exclusive looks behind the scenes of my work, and reader competitions.

If you have the time and would like to share your thoughts about this book, do please leave a review. I read and appreciate each one as it's wonderful to hear what you think. Reviews also encourage other readers to try my books.

With warmest wishes,

Rosie

IF YOU ENJOYED DIGGING FOR VICTORY AT ROOKERY HOUSE...

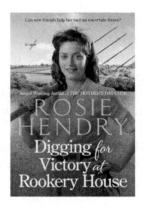

It would be wonderful if you could spare a few minutes to leave a star rating, or write a review, at the retailer where you bought this book.

Reviews don't need to be long – a sentence or two is absolutely fine. They make a huge difference to authors, helping us know what readers think of our books and what they particularly enjoy. Reviews also help other readers discover new books to try for themselves.

You might also tell family and friends you think would enjoy this book.

Thank you!

HEAR MORE FROM ROSIE

Want to keep up to date with Rosie's latest releases?

Sign up to receive her monthly newsletter at her website.
www.rosiehendry.com

Subscribers get Rosie's newsletter delivered to their inbox and are always the first to know about the latest books, as well as getting exclusive behind the scenes news, plus reader competitions.

You can unsubscribe at any time and your email will never be shared with anyone else.

Have you met the East End Angels yet?

Winnie, Frankie and Bella are brave ambulance crew who rescue casualties of the London Blitz.

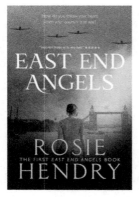

BOOK 1 - USA and Canada edition

BOOK 1 - UK and rest of world English edition

Available in ebook, paperback and audiobook.

ACKNOWLEDGMENTS

Many people have helped me with my research into wartime Norfolk — a big thank you to Reepham Archive and Aylsham Heritage Centre and Archives, Norfolk Library Service for supplying many research books, and the Imperial War Museum in London for access to recorded oral histories and documents.

My mum patiently answered my many questions about life in rural Norfolk in the Second World War — thank you.

Thanks to the fantastic team who help me create the books — editor, Catriona Robb, cover designer, Andrew Brown and photographer, Gordon Crabb.

My fellow writers are a great support and I appreciate their friendship, company, wise words and listening ears. Thank you especially to the Strictly Saga authors and my dear friends in the RNA's Norfolk and Suffolk Chapter.

Finally, thank you to David, who listens and supports me in all I do.

ALSO BY ROSIE HENDRY

East End Angels novels

East End Angels

Secrets of the East End Angels

Christmas with the East End Angels

Victory for the East End Angels

Rookery House novels

The Mother's Day Club

The Mother's Day Victory

A Wartime Welcome at Rookery House

Digging for Victory at Rookery House

Rookery House novella

A Wartime Christmas at Rookery House

Standalone novel

Secrets and Promises

Standalone novellas

A Home from Home

Love on a Scottish Island

Short story collection

A Pocketful of Stories

Rosie Hendry lived and worked in the USA before settling back in her home county of Norfolk, England, where she lives in a village by the sea with her family. She likes walking in nature, reading (of course) and growing all sorts of produce and flowers in her garden — especially roses.

Rosie writes stories from the heart that are inspired by historical records, where gems of social history are often to be found. Her interest in the WWII era was sparked by her father's many tales of growing up at that time.

Rosie is the winner of the 2022 Romantic Novelists' Association (RNA) award for historical romantic sagas, with *The Mother's Day Club*, the first of her series set during wartime at Rookery House. Her novels set in the London Blitz, the *East End Angels* series, have been described as 'Historical fiction at its very best!'.

To find out more visit **www.rosiehendry.com**

Printed in Great Britain
by Amazon